Dear Ke
Best wish
to my neighbor
Enjoy the read

MOTIVE TO KILL

Elliot Ayt

MOTIVE TO KILL

BY ELLIOT AZOFF

ARCHWAY PUBLISHING

Copyright © 2015 Elliot Azoff.

All rights reserved. No part of this book may be used or reproduced by any means, graphic, electronic, or mechanical, including photocopying, recording, taping or by any information storage retrieval system without the written permission of the publisher except in the case of brief quotations embodied in critical articles and reviews.

This is a work of fiction. All of the characters, names, incidents, organizations, and dialogue in this novel are either the products of the author's imagination or are used fictitiously.

Archway Publishing books may be ordered through booksellers or by contacting:

Archway Publishing
1663 Liberty Drive
Bloomington, IN 47403
www.archwaypublishing.com
1 (888) 242-5904

Because of the dynamic nature of the Internet, any web addresses or links contained in this book may have changed since publication and may no longer be valid. The views expressed in this work are solely those of the author and do not necessarily reflect the views of the publisher, and the publisher hereby disclaims any responsibility for them.

Any people depicted in stock imagery provided by Thinkstock are models, and such images are being used for illustrative purposes only. Certain stock imagery © Thinkstock.

ISBN: 978-1-4808-1695-4 (sc)
ISBN: 978-1-4808-1697-8 (hc)
ISBN: 978-1-4808-1696-1 (e)

Library of Congress Control Number: 2015904430

Print information available on the last page.

Archway Publishing rev. date: 4/21/2015

A LEGAL MYSTERY THRILLER
A LAWYER PLACES HIS LIFE ON
THE LINE TO SOLVE THE MURDER
OF HIS BEST FRIEND.

ACKNOWLEDGEMENTS

First, I want to acknowledge and thank my Muse. When I first sat down to write a murder mystery, I did not follow any of what I have learned are the general procedures for writing such a book. No plotting out chapters, outlining the story or character sketches. I did not even know who committed the murder or what problems would arise in solving the crime. I put my total trust in my Muse to show me the story that I recorded as it played out in my mind. And, indeed some 80,000 words later, everything came together: the murder was solved and the story was completed.

I need to thank Mary McFarland and Marcy Gaige for their valuable assistance. I am particularly grateful to Elaine Geller who encouraged me to revisit the manuscript, which had been set aside, and to arrange for its publication. She also provided some pithy suggestions for improvement. Sharon Schnall added her editorial expertise to make sure that editorial conventions were followed and that references were accurate. And last, but certainly not least, I must thank Roberta Crawford who carefully proofread the copy, provided advice, researched and prepared the mockup for book covers, and brought together the many requirements for publication.

And finally there is my friend, since high school, law school classmate and law partner Tom Seger.

DEDICATION

For my children, Ben, Rachel, Jon, Danny, and Andy Azoff

CONTENTS

PART ONE
Death
1

PART TWO
Secrets
57

PART THREE
Entanglements
119

PART FOUR
Escape
175

PART FIVE
Solutions
229

EPILOGUE
273

PART ONE
DEATH

1

I have never been overly superstitious. Black cats, a hat on the bed, a ladder across the sidewalk; those things don't bother me. So I didn't pay much attention to the fact that it was Friday, April 13th.

Until the phone call, the day had been routine. As a sixty-year-old lawyer at one of those big law firms that runs the city, I have few days that don't blend one into another. I'm a labor lawyer. I go all over the country negotiating bargaining agreements with unions. I'm Mr. Fix-it. If you have a problem, whether it be with a union or an individual employee, you come to me and I'll solve the problem for you, or try to. Most of that day, I spent at my desk, dispensing legal advice over the telephone at five hundred dollars per hour in a large corner office of the fifty-fifth floor of the Union National Bank Building.

The high point was Max Cohen, a longtime client who owns a factory in Kalamazoo, Michigan, calling to complain about a four-hundred-pound delivery driver. Max wanted to fire the driver, who was frequently missing work, as a preemptive strike before the inevitable accident and workers' compensation claim, but was afraid, if he did, he'd violate some law.

Max was right. In today's world, you can't fire anyone anymore without being sued. But I shouldn't complain. That's why I make the big bucks. So, for the next four hours, I worked my magic, engaged in what my time records will reflect as two thousand dollars' worth of employment law strategy. Suffice it to say, all parties were happy, but my day was no more thrilling than the one before.

After transmitting all the necessary documents to Max, I looked over at the grandfather clock that stands in my office, next to a lithograph of Justice Louis Brandeis—an original Andy Warhol—and saw that it was already 4:00 p.m. Without hesitation, I decided that for a partner, my billable hours were sufficient to call it a week. McGinty's Pub was beckoning. The Back Room at McGinty's is the favorite—and exclusive—watering hole of the most influential attorneys, politicians, and judges in the city.

It's not exactly clear how you first get invited into The Back Room. There is no election or formal application process. I guess it just happens when you become the right kind of person. By that I don't mean that you have to be a WASP, rich, or a partner at a top law firm. Actually, on any given afternoon or evening, the group assembled in The Back Room has a positively politically correct kind of rainbow diversity: Black, White, Jewish, Protestant, Italian. The single common denominator? Influence.

On first walking in, it's unremarkable. A long, old-fashioned wooden bar fronted by a dozen bar stools on the immediate right. To the left, a half dozen equally uncomfortable wooden booths line the wall. Straight back from the doorway Charley presides over the kitchen. Looking about eighty years old, Charley has a perpetual two-day beard and food stains cover his cook's whites. He wears a New York Yankees cap with a half-smoked cigarette dangling from his mouth. If he has a last name, no one knows it.

Ruling from behind the bar is James McGinty. At first glance, you might see him as just another barkeep and not pay him much heed. That would be your mistake. McGinty, as he is known to practically everyone, has an unruly shock of white hair and Paul Newman-like piercing blue eyes. Not a tall man, perhaps five feet seven inches, McGinty exudes authority. And, he is the gatekeeper. He alone decides who may enter through the wooden door leading into that inner sanctum — The Back Room. You don't challenge McGinty or his decisions. The occasional patron, generally drunk, who foolishly disregards McGinty's suggestion that The Back Room is off limits to the general public, finds himself removed, and not necessarily gently.

I've been drinking in The Back Room now for nearly three decades; yet, I still vividly remember that April evening, in 1983, when Paul Martin, my law partner and best friend since high school, and I were sitting with the wannabes at a booth in the front room, and McGinty approached our table.

"Gentlemen," he said ever so softly, "why don't you come with me?"

With no more formality than a flight attendant upgrading a worthy road warrior from coach to first class, McGinty ushered us into The Back Room to a corner table where two other men were already seated.

"Mr. Jackson, Judge Black, I'd like you to meet Mr. Stein and Mr. Martin. I'm sure you'll make the introductions."

That was it. That was all he said. Now I previously had met Robert Jackson, a prominent African-American attorney and former president of City Council. And as a young associate, I'd once appeared in a case before Reginald Black, who was the Chief Judge of the Common Pleas court, which is the state trial court. With heart pounding, I looked around. The room was mahogany-lined. Seven round linen-covered wooden tables, each with six chairs, and a television mounted on one wall rounded out the furnishings. Besides the single television, the walls were bare. Our table hosts took Paul and me around to the other tables and introduced us to all present. It was now official. We were entitled to drink in The Back Room.

Since then I've been a regular.

Actually, for the last six months, I've spent most evenings drinking and eating in The Back Room. Loneliness was reducing me to one of those sad characters described in the *Piano Man* song. It's been exactly six months since my wife of more than thirty years announced she wanted a divorce and insisted that I move to an apartment. It would be an understatement to say that I was shocked. Our marriage, while admittedly not perfect, was still better than those of many of our contemporaries. The difference was that theirs were still stumbling along and mine wasn't. If nothing else, I'd always been faithful to Maxine and that fidelity had gotten me, exactly what? A chance to spend my birthday living alone downtown in a spartanly furnished two-bedroom apartment.

Since a microwaved dinner for one at an IKEA table, I'd nicknamed Smedvick, wasn't beckoning me home, most nights found me where I was tonight, sitting in The Back Room, a plate with the remnants of one of Charley's succulent rib steaks on the table, sipping my third Cranberry and Ketel One, and chatting with Vince DeMarco, a councilman and the local Democratic Party boss, and Billy Gold, a millionaire trial attorney.

Billy is a classic American success story. While working as an electrician's apprentice, he went to law school at night, graduated, and passed the bar examination on his third attempt. Billy's not, and never has been, a particularly good lawyer. But his brother Solly was first elected Business Agent and then President of the local Electricians Union. In a touching demonstration of fraternal loyalty, and a finder's fee, Solly referred brother union members who had been exposed to asbestos to Billy. You don't even have to try the cases. As Billy proudly explains to anyone who will listen, the key to success is a panel of malleable doctors on retainer to provide the necessary diagnoses, several underpaid paralegals to prepare individualized packets describing the maladies suffered by and damage done to each client, and the patsy companies and their insurance carriers that just throw money at you. Most of the settlements are seven figures, and Billy gets one-third. Compared to Billy's piracy, my billing rate is quite reasonable.

Vince, Billy, and I were just sitting around, discussing the upcoming National Basketball Association playoffs. A meaningless, end-of-the-season NBA game graced the large plasma screen that McGinty had mounted on one wall of The Back Room; the play-by-play was muted.

In other words, it could not have been a more ordinary post-separation Friday night. Nothing more important on my mind except that Vince was wrong. LeBron James was better than Kobe Bryant or even Magic Johnson. The truth was that I was in no particular rush to return to my new home, the apartment. If I had something better to do, I would not have been sitting there talking to Billy.

When my cell phone rang, I realized I needed to change the pulsating four-ring melody to something less annoying, but I had no premonition, no creepy Friday the 13th unease prickling up my spine.

Looking back, it's hard to say whom exactly I was expecting to hear when I pressed the button. One thing's for certain, though, it was not a sobbing, gulping, hysterical woman, which is precisely whom I heard. Those are not the kind of calls I usually get.

For a moment, I imagined it was Maxine. Some unexpected tragedy had brought her to her senses and she needed me to return home. That delusion was quickly dispelled.

Between uncontrollable sobs, I heard: "Paul's dead."

"He's been murdered."

"I need help."

Finally there was recognition. The voice was Phyllis, my best friend Paul's wife. For the sake of full disclosure, Phyllis was Paul's fourth wife.

My brain was pretty much stuck on processing "Paul," never mind "dead" or "murdered." I don't know whether it was Phyllis's hysteria or my own shock, but everything else she was saying made little sense: a car in the Wal-Mart parking lot; a bullet in the back of the head; police. Those things don't happen to a person like Paul. And people like me don't get phone calls about things like this.

My mind was spinning. Just last night I ate pizza with Paul and Phyllis at their house. Nothing seemed out of the ordinary. Paul, himself, was a veteran of three divorces, and Phyllis's husband had run off with his dental assistant after more than twenty years of marriage. They sympathized with my plight.

I gasped for breath.

"I don't understand. What are you talking about? I saw Paul this morning," I stammered.

"The police, they're here. They're asking questions, so many questions."

More sobbing.

"I don't know what to do."

"I'm at McGinty's. I'll get over to your place as quickly as I can."

"Please, please do," she pleaded and hung up.

2.

I was too stunned to offer a single word of explanation to Vince or Billy. I didn't care what they thought as I bolted out of The Back Room, leaving my Hickey Freeman suit jacket still hanging over my chair. I sprinted the eight blocks to the garage adjacent to my apartment where my car is typically parked. Even in light traffic, it's a thirty-minute drive from my current apartment in the city to Paul's house in the eastern suburbs. I don't even remember the drive. I know I must have started the car's engine, pulled out of the garage, and headed east, but I was somewhere else completely.

I'd first met Paul in Mrs. Henderson's tenth grade Honors English class at South High School at the start of the 1961 school year. With coal-black hair worn fashionably long and matching coal-black eyes, he was what kids today call a chick magnet. Dressed in a T-shirt, tight jeans, and loafers, he sat in the back of the class surrounded by the best-looking girls; probably bright, but not one of the real smart kids – like me. He had no interest in Mrs. Henderson's explanation of *Moby Dick* and the symbolism of Captain Ahab's pursuit of the Great White Whale. I wondered what someone like Paul was doing in Honors English.

About three weeks into the semester, much to my surprise, Paul seated himself next to me during lunch period and began talking in that self-assured, cocky but friendly tone I would come to know so well.

"Stein," he began without even introducing himself, "you gotta help me. This *Moby Dick* stuff is heavy. I understand the story. It's simple enough. A guy in a boat is chasing a white whale across the ocean and trying to kill it. But I don't see any of the symbolism crap that Henderson is talking about."

I was startled, unsure where this kid, whom I'd never before spoken to, was going. I didn't know Paul at all since we'd gone to different junior high schools. His type didn't ever much pay attention to me except to give me a hard time in classes like gym or shop. What his type was doing reading *Moby Dick* in Honors English in the first place was puzzling.

"How can I help?" I responded reluctantly.

"I can see you're smart," he continued, oblivious to my discomfort. "You're going to work with me and explain what Henderson is talking about, help me study for tests, and edit my papers. And then we're going to be good friends. You're going to be my little buddy." As I gaped in awe, he confidently outlined a plan for our future together; the matter had been predetermined, with me having no choice but to agree.

That day, Paul shared with me the explanation for his unlikely presence in Honors English. "I need an 'A' in Henderson's class because I'm gonna go to Barton College just like my father. You gotta get good grades in honors courses to get in there. It's the 'Yale of the Midwest,' you know?"

As I'd learn would most often be the case, Paul got what he sought. I helped him understand *Moby Dick*. He got his "A" in tenth grade Honors English. And, in the end, we became good friends. The friendship turned out to be more of a two-way street than I could have imagined. Being the smartest boy in the grade was an albatross around my neck. I sought acceptance by the other guys and especially wanted a girlfriend. Paul helped on both counts.

Innately understanding that athletics was key to the social acceptance I craved, Paul insisted I run track with him. "You need a varsity letter," he explained. Track, he said, was a sport where someone minimally talented – like me – could become competent through hard work. And hard work is something I've understood my whole life. Quite simply, Paul was right. With hours and hours of practice, I developed the stamina to run fast enough to be competitive and earn two varsity letters. Paul's sociological analysis of his peers also proved correct. Athletics really did help with social acceptance, as did being his friend.

In senior year, Paul came through with flying colors. I desperately needed a girlfriend to take to the senior prom. Magically, Paul arranged for me to begin dating Ellen Cohen, a girl he was dumping in favor of Jane Berke. Jane was the sexiest cheerleader in school. Years later, she became his first wife. With awe, I watched how easily he orchestrated the date without insulting Ellen. She remained his good friend. Charming women, I learned, was a natural gift Paul possessed.

Our friendship waned after high school. Paul did attend Barton College, the so-called "Yale of the Midwest," while I attended the real Yale in New Haven, Connecticut. When, over summer breaks, our paths eventually crossed, we greeted each other warmly, always promising to get in touch. We never did. You can imagine my surprise, when on my first day at Harvard Law School, in the fall of 1968, I saw Paul walk down the hall in my dormitory. During his four years at Barton College, Paul had gotten in touch with his intellect which, it turned out, was substantial.

We became best friends, in 1968, that first year at Harvard Law School. In those days, "The Law School," as it was known, was an intimidating place, accurately immortalized in the film *The Paper Chase*. Flaunting their knowledge and intellect, the professors embarrassed and humiliated their students on a daily basis. The experience of the first-year student, 1L is what we were called, was designed on the premise that the practice of law is a jungle – only the fittest would survive or, more importantly, prosper. All students took five full-year courses with such exciting names as *Contracts, Torts, Property, Civil Procedure,* and *Criminal Law*. Single examinations, in the spring, in each course, established your grade and your future. That was the Harvard Law School, the trial by fire that forever cemented my bond to Paul.

Also of concern was The Vietnam War, and the real possibility that Uncle Sam would send us off to fight the Vietcong. This cast an ominous shadow over our first year. The draft lottery wasn't in place then. Classified 1A, the group eligible to being drafted at any time into the army, by our Draft Board, Paul and I were potential cannon fodder. Unhappily, no apparent alternatives existed. You couldn't get into the Army Reserve or National Guard unless you were a professional athlete or had a last name like Roosevelt or Bush.

I still smile, remembering that life-altering Saturday night, the banging on my dorm door at three in the morning. Pulling myself out of bed, half asleep and none too pleased, I opened the door. Paul, bombed out of his mind with a big sheepish grin pasted across his face, stood, disheveled, in the doorway, holding a bottle of Budweiser in his right hand and a shoe in his left hand.

"Hey, Stein," he yelled loud enough for all my hallway neighbors to hear. "We're in, little buddy. How do you like that? Come on, let's drink to it." He pushed the half-filled bottle of Bud into my face.

Even partially awake, I knew Paul wasn't making any sense.

"What in the world are you talking about?"

Doors were opening around us. Fellow law students, clearly none too pleased at the interruption to their sleep, were staring at us. "He's drunk," I announced loudly, hoping my declaration would somehow placate my irritated neighbors.

"God, Stein," Paul retorted, "I always knew that you had a keen sense of the obvious. Listen, little buddy. I was at a party at Boston U. This foxy brunette; well, she dropped her purse and I noticed birth control pills. I notice things like that." He was slurring most of his words. "Anyway, I got her in bed. God, she was a hot one; and intelligent. Afterward, we actually started talking, at least until her boyfriend showed up. She has this boyfriend getting an MBA at BU; said he doesn't fuckin' like me."

"Paul," I interrupted as I pulled him into my room, "get to the point, if there is one. It's three in the morning. You're drunk and making a total ass of yourself.-- and me."

"Did I tell you the boyfriend was joining an Army Reserve unit in Concord that doesn't have a waiting list? You know, shot heard round the world. I'm saving your ass, again, little buddy. God, I'm quick on my feet," he said proudly. Abruptly he pushed me aside, took two steps and collapsed fully clothed in my bed where he immediately fell asleep, leaving me just as unenlightened as I'd been before his arrival. It was a long rest of the night, for me, sleeping on the floor.

The next morning we learned that Concord, the Massachusetts city where the Revolutionary War began, was not the only Concord in New England. Another Concord, the capitol of New Hampshire, was where the Army Reserve unit was located. We rented a car, drove to Concord, and returned to Harvard Law proud members of an Army Reserve unit: the 167th Direct Support Group whose insignia was a pilgrim with a blunderbuss.

No question about it, Paul had saved my ass. I would avoid Vietnam. I prayed that the foxy brunette's boyfriend hadn't joined the unit, too, so I wouldn't have to save Paul.

A fleeting shadow darted across the street in front of my car and broke my reverie. Swerving hard, I avoided hitting what looked like a black cat. Thirty minutes had passed since leaving my downtown garage; I was five minutes away from my destination, approaching the corner of Westwood Avenue and Blackburn Road. On autopilot, I turned left on Blackburn then right on Sittingbourne Lane; five more houses to go.

An unsettling thought flashed through my mind: tomorrow was Saturday. Paul and I had played tennis together every Saturday morning for over thirty years. Now Paul was dead, murdered. It didn't seem possible.

The clock on my dash, displayed 9:25 p.m. I parked my Volvo in the circular driveway behind two black-and-white-police cars. At the sight of them, incongruous behind the silver Mercedes-Benz CLK-Class convertible that told me Peter was already there, my dinner felt like it was rising dangerously in my throat.

Peter is Phyllis's son from her former marriage to a wealthy orthodontist. A successful broker with Merrill Lynch, Peter is gay. Now Peter came out of the closet about five years ago, leaving a wife and three-year-old son for Matthew, whom he introduces as his life partner.

I knocked on the front door. A short stocky man opened the door;

he had cropped black hair and a bushy mustache and wore a rumpled light brown suit that had seen better days.

"You Steve Stein?"

"Yes."

"I'm Detective Robert O'Brien. We've been waiting for you. Come on in."

The detective ushered me through the entryway into the formal living room, where Phyllis sat on a white couch next to a uniformed policeman. Despite eyes puffy from crying, she looked fantastic. Tall and statuesque, her dark auburn hair was fashionably colored and cut short; she wore a green sheer silk blouse, black designer slacks, and low-heeled black pumps. No one would ever guess that Phyllis had crossed the half-century mark last year. She looked far too attractive to be a widow, more like a model straight out of the pages of *Vogue*.

Phyllis rose from the couch to embrace me. She hadn't taken two steps when she collapsed into my arms sobbing hysterically. "He's dead, he's dead. I can't believe he's dead," she kept repeating between sobs.

I hugged her, patting her on the back while mumbling, "It'll be all right. It'll be all right." Of course, it wouldn't, but I didn't know what else to say.

With Phyllis clinging to me, I looked around to see who else was in the room. Besides Detective O'Brien and a uniformed cop, sitting on the couch, Peter stood next to the fireplace, to the right of the couch. He wore a starched white shirt, faded blue jeans, a belt with a silver buckle, and alligator cowboy boots. His unbuttoned shirt revealed a thick gold chain around his neck. The expression on his face graphically telegraphed that this living room was the last place in the world he wanted to be.

At that moment a second uniformed cop entered the room, carrying a coffee mug, followed by a middle-aged, – possibly another detective – nattily dressed in a blue blazer and gray slacks. Without uttering a word, the two men walked ceremoniously across the room and sat down on two chairs across from the couch.

The living room, actually the entire house, is decorated very Phyllis — that is, expensively, a trifle gaudy, but overall in good taste. The modern furniture, constructed mostly of glass and chrome, reflects her lively stylishness. Paul's contribution was limited to signing the checks. And there had been a lot of them. Still he never complained about Phyllis or her penchant for the expensive. After three unsuccessful marriages, Paul had found a woman who totally charmed and captivated him and loved him unconditionally.

From behind, came Detective O'Brien's voice, "Mr. Stein, we need to ask you a few questions before we head to the morgue to identify the body."

The detective's businesslike manner had a calming effect on Phyllis. She stopped sobbing and let go of me. Peter placed his arm protectively around his mother. He reseated her on the couch and, holding her hand, sat down next to her.

"Has Mrs. Martin told you what happened?" As he spoke, Detective O'Brien intently gazed at me, making certain to establish eye contact. I looked back at him, noticing that had no apparent neck.

"Not really," I replied. "She said something about Paul being killed. She was so upset, I'm not sure I understood much more, except that I needed to get over here fast." Before responding, O'Brien hesitated for a moment, either registering that information, planning his strategy, or both.

"Mr. Martin was found late this afternoon, dead in the driver's seat of his car in the parking lot of the Wal-Mart on Northern Boulevard, bullet through the back of the head. Does that surprise you?"

I swallowed hard, a bit unnerved both by the question and the detective's abrupt accusatory manner. "I'm shocked," I finally answered. "I can't imagine anybody who'd want to hurt, let alone kill, Paul."

O'Brien jotted this answer down on a small notepad. "We understand that you're his closest friend and law partner. Did you see him today?"

I paused, thinking about the question. It felt odd that he was my partner and my best friend and he was dead. It had been so routine, seeing him every day that I was having trouble remembering exactly when the last time had been. The last time. The thought hit me like a punch. "He stopped in my office at about ten this morning with a cup of coffee. We chatted about five minutes, mostly about sports. That was the last time I saw him."

"Did he mention what he was planning to do today?"

"Only that he was having lunch with a potential new client."

"Can you tell us who and where?"

Forcing myself to maintain eye contact, I told him the absolute truth. "He didn't say and I didn't ask. He just mentioned the lunch in passing."

"Mr. Stein, you can understand that we're going to have a lot of questions. I know you're very upset, losing your best friend. It's probably hard for you to process right now. We're going to want as much detail as you can remember." The gray-haired detective in the navy blue blazer was now talking. His voice was friendly. His slow cadence and overly solicitous mannerisms reminded me of Columbo, the television police detective.

"We're going downtown to have Mrs. Martin identify the body at the morgue." Detective O'Brien continued talking as he got up from his chair, moved in my direction, stopping about five feet from me. "Think about what you can tell us, about whom Mr. Martin has been seeing, anything he might have said about concerns or problems. Think about who might have a motive to kill him. We'll meet with you first thing tomorrow morning."

At this point Phyllis, who'd been listening quietly, interrupted. "No he won't." Her voice was polite but firm.

Everyone in the room stared at Phyllis. No longer the weeping helpless widow, she stood up and, with all eyes on her, assumed control of the men surrounding her. This was more like the Phyllis that I knew.

"Tomorrow morning, Steve is coming with me to make arrangements at the funeral home. I'm sure you will be sensitive to my needs.

Motive To Kill • 17

You'll have to interview him afterward. That will work for you, won't it, detective?" She smiled at Detective O'Brien.

As a professional labor negotiator, I take pride in my ability to read people. It's my livelihood, but at this moment, Phyllis's sudden transformation was confusing. And I knew her well. One minute she was the tear-stained, grieving widow, the next minute, the take-charge organizational woman who once ruled over the city's Junior League. But she was Jewish. And they're emotional people. Strange. Very strange.

The Detective, whose name I still didn't know, responded with equal politeness, bringing me back to the present. "All right ma'am. We understand. We'll work our schedule around yours." O'Brien just stared at Phyllis. I wasn't sure if he admired or resented her transformation, but he was surprised.

Now Phyllis turned her attention to me. She walked over and put her hand on my arm. "Steve, you stay right here and make phone calls while I'm downtown with the officers. Call Marti first, and let her and the girls know what happened." Marti was Paul's third wife, the mother of his three daughters. "You may also want to let Babs know. If you decide to call her, she can telephone John. But,"— she gave me a significant look —"I'll let you decide if that's necessary." Barbara, nicknamed Babs, was Paul's second wife, and John was Paul's estranged son by Babs. He lived somewhere in Chicago.

I nodded. "Is there anyone else who needs to— " I almost couldn't get the words out. This was my oldest friend. "— to know?" My mind kicked into gear as I said it. Of course there was. "I'll let people at the firm know."

Her eyes met mine. "You're right. We don't want them to read it on the front page of tomorrow's *Chronicle*." I nodded again.

Her hand had slid down my arm and now grasped my hand and squeezed so tightly I knew my fingers would be white when she let go. "Steve, I don't want to be alone tonight. I need you to spend the night in the guest bedroom. Besides, we'll be able to get an early start tomorrow on making the funeral arrangements."

I saw O'Brien raise his eyebrow. Peter spoke. "There's no need for that." I'd almost forgotten Peter was still sitting on the couch until he spoke. "I'll stay with you tonight, Mom. Matthew won't mind. Steve probably has to go home to his wife."

It struck me that he was uncomfortable, maybe even embarrassed, by his mother soliciting support from someone other than him, especially in a room full of strangers. Phyllis didn't seem to care. I knew she hadn't fully accepted that her son publicly, to use her words, "had abandoned" her grandson to live a gay lifestyle with Matthew. The only subject of contention I even remember between Phyllis and Paul, had been Phyllis's treatment of Peter. Paul had sought, I thought with some success, to reconcile his wife and stepson. I guess things were still not perfect.

"That won't be necessary dear. Steve is fully available. He and Maxine are separated. But you can come with me to the morgue. I don't want to do that alone."

Detective O'Brien glanced at his partner and nodded ever so slightly. He pulled out his notepad and jotted something down and then smiled at me.

My face reddened. My best friend was dead and now the investigators were thinking I was shacking up with the widow. But what to do? I looked over at Peter who had no more choice than I did. Phyllis was a force of nature. He nodded; just as I had. "Of course."

Without waiting to hear our replies, Phyllis turned to the detectives. "You'll drive Peter and me in one of your cars and then bring us back here. I don't want to drive into the city at this hour in Peter's convertible."

The two uniforms looked at each other strangely. Phyllis wasn't asking. The gray-haired detective winked at O'Brien and asked with concern, "Mrs. Martin, should we arrange to have sandwiches served at the morgue just in case you're hungry?" He spoke softly without a trace of sarcasm.

"No. That won't be necessary. I couldn't eat at a time like this." The two detectives looked at each other. I couldn't think of anything to say.

Phyllis, as always, was firmly in control. We all obeyed. Within five minutes, the uniforms had departed and the detectives, with Phyllis and Peter in tow, left for the morgue to officially identify Paul's body. I remained alone in the kitchen with Phyllis's address book, a mug of coffee, and my memories.

O nce safely a member of the Army Reserve, a dark storm cloud no longer shadowed me. Although the monthly training in Concord was inconvenient and I faced six months of future active military duty, and a total six-year commitment, I had avoided a fully government-financed and directed sojourn in Vietnam. First-year life at Harvard Law School passed in a blur of excitement. As Paul and I studied and partied together, our friendship blossomed. The only hiccup occurred in the last week of April, when we both received orders to report to basic training to begin our active duty. The reporting dates conflicted with the beginning of final exams, placing our entire first year of law school in jeopardy.

We drank heavily that night at a pub on Massachusetts Avenue. Fortified with courage, supplied by a half dozen boilermakers, we decided to pay a visit the next day to the dean of the law school to explain our problem. We had it all figured out. When he learned we would miss exams as the result of military service, he would undoubtedly excuse us from taking the tests, especially when we explained we would ace them anyway. In retrospect, it's amazing how alcohol can addle two supposedly intelligent brains.

Actually, it wasn't until noon that we had sufficiently recovered from our hangovers to walk the hundred yards separating our dorm from the dean's office in Langdell Hall, the ancient building in the

Law School quad that housed the Law School Library, most of the professors' offices and several classrooms. Sometimes fools succeed by venturing where wise men never would tread. This was clearly the case. After listening to our plea, the dean's secretary ushered us into his cavernous office. Wearing a tailored charcoal gray pinstripe suit, Dean Bok, a handsome man with not a strand of his wavy brown hair out of place, sat facing us in a large, brown leather desk chair. The impeccably furnished office was decorated with pictures of the dean with various politicians and dignitaries. I noticed on a wooden shelf immediately behind the enormous mahogany desk a picture of him playing touch football with both John F. Kennedy and Bobby Kennedy.

"Well gentlemen, what can I do for you?"

My mind went blank. I was tongue-tied. Paul stepped into the breach without missing a beat.

"My name is Paul Martin and this is Steve Stein. We're 1Ls and, Sir, we have a problem."

He spoke with confidence as if he knew that the Dean of the Harvard Law School would obviously help us if only he understood the particulars of our distress, which he was about to explain.

"We joined the Army Reserve so as not to interfere with our law school education. We've been studying so hard and now just before our final examinations, we've received orders to report to basic training the last week of April." The words were flowing as Paul made his final impassioned plea. "And, so you see Dean, as we go off to do service for our country, we need to be excused from final examinations. It is the right thing to do!"

The dean flashed a smile. He seemed genuinely amused.

"Son, this is Harvard Law School. No one, not Justice Louis Brandeis, not Justice Felix Frankfurter, and certainly not Paul Martin is excused from final examinations. But you and Mr. Stein do have a real problem. I can see that. The question is, 'What to do?'." For a fleeting second, I thought I saw him wink at Paul. Still looking at Paul, he pressed the intercom that connected his office with that of his secretary.

"Betty, get General Lodge at the Pentagon. His phone number is in my rolodex." He picked up a pen and smiled at us.

"All right, —let's see what we can do to fix your problem."

Time stood still. The dean was engaged in paperwork. A beaming, serenely confident Paul silently surveyed the photographs and memorabilia that filled the office. Several times, he nudged me in the ribs to point out some object. I shook my head signaling I wanted to be left alone, and gazed at my fingernails. To Paul, we were part of a great adventure that was bound for success. I, on the other hand, saw the glass as half empty and half expected that we would be ordered to Vietnam for our impertinence.

Not even two minutes later, we heard Betty's voice telling the dean that General Lodge was on line one.

"Hello General, Derek Bok here."

"Derek, it's been a while. I don't think I've seen you since the funeral."

"General, two of my boys here have a little problem and we need your help. They've received orders to report to active duty the last week of April. April just doesn't work. It would interfere with their first-year examinations and could ruin their legal careers. We can't let that happen."

General Lodge, agreed with the dean, requested our social security numbers, and promised that new orders would be issued, ones that would not interfere with examinations.

From that point on, I always considered Paul's plea to the dean as the harbinger of his future success as a trial lawyer.

Classes finished, exams were completed, and Paul and I reported in July to basic training. Although a sad sack soldier, I somehow survived the experience as did Paul. By January 1970, we were back in Cambridge hunting for work since we couldn't re-enter law school until the fall.

I did ace the first-year exams and was invited to join the *Harvard Law Review*, which after graduation, translates into a gold-plated employment invitation to any law firm in the country. On the basis of that credential, a single phone call resulted in an offer of an eight-month internship at the most prestigious – and possibly the stuffiest – law firm in Boston. The offer was extended over what was also the stuffiest lunch of my life. Paul had not done as well grade-wise, but, after a morning of telephoning law firms, the cachet of Harvard Law School worked its magic. He received a job offer from an aggressive group of plaintiff personal injury lawyers, a firm my new employers derided as ambulance chasers — albeit very rich, successful ambulance chasers. And, Paul didn't have to go to lunch.

Flush with our newly acquired wealth and credit, we bought wheels. An eight-year-old beige Plymouth for me and a ten-year-old green Volkswagen Bug for Paul. We moved into a two-bedroom apartment on Beech Street behind Porter Square in Somerville, Massachusetts. Every night, the winter and spring that followed, was party night. Paul managed to arrange a never-ending supply of good looking co-eds from Boston's several dozen colleges. Women were always at our apartment, and while Paul always did better, I didn't exactly do badly. Living with Paul had its benefits.

That was the spring of the 1970 American invasion of Cambodia, demonstrations on college campuses throughout America, and the massive anti-war March on Washington. That was also the spring that, responding to campus unrest, Harvard Law School cancelled final examinations and instead allowed take-home exams over the summer. And, it was the spring that irrevocably changed Paul's life and, ultimately, may have caused his death. His first forays into gambling and marriage would become lifelong addictions.

Until then, Paul never gambled more than a few dollars on parlay cards during the football season. He refused to play poker with our classmates, something I excelled at and enjoyed.

Women. Paul always loved women, but never for more than a

month at a time. Serious relationships, he used to say, were for suckers. The word marriage was taboo.

That spring changed everything. Sweeney and Cohen, the personal injury or P. I. firm where Paul was interning, won a $10 million jury verdict for an injured railroad worker who'd lost both his legs because of a bug bite. The company negligently allowed a pond in one of its railroad yards to become infested with mosquitoes resulting in the bug bite. Having lost the jury verdict, the railroad settled with Sweeney and Cohen that summer for $7.5 million. With his firm's one-third take in hand, Martin Sweeney gave Paul a five thousand dollar bonus, a pre-paid two-week stay at the Riviera Hotel & Casino in Las Vegas, Nevada, and a round-trip airline ticket as "thanks" for his help in winning the case.

In August, I reported to the *Harvard Law Review* to spend sixteen-hour days working on the annual edition of the Supreme Court's recent term. I was convinced my sacrifice would contribute to future jurisprudence. At the same time, Paul arrived at Boston Logan International Airport to catch a flight to Vegas. In retrospect, my August impacted nothing other than a developing disillusion with the *Law Review*; Paul's sojourn, on the other hand, had long-lasting consequences.

I'll always remember the early Sunday morning call that followed, and the excitement and pure joy in Paul's voice. Paul's speech was manic; he spoke with machine-gun-like speed. "Steve. You won't believe what's been happening. I can hardly believe it myself. I won. I'm married. I'm one lucky son-of-a-bitch. It's all so amazing."

I was confused. He didn't sound drunk. "Married? What are you talking about? Won? What did you win?"

I heard him take a deep breath. "Do you remember Jane Berke, the cheerleader I dated in high school?"

Yeah, you began dating her in senior year when you dumped Ellen. I still owe you for that one."

"Well, I met her at this club in Vegas where she was performing. She's a . . . a showgirl. She's drop-dead gorgeous. And she's my good luck charm. We hooked up and she was by my side the whole time, blowing on the dice. We won! It was unbelievable."

He paused to take another breath. I used the pause. "Won what? You're not making much sense."

"Let me try and start from the beginning."

It didn't take long to piece together what had happened. Paul met Jane at a club where she worked as a stripper. They hooked up after the show and she immediately moved into Paul's hotel room. Jane introduced Paul to the game of craps. When they weren't drinking or fucking, they played craps at Jane's favorite hangouts on the strip using Paul's bonus as their stake. At some point, Paul threw or made his points for twenty minutes straight. When the winning streak ended and he finally crapped out, Paul's bankroll exceeded fifty thousand dollars. On this high, Paul and Jane left the craps table, and returned to the hotel room. After a night of drinking, sex, and smoking pot, just to make the night, or more accurately by then the early morning, complete, they married at an all-night chapel. Now they were calling me with an assignment.

"Jane and I need your help."

"You seem to have done quite nicely by yourselves." I knew I sounded petulant. I wasn't sure why, but I felt betrayed and hurt.

"Come on, Steve. It's going to be great: the three of us. We're all three going to be best buddies." As usual, Paul spoke with absolute certainty.

"What do you want?" I never was able to stay peeved at Paul for long.

"We'll be back in Cambridge in three days. We need you to rent us an apartment and buy us a bed. Jane will do the rest of the decorating. And, I promise we'll celebrate at Locke-Ober's."

The apartment I found was on Massachusetts Avenue, two blocks from the school. The queen-sized marital bed, I bought at the Sears store in Porter Square, was delivered in time to be waiting for the newlyweds on their arrival.

Not surprisingly, the marriage failed.

A tall, willowy blonde with long legs and a curvaceous body, Jane magnificently filled out a sweater. When she sauntered around campus, heads invariably turned. But marriage to a Harvard Law School student stifled her. She found Cambridge life boring and considered Paul's classmates immature. Her reaction was a defense mechanism. With only a high school diploma on her résumé, she felt inferior to the high-achieving intellectuals surrounding her, unaware that they, in turn, viewed her as an unattainable goddess.

As Paul had prophesized, Jane and I developed a friendship. She remembered me as a high school friend of Paul's and felt comfortable around me. I became the confidant with whom she shared her side of the continual quarrels with Paul. For his part, Paul did try. First, at Christmas, and then at the end of our second year of law school, he took Jane for two-week vacations to Vegas to visit her friends and gamble. Looking back, Jane was Paul's good luck charm. With her at his side, he invariably walked away a winner as he diversified his gambling from craps to betting on professional sports and horse racing. Whether in Vegas or with his bookie from South Boston, Paul regularly won large sums of money. And the more he won, the more he gambled.

During Christmas vacation of our third year at law school, Paul and Jane split up in Vegas. Paul's bankroll at the time stood at seventy-five thousand dollars. He wrote Jane a check for sixty thousand dollars and they divorced, but as friends. For years, regardless of his marital status, Paul and I made an annual trip to Las Vegas, the first week of January, to commemorate his first attempt at matrimony. He lost sizeable sums of money, but always looked up Jane. But, "What happens in Vegas stays in Vegas," and it always did.

Sitting at the kitchen table clutching a mug of coffee and daydreaming about the past, I procrastinated, not wanting to notify former wives and friends that Paul was dead. Avoidance is my personal form of denial. By not telling anyone Paul was dead, I was forestalling coming to grips with the horrible truth. But I had to begin calling because I couldn't take the chance that Marti, the girls, or Paul's closest friends would learn of his murder on the 11 o'clock news. I dreaded having to tell Marti and I dreaded Babs.

After law school, Paul and I returned home to join the city's largest law firm, Hays, Harris and Dodge, spurning offers in New York City and Washington D.C. He became a litigator while I became a labor lawyer, a strange choice for a *Harvard Law Review* alumnus. Enough entanglement with the esoterica of law, I wanted to bring practical solutions to the everyday problems of the workplace.

With his good looks and natural charm, Paul was considered one of the city's most eligible bachelors. *The Chronicle*'s gossip column repeatedly connected him with the daughters of the city's moneyed elite. He was a regular at the city's trendy clubs. I was tagging along with him at one of those nightspots, Redux, when I first met Maxine, my now soon-to-be ex. Our introduction was auspicious. She spilled a Bloody Mary over my recently purchased Armani sport jacket.

"I'm so sorry. Let me treat the jacket with club soda before it permanently spots." I gazed at the spoiler of my prized possession. She was a busty twenty-something with red hair and freckles, barely over five feet tall.

The next thing I knew, my tormentor had a glass of club soda and a napkin in hand.

"That won't be necessary. I think you've helped enough."

"No, no. I want to help."

"You klutz," I screamed as she spilled the glass of club soda all over the crotch of my slacks.

"Oh, my God! I'm so sorry."

That was my introduction to Maxine Sachs, an OB/GYN resident at Mt. Sinai Hospital. Not a conventional beauty, she never wore makeup – lipstick, rarely. But her green eyes sparkled, especially when she laughed. And she laughed a lot at my jokes, at least in the beginning. Paul was the best man.

Less than a year after Maxine and I tied the marital knot, Paul met his second wife while sick in bed with the flu. He was thirty years old and the rising star in a nationally recognized litigation department. He enjoyed playing the field, bedding a different beauty every weekend.

But it was the flu that brought him to his knees. Or more accurately, to his bed, from where he first glimpsed Barbara "Babs" Brown on Channel 7, co-hosting the *Coffee Klatch*, one of those chatty morning shows targeting housewives.

"Stein. I found her. She's beautiful, intelligent and funny."

"Paul, what in the world are you talking about? I think maybe you got a problem. It's too early in the morning to be hammered."

"I'm in bed with the flu. I am on nothing more powerful than Robitussin. I've been watching this program on Channel 7. There's this woman on the show, Babs Brown. I tell you, I've fallen in love with her. She's gonna be the next Mrs. Martin."

I didn't even think that dignified a "You're nuts" before I hung up.

Nuts or not, Paul managed to arrange a date with Babs. Four years

Paul's senior, Babs was nearly six feet tall, had a model's body, very thin with long legs, and blonde hair. *Coffee Klatch* was local daytime television, but Babs saw herself as a star, demanding all the prerogatives of celebrity including the right to throw tantrums. Recognition of her star status was important. Waiting to be seated at a restaurant was a totally unacceptable experience, as several maitre d's chastened by Babs can attest. She firmly believed that wardrobe makes the person and she dressed accordingly. She wore haute couture exclusively—Dior, Chanel, Hermès.

Paul and Babs became an exclusive pair, attending benefit after benefit, vacationing in the Caribbean, and even attending fashion week in Paris. Maxine accepted Paul as my best friend; Babs left Maxine cold. While I tolerated Babs, it would have been fair to say then, and remains fair to say now, that she was my least favorite of Paul's wives.

In a single two-week period, Paul turned thirty-two, was elected a partner at the firm, and married Babs. The wedding had several firsts. It was the first wedding where I was best man as I was to be at all of Paul's subsequent marriages. It was also the first and only one that Maxine attended. The couple honeymooned in Hawaii, then returned and began house hunting, finally purchasing a five-bedroom colonial on a five-acre lot in Sycamore Heights, the city's most exclusive suburb.

I didn't know exactly how much Babs and Paul were earning, but it was clear to Maxine and me that the couple was living beyond their means. Paul seemed to be under intense pressure to make more money. With increased regularity, he placed large wagers on sporting events, football, baseball, and basketball, depending on the season. But, without Jane at his side, Paul's luck soured and he lost far more often then he won.

Whatever financial pressures Paul was feeling was lost on Babs. If anything, her thirst for expensive baubles increased, literally. She decided at one point to start her own line of jewelry and spent nearly one hundred thousand dollars during one trip to New York buying antique jade and colored gemstones. She sold half a dozen pieces before tiring of the venture.

Given the tension in the marriage, I was surprised when I learned

Babs was pregnant. Paul confided the pregnancy was planned. Babs's biological clock was running out and she wanted a child. I guess Paul just never learned to say, "No," to Babs. Babs remained on the *Coffee Klatch* until two weeks before John's birth, sharing every aspect of her pregnancy with her television audience. Every detail of Babs's pregnancy was followed by housewives throughout the city. Every daytime viewer had an opinion on whether Babs should use an epidural, Lamaze, Bradley, or a combination. Breast or bottle became a burning question in salons throughout the metro area. You might have thought Paul would have been amused when he learned that a poll organized by the firm's secretaries supported breastfeeding 2 to 1, maybe try to place a bet. Instead, he was outraged. There was nothing about Babs anymore that he found humorous.

By the time John was born, Paul and Babs spent little time together. Their marriage and finances were on terminal life support. Paul immersed himself in work, seldom coming home until midnight, often later. John's birth didn't slow the downward spiral of the relationship; indeed every aspect of the birth became a source of aggravation to Paul. The night that John was born, I went to see Paul at his home. I let myself in the side door. Paul was sitting alone in the kitchen, drinking a bottle of Miller Lite. I walked in to join him.

"Mazel tov!"

"That hypocritical bitch." He popped the top on a second beer with an economical motion. I could tell by how carefully measured his movements were that he was furious. "She hates pain – couldn't get that epidural needle in fast enough. Then to suck up to her audience, Channel 7 issues a press release describing her delivery by natural childbirth."

"Who gives a damn?" I couldn't figure out why it mattered to him. After all, Babs and hypocrisy were hardly recent acquaintances, and he hadn't cared before. "You have a son. Enjoy."

"That bitch has drained every last ounce of pleasure out of the experience. God, I hate her."

Paul's voice was barely above a whisper. Color drained from his face; his angry expression was replaced by a sad look of resignation. I didn't fully empathize with Paul at the time, as I certainly would now. Maxine was already spending inordinate time at the hospital and her practice. I thought it was a phase that would pass. It never did.

Paul and Babs were divorced within the year. It was not divorce "lite." They fought over everything—money, custody, even furniture. The litigation lasted two years, and even after the final divorce decree, endless issues arose as Babs challenged Paul's visitation rights and his payment of child support.

And the relationship didn't improve with Babs's remarriage to Ken Simon. Ken was the beneficiary of a substantial trust fund set up by his grandfather, a shipping magnate, and had no need for a day job. His full-time occupation became satisfying Babs's every whim.

Not surprisingly, Babs did everything possible to estrange John from his father, portraying Paul as uncaring. If Paul arranged to pick John up at 2 p.m., for a Sunday afternoon movie, she would tell John his dad was arriving at noon. By the time Paul arrived, at best John was disappointed, but more often had been sent by Babs to play with friends, believing his father once more forgot about him. Confronted, Babs always claimed a misunderstanding, a failure to communicate. I remember one summer John was to spend a whole month with his father. In anticipation, Paul rented a fishing cabin in Ontario. Babs, in yet another "misunderstanding," enrolled John for the same month in an enrichment program at M.I.T. for twelve-year-olds interested in science. The father-son fishing vacation never materialized. Paul could never win. By the time John left for college, in California, he wanted no further contact with his father.

6

Marti's telephone number was listed in the phonebook Phyllis had provided me. She was still married to her soul mate, Dr. Thomas Winthrop Lowell, the cardiologist with three kids who had been the cause of Marti divorcing Paul. I felt queasy. I took a deep breath and was about to dial. Suddenly I found myself dialing Babs instead. I was shocked at myself since I'd been toying with not calling her. The passing years hadn't improved either her relationship with Paul or her disposition. But, John, Paul's son, needed to learn of his father's death, even if they were estranged, and I didn't know how to contact him except through her. I knew he lived in Chicago but didn't know what he was doing there.

"I always figured his whoring and gambling would catch up with the son of a bitch one of these days," she said, true to form.

Hearing Babs's diatribe unlocked something in me other than the overwhelming grief: it was anger.

"Paul was my best friend, so I strongly suggest you shut the fuck up. I only called so you'd be able to tell John. I consider my duty done."

I was about to hang up. Hard. But before I could, Babs uttered the two words I never thought would pass through her lips, "I'm sorry." I was busy trying not to drop the phone in my shock when she went on, "I really am. My comment was totally inappropriate and disrespectful. I apologize. I'm so used to being negative about Paul, I don't know when to keep my mouth shut."

"Apology accepted," I lied. "I'm sure if you or John are interested, the details of the funeral will be in the paper, or you can call my secretary."

"Would you consider calling John if I give you his phone number in Chicago?" Babs asked. "John and Paul had been in touch lately. Since John knows how I feel about Paul, he's never told me the details, but I believe they worked out their differences. Hearing that his father died from me wouldn't be constructive; it would be much better for him to hear that news from you."

I didn't know anything about a rapprochement between father and son. For a moment, I felt a surge of anger followed by disappointment and then hurt. How could Paul have kept a secret from me, his best friend?

Flabbergasted by the news of Paul and John's renewed relationship and Babs's civility, I didn't know how to respond. Calling John after not seeing him for more than ten years was not a task I particularly wanted to assume.

"Please, please," she implored. "Do it for Paul."

I never have been good at saying "No," especially when friendship is involved. Reluctantly, I agreed to call John.

Shocked to learn of his father's death, John confirmed that he'd been in communication with Paul.

"About six months ago, Dad called totally out of the blue," he explained. "He told me his single greatest regret in life was being separated from me. He said there was more to what had happened than I knew, another side to everything. He asked if he could fly to Chicago and take me to dinner. I refused at first. He hadn't been with me as a kid when I'd needed him, and I sure didn't need him now. But Dad was persistent and convincing. After his third call, I agreed to meet."

"Dad was in a difficult position. He knew Mom had caused much of the problem between us, but sensed that bad-mouthing her would only turn me off. I then experienced firsthand why Dad was such an effective trial lawyer. He won me over the same way he always won over a jury. I saw a side of him that I'd never appreciated. Anyway, after that first meeting, we started talking and he took three trips to Chicago to visit me. I just can't believe it. Now that we were finally beginning to know each other, he's suddenly gone. Life just isn't fair."

At this point, John lost his composure.

"God it hurts. I grew up believing Dad had abandoned me, that I didn't have a father. Now I've lost him." His voice cracked. "It makes me want to hate him all over again. Why did he wait so long?" His hurt sounded real.

"Your dad was a great guy," I assured him. John was right: it wasn't fair after finally rediscovering his father to lose him so quickly.

"You never knew it, John, but you were important to him. He always wanted to connect with you. His difficulties with your mother made that impossible."

As best I could tell over the telephone, my words seemed to comfort John. Regaining his composure, he announced with surprising assurance in his voice, "Dad had a premonition something bad might happen."

"What do you mean by premonition?" This was strange. Paul hadn't exactly been a premonition kind of guy.

"I last saw Dad three weeks ago in Chicago," John explained. "He had a day meeting and arranged to stay overnight so we could have dinner. We were kicking around the idea of going to Europe together on vacation. Then, all of a sudden, he gets agitated, said he had major issues involving work to resolve and was worried about making plans and then not being around to see them through. He didn't want to disappoint me again. I distinctly remember him using that phrase 'not being around.' He promised I'd be taken care of if anything should happen to him."

I was certain I heard a tremor in John's voice; he was close to breaking down.

"Dad insisted if anything happened, he was ready. He had a large life insurance policy to provide for his wife and three daughters. He said he now realized how this division was wrong and hurtful. He wanted all his children to share equally in his insurance trust. I thanked him and told him how much what he was saying meant to me, but having just found him, I had no intention of letting him leave me. I made a joke about it."

At this point, John lost it and began sobbing.

"He told me. . . . he told me that . . . that you can't count on anything but . . . but death and taxes, and that he had paid his taxes."

I didn't know what to say. I knew Paul had a large life insurance policy, but he hadn't mentioned changing the beneficiaries. The reference to issues at work was also puzzling because despite being best friends and colleagues—and in fact, sitting together through weekly partners' lunches—Paul had never mentioned having any particular problems or concerns.

"Do you have any idea what your dad meant when he said he had 'major issues involving work'?" Whatever they might have been, it didn't seem possible that any aspect of a big law firm practice could result in murder. I mean, we were about as far removed from the world of criminal law practice as you could get. Our cases, in one way or another, almost always boiled down to money. Although, come to think of it, money is as good a motive for murder as any.

"He never discussed his cases in much detail. It was a lawyer-client privilege thing with him. That night I think he mentioned he was working on a white-collar crime matter involving a bank. I don't remember him saying much more than that."

John's words once again flowed smoothly and coherently.

It was almost ten o'clock. I hadn't called Marti and still had other calls to make, but I felt bad about cutting John off. "Let me give you my home and work numbers," I offered. "You can call and we'll talk in more detail about your dad whenever you want. He was a wonderful man."

"I'm coming to the funeral," John announced. "When will it be?"

"I'm not sure yet. Tomorrow morning I'm going with Phyllis to make the arrangements. I promise I'll call to let you know the details."

Hanging up, I had a warm feeling. Paul would have been pleased to hear John's words and know his son would attend his funeral. And, what was a real first, for a fleeting moment at least, I felt positively toward Babs who, after all, had been the one who insisted I call John.

After the bitter divorce, and in the face of Babs's continued efforts to keep him away from their son, Paul threw himself into work with a fervor not previously seen. And, apparently, much of the work was with Marti Leonard, a second-year associate who was assigned to work with Paul on a major tobacco case.

To me, she was just another hardworking associate, certainly an attractive one, although, not the type of woman Paul usually found attractive. Sporting short brown hair and piercing blue eyes, Marti seldom wore makeup. Most noticeable about her appearance was a perpetual smile. She was exactly what she looked like: a sweet girl from Wisconsin, and an exceptionally smart one. Her father owned a small town hardware store whose customers were almost exclusively farmers.

Paul's work and dedication paid off, resulting in a spectacular victory in one of the earlier tobacco cases. And with this win came more than the usual fifteen minutes of fame. *The New York Times* profiled Paul; next, he was the subject of a flattering *Sixty Minutes* television news profile. More importantly, for his career, he was placed on that short list of Super Litigators from which general counsels of Fortune 500 companies select their lawyers.

Maxine, meanwhile, continued to spend more time at the hospital with her patients than with me. As a couple, we did little with Paul. But we were together when Paul announced he was giving marriage a third try.

We had invited Paul to Morton's, one of the city's best steakhouses, to celebrate his victory in the tobacco trial. We even sprung for a bottle of Chateau Lafite Rothschild. Lawyer after lawyer came to our table to pay homage. He loved the adulation. As we sat sipping wine, Paul said, "I think this case was a watershed event. My life is finally beginning to turn around."

"Hey, it's not every lawyer who gets profiled in *The New York Times*, picture and everything. You're big time now."

"I'll bet when you get to the Big Apple, you'll have to fight to keep the women off of you," added Maxine. "You looked like a movie star in the newspaper."

Paul smiled. "That's all exciting. But I think something even more exciting is going to happen."

"Let me guess. You're leaving the firm to become general counsel of one of the big tobacco companies" I suggested only half-jokingly.

"No," he said swirling the wine in his glass, while Maxine kicked my leg, signaling me to hush. "But you can take your tux out of the mothballs."

To say this comment caught me by surprise would be an understatement.

To my knowledge, he wasn't even dating. He'd never even hinted there was a woman in his life. Admittedly, I'd seen little of Paul for the last three months. He'd been out of town. Was he serious? I responded with sarcasm which I often do when I don't know quite what to say.

"Here I thought you sold your tux after all those benefits you attended with Babs. Or, did she get the tuxedo as part of the divorce settlement?" I looked at Paul to see if my teasing was getting the desired rise out of him.

He ignored my feeble attempt at humor. "No, I'm serious. I'm getting married."

"What are you talking about?" It seemed inconceivable that Paul would be considering marriage.

"I'm getting married in three months and I'll be in need of your services as best man unless, or course, your hourly rate has become too high." He smiled.

"You're shitting me." Despite my polysyllabic Ivy League vocabulary, that was all I could think to say. Oh, and one more thing: "To whom?"

"Marti Leonard. We're getting married at Marti's father house in Wisconsin. I'll expect both of you to be there."

Maxine leaned over and kissed Paul on the cheek. I just stared.

He wasn't, as it turned out, shitting me. Three months later, Paul and Marti were married in a small town about one hundred miles north of Madison.

And, once again, I served as best man.

A Methodist minister conducted the ceremony and a simple reception followed in the backyard of Marti's childhood home. Marti was breathtaking, sparkling in her unfussy way; her happiness was contagious to all around her – except her father. Perhaps, like all fathers of the bride, he was unhappy about losing a daughter, but something more was involved.

Bill Leonard was unsure whether Paul, ten years his daughter's senior and divorced with a child, was worthy of his daughter. Bill bluntly shared these sentiments with me shortly after the wedding ceremony, when I found myself alone with him waiting to use the bathroom by the family kitchen.

"Tell me, Best Man, what kind of husband will your friend be to my daughter? He doesn't seem to have much of a track record." I was uneasy. This was not a conversation I wanted to pursue.

"I think they're made for each other. They really are in love," I finally sputtered.

"Well, 'Best Man,' I'm real concerned." He lowered his voice. "My sources tell me he has a real hard time keeping his dick in his pants."

I was at a loss for words. This description, albeit true, was coming no less from the father of the bride about my best friend. I felt like someone had punched me in the solar plexus.

Now his voice was so low I had to strain to hear. "'Best man,' make sure your friend knows that if he ever does anything to hurt my little girl, I'll be over there with my shotgun and hunting knife. Cutting off his dick will be the least of his worries. You be sure to tell your friend that for me, 'Best Man'." Then he winked at me and stepped back. "Hope you enjoy the reception, Mr. Stein," he said over his shoulder as he headed back to join the guests. "And be sure to try my wife's Bundt cake. It's the best in the county."

Despite Mr. Leonard's concerns, a subject I never repeated to anyone, Paul's luck in marriage appeared to finally have turned the corner. Although stretched financially, Paul purchased another large suburban home. Within seven years, three daughters, Sara, Jennifer, and Lisa, were born and filled that house . Maxine delivered them all. And, along the way, Maxine and Marti became friends. Marti and her growing brood would routinely meet Maxine for lunch, at the group's favorite restaurant across from the hospital.

Paul's legal career blossomed. After the tobacco case victory, Paul's litigating skills were in high demand. He accepted only high-profile cases. He represented clients willing to pay a hefty premium for his services. His salary soared to seven figures. Meanwhile, the disruption of her first two maternity leaves made it difficult for Marti's legal career to advance. Secure in the knowledge that the family did not need her second income, when she became pregnant the third time, Marti left the firm permanently to be a stay-at-home mom.

One year after Lisa's birth, Maxine reported that Marti had said she was tiring of "scintillating high-level discussions concerning the pressing issues of the day" with her three young daughters. Shortly after, Marti hired a nanny and returned to work as associate general counsel of the Mt. Sinai Medical System, one of the city's two surviving hospital systems—a job Maxine helped her to find.

Two potential dangers loomed on the horizon. Maxine shared that

Marti was concerned with Paul's compulsive gambling. He'd cut back some, but I knew during the football season he was betting several thousand dollars each week with his bookie. When I raised the issue, Paul brushed me off or countered with a joke. He was clear: the subject was off limits for discussion. But I also had heard enough from the guys at McGinty's Pub to be alarmed. The tip of the iceberg was visible but I wasn't sure what was below water out of view.

Also, given the nature of his flourishing practice, Paul was traveling with increased frequency. Knowing Paul as I did, I hoped with little optimism that he wasn't doing anything foolish on those business trips that might invoke the wrath of his father-in-law. I knew that on our annual Las Vegas trips, he continued to spend at least one night with Jane. Since discussion of matrimonial fidelity was also taboo, ignorance and silence, on my part, were best practices.

To my surprise, and I'm certain much to the chagrin of old Mr. Leonard, the marriage didn't fail because of any dalliance on Paul's part. It was ultimately Marti who devastated Paul when she confessed to falling in love with a Mt. Sinai doctor, a cardiologist.

We were sitting in The Back Room when, when after two martinis, Paul said, "I can't believe it. It's happened again." The look on his face told me something had gone wrong, very wrong. But I never thought of the marriage.

"You've been gambling again?" I knew it. "How much did you lose?"

"No, it's not that." He sighed and took a swallow from the fresh martini that had materialized on the table. "Marti is leaving me."

He said nothing more. His lower lip quivered. I waited. I took a sip from my vodka and cranberry and busied myself, stirring the ice cubes and squeezing the lime. Paul remained eerily silent.

I looked at Paul. He eyes swelled with tears. The silence became too much for me. "Do you want to tell me what happened?"

That question opened the floodgates.

"Last night, after the girls were in bed, we were sitting and watching television in the family room. It was a rerun of *Two and a Half Men*.

We're sitting on the couch watching, her feet on my lap, when she just told me: she wants a divorce. Apparently she met this doctor at the hospital and he's her soul mate. She says it isn't my fault, that she still cares for me, and I'm a good father. I'm just not her soul mate. What the fuck is a soul mate?"

The news was totally unexpected. I was stunned. I just stared at him, my heart pounding. "What the fuck is a soul mate?" he muttered to himself over and over.

How do you answer a question like that? Probably wasn't even meant as a question. Desperately I tried to think of something comforting to say. I could think of nothing. Everything seemed so trite.

"Who's the doctor?" I finally stammered. No answer. "Do you know the name of the doctor?" God that was lame, I thought. Why had I repeated the question?

"Dr. Lowell. Dr. Thomas Winthrop Lowell. He's a cardiologist. He has three kids, too. He's going to divorce his wife. And, he's her soul mate, her fucking goddamn soul mate." With that, Paul chugged down the rest of his martini and stared off into space, repeatedly mumbling, "Soul mate, fucking goddamn soul mate."

In the days and weeks that followed, Paul's interest in his work declined – alarmingly so. He moved out of the house and spent most evenings, and some afternoons, drinking at McGinty's. His gambling escalated.

For her part, Marti, whether motivated by guilt or a genuine concern for Paul's well-being, proved most un-Babs-like. She insisted they share joint custody of the girls, constantly assuring Paul he was important to the girls and she expected his continued participation in every aspect of their lives. She telephoned him religiously about school functions or extracurricular activities he might like to attend. Financially, she asked for nothing more than generous child support. But none of Marti's overtures dispelled Paul's gloom. Each phone call from Marti was another dagger in his heart. He was no longer the Paul I'd known for years. Quite frankly, I was worried about my best friend.

"**L**owell residence. This is Lisa."

"Hey Lisa, this is Steve Stein. Is your mom home?"

"Yeah, she's upstairs. I'll get her."

After a minute, Marti picked up the phone. "Steve, what's up? Haven't heard from you for the longest time. And now? Why so late on a Friday night?"

I took a deep breath and began talking. "Marti, I don't know how to say this. Paul's dead. He was killed. His body was found early this evening."

Absolute silence. Marti didn't cry; she didn't ask questions; she didn't say anything. There was total, excruciating silence.

After what seemed like an eternity, but was probably not more than ten seconds, I broke the silence. "I'm sorry, Marti, to have to tell you this. Are you all right?"

"Steve, this is terrible. I don't know how I'm going to tell the girls. What happened? Was it a robbery? My God, I talked to him Wednesday evening. Paul, dead, I can't believe it. Where are you?" Once she started talking, the thoughts and questions poured out intermingling with each other in no particular order.

"I'm at Paul and Phyllis's house. Phyllis called about two hours ago, to tell me what happened. The police were with her. She asked me to come over."

"Is there anything else you can tell me? Was it his gambling?" Marti asked question after question without waiting for answers. She spoke rapidly, barely pausing to breathe.

"I cared for him. I really did. The girls worship him. He was coaching Lisa's softball team. What are we going to do without him?"

The telephone conversation was becoming as emotional as I feared. "Tomorrow I'm helping Phyllis with funeral arrangements." I told her. "I'll call you in the afternoon." I wanted to end the conversation, but the questioning continued.

"Do the police know what happened? What have they told you?"

"At this point, they don't know much, or at least aren't saying."

"Oh God! What about Phyllis? How's she doing?"

"It's hard to say. I only saw her briefly before she and Peter left with the police to identify Paul's body at the morgue. I promised to spend the night here so she won't be alone."

"What am I going to tell the girls?"

I had no answer. There can't be a good way to tell three doting girls their father is dead.

Less than an hour remained before the local nightly news would broadcast the story of Paul's murder and I still hadn't called a single law partner. But those calls would have to wait. Jane, Paul's first wife, needed to hear the news directly from me. Although a brief marriage, unknown to anyone but me, Jane remained a close friend to Paul; actually more than a friend. I knew Paul would want me to call her.

Not surprisingly, as it was early still in Las Vegas, voicemail picked up. I left a brief message describing what little I knew about Paul's death together with the phone number at my apartment and at work.

I turned my attention to Paul's friends at the firm. Explaining my urgent need to make multiple calls in a short period of time, I kept each conversation mercifully short, explaining Paul had been murdered, but refusing the inevitable invitation to speculate as to who or why. My fourth phone call was to Louis Callahan, a business lawyer who puts together some of the biggest business deals in the city. We'd joined the firm in the same associate class and remained friendly, eating lunch together or seeing each other at The Back Room several times a month.

"Have you told Blackjack yet?" Lou asked.

John "Blackjack" Townsend is the executive partner of the firm. To label him a tyrant would be an understatement. While the firm has, or at least pays lip service to having, a managing committee, Blackjack, and Blackjack alone, runs the show. A partner, no matter how senior or influential, who crosses Blackjack, does so at his or her own peril. The stories of Blackjack's ruthlessness are legendary. A managing partner who once voted against him on a minor issue found his pay cut by fifty thousand dollars the next year.

"No, I didn't think of it." I immediately realized this could be a devastating and financially costly blunder.

"He'll rip you a new a-hole if he hears it from someone else," Lou said bluntly. "If I were you, I'd hang up right now, contact Blackjack, and develop a convenient case of amnesia about any earlier calls." Without further comment or ceremony and in a show of sincere concern and camaraderie that only a partner at our firm would appreciate, Lou abruptly hung up.

One major problem remained: Blackjack's home telephone number. It certainly wouldn't be listed in the White Pages. Fortunately, the firm has night secretaries who work from late afternoon until the early hours of the morning preparing briefs and documents. I called my favorite night secretary. It took a little sweet-talking, promises of absolute anonymity, and a box of her favorite Godiva chocolates, but she eventually gave me the number. I prayed my luck would hold and no one would be home so I could leave a message on an answering machine.

No such luck. Blackjack was not only home, but he answered the phone. In the fewest words possible, I told him of the murder, that I was at the house notifying family, and Phyllis was identifying the body at the morgue with the police. To my horror, Blackjack was interested.

"Did the police question you?" Sweat materialized on my brow.

"This is not good. Not good at all," he mused. "The lead-in on every

TV report and newspaper article will identify Paul Martin as a major partner at the firm. Too big a story to kill I suspect. Maybe those useless P.R. gurus can finally earn their keep." He was mumbling to himself, not to me. At least he was no longer asking me questions.

"The police. You still haven't told me. Did the police question you?" Panic. I felt actual panic.

"A few superficial questions about what Paul was doing today." I answered carefully, trying to remember the specifics of what the police had asked, but under Blackjack's scrutiny, failing to do so. My memory is usually sharper than a Great White's incisor. I can vividly recall entire transcripts of arbitrations. I can reel off the names, credentials, and office phone numbers of the presidents of the five largest international unions in the country. I could tell you, to a penny, how much the strike at the *Chronicle* reduced its 1998 bottom line profits. But I couldn't remember more than three words the police had said to me. That is what fear will do to you.

"Stein?"

"Um." I dragged my attention back to Blackjack, who was making little irritated breathing noises on the other end of the phone.

"They were in a hurry to take Phyllis to the morgue and said they'd interview me in greater detail tomorrow."

"I don't think it would be a good idea for you to refuse to talk to them."

"I wasn't planning to."

"Not good at all."

"Er, no—" I started to respond, again, since apparently he hadn't heard me. Then I realized: Blackjack wasn't conversing with me, but dialoguing with himself as if I wasn't on the line. It was kind of fascinating, actually.

"Yes," I'd imagine it would be prudent to be cooperative with the police. Probably wouldn't look right to insist on legal representation at this juncture. Sign of weakness, hiding something. Of course, a prudent partner would be most careful about sharing anything private about the firm or its clients with the police. If Paul shared confidential information about particularly worrisome cases with his best friend, attorney-client privilege would still apply; yes it certainly would since his best friend is also his law partner. Yes, yes, attorney-client privilege. Very important. Certainly a prudent partner who possessed information he believed connected Paul's murder to firm business or any of its clients would vet those beliefs with the executive partner before sharing the information with the authorities. Otherwise, the executive partner would be disappointed and most unhappy. Yes, indeed, that would be the prudent course of action."

With my keen ability to sense the obvious, I recognized Blackjack was worried about something. "Information connecting Paul's murder to firm business." Yes, I was certain Blackjack used those words. There was nervousness in the pit of my stomach.

"Steve," Blackjack was talking to me again, "I appreciate your giving me the heads-up. What a tragedy. Please tell Phyllis our hearts and sympathies are with her. If there is anything, anything she needs, let me know and it will be taken care of." Blackjack was addressing me in a friendly, almost kindly tone of voice. Then abruptly his voice hardened. "I'll see you in my office Monday morning, 9 a.m. sharp with a complete report. Don't keep me waiting."

He hung up before I could ask, "A complete report on what, exactly?" I followed suit and clicked off the phone. At least I had until Monday to figure it out. Good thing we lawyers are used to winging it when we haven't got a corner of a clue what we're talking about. I'd done it in front of hundreds of judges and I'd done it persuasively. I could do it in front of Blackjack.

I let my breath out. Paul was dead and somehow or other I was ending up in the hot seat. It was going to be a long few days in a lot of respects.

9

I'm convinced much of life is controlled by Fate. Paul's life rapidly spiraled downward after his divorce from Marti. Just when I began considering some organized intervention, Phyllis mysteriously appeared, or as I later learned, reappeared in Paul's life. Fate provided Paul the tonic he needed most: a divorce buddy.

I left work early to spend additional time with Paul at The Back Room. Sure enough, Paul was there, sitting at a table, martini in hand, engaged in conversation with Billy Gold and Seymour Simon. Seymour is a wealthy builder turned real estate investor. A Holocaust survivor, he is the shrewdest and toughest businessman I ever met, but with a heart of gold. Recently, Seymour committed the mortal sin of using carpenters rather than laborers to perform clean up at a rehab project. The laborer steward threatened to close the project down, Seymour telephoned in a panic, directing me to "fix it." With one call I brokered a deal. The steward looked the other way. In return, Seymour hired an out-of-work laborer, who just happened to be the steward's brother-in-law. The extra expense ate at Seymour, but this was the best deal I could arrange.

I ordered my usual Ketel One and cranberry and walked over to the table where Paul was sitting. Seymour rose from his chair to greet me.

"Steve, sit down, join us," he said in his accented English. "You cleaned up that laborers' mess. It cost too much. But you did good. You're not going to charge me for one five-minute phone call, are you?"

"God damn right I am," I replied, flashing Seymour a big grin. "Five hundred bucks and you should be happy to pay. It would be a bargain at twice that. You've got my best offer."

"Five hundred for one telephone call. You're a ganef." Seymour laughed. He frequently interspersed his conversation with Yiddish expressions. I chuckled, having just been called a thief. Seymour paused, gauging my reaction, and then continued. "But, you're a smart one and I love you." We embraced.

Still grinning, as I sat down next to Paul, I looked over at Billy. "And you, Billy, what's new in the world of my favorite, and richest, P.I. Lawyer?"

"Just bought a one-third interest in a Bombadier Learjet 45. It works like a timeshare. I'm gonna use the plane to develop new business. We gotta diversify. You stand still, you're gonna die. I tell that to my law partners all the time. We gotta expand where the action is: explosions, bridge collapses, airplane crashes – that sorta thing. In the disaster business, ya gotta be Johnny-on-the spot if you wanna chance to be the lead plaintiff. You gotta sign up a victim and be first in line at the courthouse to file. I tell you, all the big players got airplanes. You guys wanna see a picture? She's a beaut." With that, Billy pulled a picture of the plane from his wallet, passing the snapshot around the table, beaming like a proud parent. Funny, I thought, I don't recall ever seeing pictures of Billy's kids.

"What about personal use?" As soon as the words left my mouth, I regretted them. I wasn't the least bit interested in Billy or his Gulfstream.

"That's privileged information between a taxpayer and his accountant." Billy chortled. "Actually, I was tryin' to convince your buddy Paul here to fly with me to Vegas. I'll call my friend Shecky. He owes me big. He'll comp us a suite. He'll take care of all our needs, and I mean all our needs." At that point, Billy gave us all a big wink. "I always say, if you fall off a horse, you gotta get up and climb right back into the saddle."

"You wouldn't know a horse's head from his ass," Seymour interjected. We all laughed.

Billy elected not to respond to Seymour. Instead, he swiveled and posed the question directly to Paul. "Well, Paul, what do you say? We'll have a lot of fun." He winked again. "And that's a promise."

I turned to Paul who was silently amusing himself, playing with the three olives in his martini. "What do you think of the idea? A trip to Vegas might be just the boost you need. You've always enjoyed yourself there."

"No, thanks. I don't want to take a trip right now. I'm having too much fun. Now that I have a divorce buddy, I'm able to deal with everything."

"What?"

Who and what was he talking about? I was Paul's best friend and he never mentioned anything about a divorce buddy to me. I said nothing further, figuring Paul would share whatever he felt comfortable saying in front of Billy and Seymour. To my surprise, Paul wasn't shy and laid out the entire story.

"Guys, it has to be Fate. There was this girl I dated regularly when I was a senior at Barton College. Her name back then was Phyllis Roth. I liked her. Actually, I liked her a lot." Paul stopped, sipped his martini, ate an olive, collected his thoughts, and then continued. "What you won't believe is that she dumped me. First time in my life that ever happened. She didn't want to get too involved with a gentile. Said it would kill her parents."

"A good Jewish girl," interrupted Seymour. "From her lips to my granddaughters' ears."

"That's the last time I saw her until three weeks ago," explained Paul ignoring Seymour's comment. "I was eating alone at Il Battuto, the little Italian restaurant on Mulberry Street. This attractive woman at the table next to mine looks familiar, but I can't place her. It bothers me. I know I'm staring, which makes me uncomfortable, especially when I notice she's staring back. She looks right at me and says, 'Paul, Paul Martin is that you?' Suddenly it clicks. I recognize the woman. It's

Phyllis Roth from senior year at Barton College, except now her name is Phyllis Orenstein."

"She slides over next to me at my table and we start talking. Right away, it's special. It's like time stood still. For the last twenty years, she's been living in town on the east side. She married this orthodontist Ronald Orenstein and they have one son. This Orenstein's a real pig. Two years ago, he divorced her to marry his floozy dental assistant. She's half his age."

"Phyllis knows exactly what I'm feeling. She's been through it herself. She says everyone getting divorced needs a divorce buddy to share innermost feelings. Well, she's my divorce buddy. We talk at least once a day. I know I'm on the mend emotionally. Phyllis is giving me the TLC I need."

"Hell, I've been divorced twice and I never had a divorce buddy," insisted Billy. "Maybe these other guys buy all this psychobabble. But if you're doing better, it's cause she's giving you some. Has she?"

Paul didn't answer; eyes sparkling, he smiled a knowing smile leaving Billy's question to be answered by our imaginations. Paul radiated happiness. I remained quiet, no longer worried about his emotional stability. Paul had found a soul mate.

I confess a pang of jealousy. On most weeks, I was on the road representing clients, especially newspapers with their union problems. If I was home on a week night, Maxine usually was at the hospital delivering a baby. We settled into a comfortable pattern. If we were both at home, we went to dinner at a restaurant. On a weekend, if she wasn't busy, we'd see a movie. Little excitement. No passion. Maxine's green eyes didn't' sparkle much anymore. She seldom laughed at my jokes.

"So is she?" No one ever gave Billy points for tact.

Seymour frowned. He didn't particularly like Billy. "You know Billy," he said in a hushed voice only those at the table could hear, "For a Jewish boy, you're not too smart." And, then looking directly at Paul, he added simply, "It was Bashert."

"What is Bashert?" asked Paul.

"Fate," I answered.

10

The coverage of Paul's murder on the 11:00 p.m. news lasted barely thirty seconds. A reporter standing in front of a car in the Wal-Mart parking lot, explained to the television audience how Paul Martin, a prominent attorney at the city's preeminent law firm, had been found shot to death in his car parked in the lot. The reporter quoted a police source close to the ongoing investigation as saying robbery was not the apparent motive.

The bantering news anchors spent more airtime discussing the origin of the superstition of bad luck surrounding Friday the 13th than reporting Paul's murder. I learned that, according to the *DaVinci Code*, bad luck has been associated with Friday the 13th since King Philip IV of France rounded up the Knights Templar for imprisonment and torture on Friday, October 13, 1307. A vital piece of knowledge everyone should know.

Shortly before midnight, I heard a car pull in the driveway and then saw the flashing lights of a police car through the living room's bay window. Minutes later, the front door opened. Pain and sorrow etched on her face, Phyllis stood starkly alone in the hallway. Within a seven-year span, she progressed from divorce buddy, to Mrs. Martin, and now to widow. Although she wasn't crying, the mascara streaks and puffiness around her red eyes hinted her self-control might be a temporary condition. Instinctively, I stepped toward her.

Phyllis's entire body began to shake slightly and she whispered in a trembling voice, "Please, please hold me. This has been the worst day in my life. Horrible. It's been so horrible. Please, Steve, please hold me."

I wrapped my arms around her quivering body. Phyllis began to sob uncontrollably. What words comfort a woman who has just come from identifying her murdered husband at the morgue? I couldn't think of any, so I just held Phyllis in my arms and let her cry.

After several minutes, she sighed heavily, and gently pushed me away. She looked sad. "Mix me a scotch and water, and don't let me drink alone," she said.

I went to the kitchen counter where I'd seen a bottle of eighteen-year-old Glenlivet and mixed two stiff drinks. Phyllis followed and sat down at the kitchen table. Placing a scotch and water and the bottle of Glenlivet in front of Phyllis, I sat down next to her with my drink, ready to listen.

She frowned. Her eyes glistened with tears.

"Looking at Paul's body was the hardest thing I've ever done in my whole life." Phyllis punctuated her statement with a belt of the scotch.

"He was shot in the back of the head. But there was blood all over his face. It was awful. So awful." She paused and stared off in the distance. "The look of horror on his face will give me nightmares. I'm sure he knew what was happening."

I shuddered at the thought. These weren't the details I wanted to hear or the conversation I wanted to have. I problem solve with the best. Comforting is also in my repertoire. I'm good at consoling. But not this.

"Do the police have any idea who did it?" The question was my transparent effort to change the subject. Even talk of blood makes me queasy. This character flaw, according to my mother, explains why I couldn't fulfill her Jewish mother's dream that I become a doctor, a source of never-ending disappointment for her.

She responded without hesitation. "No, the police don't have any leads, or at least none they're sharing with me."

Silence followed. Phyllis looked down, her attention focused on the two ice cubes, in her drink, she was clinking together with her finger. I studied Phyllis's body language. Years of negotiating experience told me she wanted to say something, so I remained quiet, waited, and listened.

Taking another gulp of scotch, Phyllis looked at me forlornly. "There are things we need to discuss." She pursed her lips and sighed.

"For the last two months at least, ever since you guys took the trip to Las Vegas, Paul's been preoccupied, acting strangely. He'd get phone calls, at odd times, on his cell phone and walk out of the room to take them. When I asked who called, he was evasive. He said it was a rich client, a broker, I think, in a fraud case, who was fragile and needed constant reassurance; said it was a special assignment from Blackjack."

"Did he mention the name?"

"No, and that's strange in itself." Phyllis's brow furrowed and concern showed on her face. I noticed her right foot twitching beneath the kitchen table. "Paul's always careful not to discuss clients' confidences, but he's never hesitated to share names. He took pleasure in letting me know the names of the important companies and people he represented. But this time it was different. He was vague and secretive. He didn't want me to know what was going on. I could feel it."

The reference to a trip to Vegas, two months ago, resonated in my mind. Two months ago would have been February. My annual trip to Las Vegas with Paul occurred in the first week of January.

"I'm a bit confused, too," I responded. "You know we went on our Las Vegas trip, like we always do, the first week of January. I didn't know Paul went back two months ago. He never mentioned it."

"You didn't go to Vegas with Paul in February?" Phyllis looked quizzically at me. "Paul told me you were depressed, moping over your separation from Maxine. It was finally his turn to be there for you. He was treating you to Vegas for a weekend to lift your spirits. He'd arranged it with Billy's Vegas friend. That's what he told me."

"Honestly, Phyllis, this is the first time I'm hearing about the trip." The troubled look on her face told it all. This news was a bombshell.

Phyllis drained the rest of her drink like she was doing shots at a bar. She poured herself another drink. No water or ice this time. She shook her head. "I don't understand," she said. I detected a mixture of sadness and exasperation in her voice. "I thought we had the kind of special relationship where two people share their innermost thoughts and concerns. Steve, you knew him longer and better than anyone. Why would he lie to me?"

I was on the spot, knowing with absolute certainty there were things Paul hadn't shared with Phyllis and probably some he'd lied about.

My years of legal training saved me. We lawyers are skilled at the art of obfuscation.

"Paul loved you deeply." I stalled, organizing my thoughts as I talked. "I've known each of Paul's wives, and the relationship you two guys shared was something special, something he'd never experienced before. Paul told me so many times." My carefully crafted response was truthful.

"He must have believed in his heart he was protecting you by not telling you the purpose of his going to Vegas."

Phyllis smiled weakly. "I'll accept that answer for now. I don't have a choice." She sighed again and looked at me. The wan smile disappeared from her face. "Do you have any idea who killed Paul or why?" she asked.

"No, I don't. I wish I did, but I don't."

I'm not sure whether it was Phyllis's distress or my need to bring closure to a relationship central to my life for more than forty years, but I heard myself, a sixty-year-old lawyer, whose previous idea of high adventure was a Caribbean cruise, pledge, "I promise Phyllis, I'll find out who killed him." The most disquieting part about this bravado was it was a promise I intended to keep.

PART TWO
SECRETS

11

I woke up Saturday morning after a dreamless night in the Martins' guest bedroom. This unfamiliar setting served as a reality check. No, I wasn't the victim of a bad dream. There would be no tennis match with Paul today. He was dead. Murdered.

I showered, shaved, and hurried downstairs dressed in yesterday's clothing. It was nearly nine o'clock. Phyllis sat in the kitchen, dressed in a prim blue pinstripe suit and lacy white blouse. A large green jade Buddha hanging around her neck, she was drinking a mug of coffee reading the morning *Chronicle*. She looked like a businesswoman, readying herself for a day at the office, not a grieving widow preparing for a visit to the funeral home. A landline phone and her cell phone lay on the kitchen table atop a yellow legal pad covered with scribbled notes. The floor squeaked as I entered the room. She glanced up from the newspaper.

"Good morning, Steve. You slept well?"

"Yes, surprisingly so. How did you do?"

"Not so good. I was up most of the night thinking about Paul."

"You should have woken me. I'd have kept you company."

"It wasn't necessary. You needed to sleep and I needed time to prepare for this morning's ordeal. You wouldn't believe how many calls I've already received. Both phones have been ringing nonstop since before seven. Everyone's calling to offer help and sympathy."

I walked to the coffee machine, stationed on the counter, poured a mug of coffee, sat down at the table next to Phyllis.

"What's this morning's schedule?"

"I called Roger Brown," she told me glancing at the legal pad in front of her. "He agreed to meet with us at eleven."

A third-generation undertaker, Roger Brown operates the Brown and Schmidt Funeral Home founded by his grandfather, Robert Brown, and his mother's uncle, Hans Schmidt. Brown and Schmidt is the funeral home of choice of the city's elite. I knew Roger from our mutual involvement in Shoes for Kids, a local charity that supplies shoes to children in need. His advice would be important since my familiarity with funerals, and that of Phyllis, was limited to Jewish funerals.

"There's still time. Let me fix you breakfast," Phyllis suggested, as I drank my coffee. "I have all the fixings. I bought them yesterday morning at the deli." Paul and I alternated brunch at each other's home after our regular Saturday morning tennis match. Since my separation, the brunches relocated to his home.

The perfect hostess, Phyllis prepared my favorite breakfast – a toasted pumpernickel bagel and a plate of lox, cream cheese, sliced tomato, and Bermuda onion. As I ate, my thoughts returned to my first brunch with Paul years ago in Cambridge. The invitation to Sunday brunch was a thank you for finding Jane and Paul their apartment and furnishing it with a bed. The couple proudly placed a platter piled high with scrambled eggs and sausage before me on the card table that served as their dining room table. Mortification ensued. While not a super-religious Jew, I don't eat pork.

"If you don't eat sausage, what do you eat for brunch?" Paul demanded.

"Lox, cream cheese, and bagel," I answered. "Doesn't everybody?"

Neither Paul nor Jane was familiar with lox. Paul asked, in error, if lox was a type of gefilte fish, a delicacy he remembered once eating at a Jewish girlfriend's house. The next weekend I returned with a shopping bag full of fixings purchased at the local Jewish deli and prepared a proper Sunday brunch: lox, cream cheese, smoked fish, bagels, and, scrambled eggs. They loved the meal.

I smiled. For the briefest of moments, I considered sharing this memory but wisely decided against it. On most occasions, Phyllis graciously tolerated reminiscences of my experiences with Paul's previous wives. Under the current circumstances, prudence dictated keeping those recollections to myself. Instead, seeing the newspaper spread open on the table, I inquired, "What's the coverage in the *Chronicle*? Is there an obituary?"

"That's what I was reading when you came in." Phyllis picked up the paper and pointed out the different articles. "The murder is reported on the front page, but there's nothing in the article we don't already know. The obituary is beautiful. It's a half page in the back of the Metro section with a picture. It covers Paul's entire life. They call him one of the nation's foremost litigators. It's wonderful."

You could feel her pride as Phyllis handed me the Metro section. I drank a second mug of coffee and read the obituary. It captured the highlights of Paul's life. A local boy had gone from Barton College to Harvard Law School and returned home to become one of the city's foremost litigators with a national reputation. Mentioned, too, were Paul's four wives and four children.

Although admiring and well written, the obituary left me sad and angry. I'd known Paul for more than forty years and really cared about him. Now his life had been reduced to twelve paragraphs. I bit my lip to keep my composure. I didn't want to know how great Paul had been; I wanted to know who murdered him.

Brown and Schmidt is located in Lauderhill Heights, an old inner-ring suburb. On a Saturday morning without traffic, at most, it's a twenty-minute car ride. Unlike me, who is habitually late for everything, Phyllis prides herself on punctuality. By ten thirty, we were together in my Volvo driving to the funeral home.

"When I leased the car, the dealership installed Sirius radio as part of the package." I knew Phyllis had no interest in what I was saying, but

I didn't want to talk about Paul or drive in silence for twenty minutes. I continued. "It's commercial-free. It has several hundred channels, with every imaginable type of music and programming. My favorite is a jazz channel that plays all the classics. Want to listen?"

"I'd rather not." She hesitated for a moment. "There's something important I need to ask you." I could sense nervousness in her voice.

"Go ahead." I wondered why she hadn't raised this important "something" earlier at the kitchen table.

"I've been trying to get up the courage to raise the subject all morning." Glancing over at her, I noticed her lower lip quiver.

Several seconds passed. She breathed deeply, and continued. "Has Paul been having an affair? Has he been seeing anyone? I need to know, Steve, I really need to know."

This was not a question I expected nor wanted to answer. I gulped, now on the spot. Paul hadn't been completely faithful to Phyllis during their marriage. That I knew. But other than Jane and a few out-of-town one-night stands, I wasn't aware of anything. Under Paul's value system this constituted monogamy. Phyllis, though, would never understand.

"Not that I know of," I hurriedly answered. Realizing the inadequacy of the response, I quickly added, "I'm sure I'd know if he was. What makes you ask?"

"Remember last night I told you how strange Paul's acted the last few months?"

"Yeah."

"There's more. Back in December, I found a receipt for a dinner at Morton's in the pocket of one of Paul's suit that I was sending to the dry cleaner. It was for a night Paul told me he was working late on a brief and eating dinner at his desk. In the same pocket, I found one of Paul's business cards. On the back, the name Elizabeth Caldwell and a phone number were scrawled in Paul's handwriting."

"Elizabeth Caldwell is an executive at First Mutual," I interjected.

"I know that. I Googled her. She's the vice president of human resources and technology at First Mutual Savings and Loan, forty-five years old and attractive. I saw her photo. Paul never mentioned her or even doing work for First Mutual. I've been through the drill before with my first husband. When I add Elizabeth Caldwell to the phone calls, the trip to Las Vegas and Paul's secretiveness, it totals an affair. I should have confronted Paul about the receipt, but I was afraid of the answer. Now it's too late. I'll have to live with suspicion."

"I met Elizabeth Caldwell about three months ago," I volunteered. Since I didn't know of anything going on between Paul and Elizabeth, I felt safe in telling Phyllis everything I knew about the woman. Maybe it would help. It couldn't hurt.

"The firm does First Mutual's corporate work and to my knowledge nothing else. It's Blackjack's client. About three months ago, he asked me to pitch Elizabeth for First Mutual's labor and employment work. We did a lunch and have talked a few times since on the phone. That's about it. She's promised to send some work my way. So far, nothing's materialized."

"Elizabeth's good looking all right, but not Paul's type at all," I added. That was inaccurate: any attractive woman was Paul's type, but I knew it was what Phyllis wanted to hear.

"I know nothing about her and Paul. I didn't even know they knew each other. Maybe Blackjack asked Paul to pitch her for some of First Mutual's litigation work. I'm sure there's a perfectly innocent explanation. I'll check it out and learn why her name was on the card."

Phyllis didn't respond. For several minutes she sat silently looking straight ahead before replying quietly, "I don't know what to think any more. Nothing makes any sense. One minute Paul's here and then he's gone. I don't know what to think about anything."

She looked out in the distance while I drove in silence. I heard her sigh. Her eyes suddenly lit up signaling the conversation was over, at least for the moment.

"Now why don't you turn on that jazz station you were bragging about," she told me.

12

Dressed in a funereal black suit expertly tailored to hide his middle-age paunch, Roger Brown welcomed us to Brown and Schmidt Funeral Home. Housed in a large white-framed house with freshly painted black-shuttered windows, the funeral home is prominently positioned on a rise in the center of Landerhill Heights surrounded by a manicured lawn and neatly clipped hedges. A tall, balding man with a pronounced aquiline nose, Roger ushered us into his office where he engaged in exactly the right amount of genteel, superficial banter to set Phyllis at ease. Every nuance of language and style was in perfect taste. In a soft, somber voice, the third-generation funeral director outlined the numerous decisions to be made, discussed the various options, and guided Phyllis to the alternatives he favored. Watching Roger in action convinced me that professional aptitude can become genetic after three generations. It certainly had for Roger.

Riverview Cemetery, one of the city's oldest cemeteries, remains the most prestigious in which to spend eternity. Or so Roger told us, volunteering that his grandparents and father were buried at Riverview. Phyllis selected a plot, located on a hill, which Roger assured us would offer a spectacular view of the city's skyline. I learned, as with most real estate investments, the key to selecting a home for eternity is "location, location, location."

A detailed discussion of the relative merits of bronze, copper, stainless steel, and carbon steel versus hardwood caskets tested the depths of my patience and resulted in Phyllis going with hardwood mahogany; top of the line, expensive. Admittedly the craftsmanship was exquisite, but that was to be expected, Roger explained, of a casket produced by the Batesville Casket Company of Batesville, Indiana, a small town with strong Midwestern values. I enjoyed a silent chuckle, knowing that the casket's future occupant didn't share those values.

The need for an autopsy complicated the remaining task of setting dates for the funeral and visitation. Roger again proved his worth. He personally knew Dr. Sperber, the county coroner. With us listening, he extracted a promise from the coroner to release, as Roger repeated aloud, "the remains of the deceased" to the funeral home no later than Wednesday morning. After performing a quick calculation, Roger suggested, and Phyllis agreed, to hold visitation on Thursday, between 2 p.m. and 4:30 p.m. and 6 p.m. and 8:30 p.m. with the funeral service at 11:00 the next morning at the First Methodist Church, followed by internment. I breathed a sigh of relief when Roger suggested the casket remain closed at all times and Phyllis agreed.

Two hours after arriving at the funeral home, we were back in my car returning to Phyllis's home. The primary details of Paul's last rites were arranged. Emotionally, I was exhausted. Cemetery plots, caskets, funeral services; everything was so final, so distant from Mrs. Henderson's tenth grade Honors English.

"I never could have handled this morning without you." Phyllis's words interrupted my thoughts as we pulled out of Brown and Schmidt's parking lot.

"You're an awesome woman," I remarked. "I marvel at how you dealt with those gut-wrenching decisions. I'm emotionally drained just from watching."

She gave a little laugh, the nervous kind. "Appearances are deceiving. The thought of Paul lying in that casket forever made me want to cry. I just kept squeezing your hand, telling myself to be brave. I was on the verge of tears several times, but I willed the tears away. But, Steve, I don't know if I have the strength to keep it up. I don't know how I'm going to make it through the next week. I just don't."

She bit her lower lip. Tears welled up in her eyes.

"I'll move into your guest room for the week," I heard myself offer. I'm not sure where those words came from, but having heard them, I knew I'd done the right thing. I now understand that Phyllis's take-charge attitude was her means of coping. "With me separated from Maxine, there's no reason I can't."

"That's kind of you." Her hand for a brief moment gently touched my right hand that was gripping the steering wheel. "You've been a wonderful friend to both me and Paul. But it won't be necessary. Not anymore.'"

"What do you mean, 'not anymore'?" "This morning," she explained, "while you were sleeping, Peter called. He was hurt I'd asked you, not him, to spend last night with me. He said I'd never accepted his being gay and I was embarrassed to have him and Matthew around. I couldn't deal with a big fight. I couldn't. So, I agreed to let him and Matthew move in with me – at least until after the funeral."

I listened without interrupting, remembering Phyllis's devastation and anger when Peter announced he was gay, abandoned his wife and his son, her grandson, Brent, to set up housekeeping with Matthew. She'd been embarrassed. And she'd been resolutely unforgiving, at least initially.

Phyllis paused for a moment, again reading my mind. "Peter's absolutely right, you know. His lifestyle and cavalier behavior did embarrass me. You don't walk out on your wife and child. Never." Even now, as she spoke, I saw anger momentarily flash in her eyes.

"Paul brought us back together," she continued, calmness returning to her voice. She spoke with a furrowed brow and closed eyes. "He was an accepting, perceptive man. He warned me I was making a mistake. I'd regret cutting Peter out of my life. He was right. And he cared about Peter. He convinced Peter how important it was to remain a father to

Brent. Paul's own separation from John still hurt him. Thank God Peter listened. He's worked at being a good father. I was so proud of both my men. Sometimes, though, I'm still uncomfortable with Peter's decision. It's so hard." Her voice trailed off into silence.

We drove along in that silence, neither one of us sharing thoughts, until I parked in her circular driveway.

"Do you want me to come in?" I asked. Peter's silver Mercedes, parked in front of the garage, announced he was waiting inside the house for his mother.

She hesitated, and then leaned over and pecked me on the cheek. "Honestly, no. You can see Peter's here already. He said he'd come over first by himself so that we could talk. We need some time together. Matthew won't move in until later this afternoon. Please, just walk with me to the front door." Phyllis's words were music to my ears: I was relieved that my tour of duty was over.

As I left her at the front door, Phyllis extracted a final commitment. "Yes," I promised, "I'd be honored to deliver a eulogy at Paul's funeral." Truth be known, I'd begun to wonder if she would ever ask.

I returned to my apartment to find more than two dozen messages of sympathy and condolence jammed onto my answering machine. One of the messages was from Jane Berke. She asked me to call back, after 6:00 p.m., Las Vegas time.

I opened a bottle of Sam Adams Light, anticipating a quiet afternoon that would give me the opportunity to be alone with my thoughts. The Yankees were playing the Orioles on the tube in the Fox Saturday game of the week. Baseball is my spectator game of choice. In this meaningless early season game, I'll root for the Orioles for no other reason than they're playing the Yankees and I'm a lifetime Yankee hater. In another age and time, I'd have rooted for David and his slingshot to upset the well-armed Goliath.

The Yankees were at bat in the first inning when the phone rang. The caller identified himself as Detective Robert O'Brien.

"My partner and I'd like to interview you at your apartment this afternoon. If it works for you, it would be helpful to meet as soon as possible."

After an entire morning at the funeral home talking cemetery plots and caskets, I had no desire to spend the afternoon answering Detective O'Brien's questions. The detective's hostile style was still a vivid and unpleasant memory and I doubted that O'Brien had undergone a personality transplant since last night. But I remembered Blackjack's admonition: cooperate with the authorities and report to him the details. Fear of Blackjack prevailed. Meet with O'Brien, I would.

"I spent the entire morning with Mrs. Martin at the funeral home planning Paul's funeral, looking at coffins, purchasing a cemetery plot. Right now, I'm watching the game of the week. It isn't much of a game. The Yankees are already clobbering the Orioles and it's only the first inning. I guess my afternoon will belong to you." I hoped this explanation of sacrifice would establish some level of empathy with the detective.

"When are you planning to come?"

"Actually we're across the street. We'll be there in five minutes."

True to his word, Detective O'Brien and his partner were almost immediately standing outside the door of my apartment. To my surprise, the detective was wearing a rumpled light brown suit. I wondered. Was this the same rumpled light brown suit he wore yesterday or does the detective have a dozen identical rumpled light brown suits hanging in his closet? Having often learned the hard way that discretion is the better part of valor, I kept this poignant observation to myself.

"Come in gentlemen. Have a seat in the living room." I motioned them in while turning off the ball game with the remote.

"Can I get you something to drink –beer or soft drinks?" I planned to finish the Amstel Light I held in my left hand.

"Can't do the beers. We're on duty," O'Brien replied. "A soft drink would be good. Do you have diet?"

"Will Diet Pepsi work?"

"Yeah."

"Works for me, too," added O'Brien's partner, the same gray-haired fashionably dressed detective I'd seen the previous evening at Phyllis's home. He was well dressed this day, wearing a herringbone tweed sports jacket with neatly pressed black slacks and a well-starched white shirt open at the neck. Quite a contrast from O'Brien.

"Two Diet Pepsis coming up."

I returned to the living room with drinks in hand, to find the two detectives strategically positioned, forcing me to sit between them. Detective O'Brien had selected the room's only chair while his partner sat on the couch across from him, leaving room on the couch for me. As I mentioned, the motif of my furnished apartment is early Spartan. The furnishings are utilitarian, new, and austere. The focal point of the apartment is my large television set.

"Nice digs," O'Brien commented. "A real bachelor pad. How long you been living here?"

"About six months."

"You married?"

"Technically, yes. I've been separated from my wife for six months."

"Interesting." O'Brien jotted something on his notepad. I remembered the look he gave me when Phyllis asked me to stay at her home last night. Already, I felt on the defensive.

I wanted to change the subject. I looked at O'Brien's partner and flashed my winningest smile. "You'll have to forgive me. Since turning sixty, my faculties, especially memory, have become suspect. If we were introduced last night, I don't remember your name."

"The name's Frank Mancini. I'm O'Brien's quieter, better-looking half."

"O.K. girls," O'Brien interrupted with a trace of impatience or was it belligerence in his voice. "Are you finished making nice?" He glared. "We have a murder to investigate, and unless my memory is becoming suspect, I seem to remember the victim was your best friend, Mr. Stein."

These guys probably do a great good-cop bad-cop routine I reflected. Again, considering the detective's attitude, I also kept this observation to myself.

"Ask away. Paul was my best friend. I want you to catch his murderers."

O'Brien paused, considered what I had said. He then established eye contact as he had the previous evening. "What makes you so sure, Mr. Stein, there was more than one murderer?" He beamed with just the trace of a smile. I half expected him to shout "Gotcha!"

The detective's gamesmanship flustered me for a moment. Use of the plural "murderers" had no significance. I hadn't given the phrase the slightest thought. As I reflected on the question, I wondered why the detective was so hell-bent on being hostile and making me uncomfortable. But I knew I could handle O'Brien types. I'd transform into labor lawyer mode, visualizing the two detectives as the union negotiating team. Superficially, I'd cooperate with the detectives, working to reach our mutual goal of identifying the murderer. But I'd measure each word carefully, knowing the slightest improper characterization would be thrown back at me. No way could I safely go "off the record" to talk "straight" with Detective O'Brien, as I might with a union representative. There was no level of trust that an "off-the-record" remark would remain "off the record."

"That phrase was used without any thought," I replied. "But thinking about it, I'd guess that more than one person was responsible for the murder. Paul was shot in the back of the head. Yet, you guys say that robbery wasn't a factor. Doesn't that point to a professional hired hit man?" Gotcha, I told myself.

"Could be," volunteered Mancini, flashing me a smile.

Scowling at his partner and me, O'Brien, voice dripping with sarcasm, challenged my analysis. "So tell us, Mr. Detective, have you figured out how this professional hit man of yours got into the back seat of your best friend's car in a Wal-Mart parking lot?"

I winced. The interview was spiraling out of control. For whatever reason, Detective O'Brien had a monumental chip on his shoulder and my butt had target written all over it. Tempting as it was to respond in kind, I held my tongue. A dose of conciliation was needed.

Looking straight at O'Brien, I addressed him in an even tone, "Detective, you and I seem to have gotten off on the wrong track. I don't know what it was. But if anything I said offended you, I assure you it was unintentional and I apologize."

The word "apologize" must have been the magic potion. O'Brien visibly relaxed and his scowl vaporized. Encouraged, I plunged on.

"I think part of the problem, Detective, is your style makes me feel uncomfortable, like you are accusing me. I do want to help you catch whoever killed Paul."

To my surprise, there was no seismic eruption. Not even a hint of sarcasm.

"Mr. Stein, let me explain. At this point in the investigation, everyone is a suspect. I know you think I'm picking on you, but I'm not." The detective's demeanor became professorial as he explained himself. "If I presently believed you were involved in your friend's death, I would have Mirandized you. But I haven't eliminated the possibility."

"If my manner offended you, get over it. I don't give a damn. But you're right. We should start over. Why don't you begin by telling us about Mr. Martin's four wives." That was as friendly as O'Brien would become.

I talked with the detectives for more than an hour, describing Paul's relationship with each wife. Detective O'Brien proved adept at eliciting information. I gave him a much more candid portrayal of the wives and Paul's successive marriages than intended. He asked a lot of questions about Phyllis. Spouses, I learned, are always the Number One suspect. In this case, I told him he was barking up the wrong tree. He should move on to suspect Number Two. He jotted that in his notebook.

When the questioning turned to Paul's career and the firm, I spoke cautiously, remembering Blackjack's unspoken warning. I discussed only facts in the public domain, not gossip or the firm's internal workings. I dumbed up when the questioning turned to Paul's current cases and clients, deciding if that information were relevant to the police investigation, it best come from others. My reticence displeased O'Brien.

"I sense you're hiding something Mr. Stein," he said and shook his head. He jotted that in his notebook as well.

The detectives knew about Paul's gambling addiction. Detective Mancini bluntly raised the issue with me.

"What can you tell us about Mr. Martin's gambling?"

"Paul's been an incorrigible gambler since law school."

"More than he can afford?"

"His gambling is cyclical. At times, it's been a problem. He's lost money he didn't have. But, he's earned a lot of money and things always worked out."

"What about recently? Any big losses?" Mancini pressed for specifics.

"I'm sure he's been betting NBA basketball, and maybe some baseball. I didn't notice anything unusual."

O'Brien responded in apparent disgust. "Tell us something we don't know, Steve. At least give us the name of his bookie."

"I don't know," I confessed. "He never told me and I never asked. Gambling doesn't interest me. Never has." O'Brien pursed his lips and shook his head. I guess he didn't like my answer.

"You guys gotta understand," I pleaded. "In all the years, I've known Paul, I never asked him to place a bet for me; not even in a football pool. Except for playing some roulette and blackjack once a year in Las Vegas, I don't gamble."

"You're a disappointment," O'Brien commented, again jotting something in his black book.

"If you want the name of Paul's bookie, I'll ask around," I volunteered. "I'm sure one of the guys at McGinty's knows."

"That would be appreciated," Mancini said.

Detective O'Brien closed his black notebook and stood up, signaling the end of the interview. "Yes," he said, "the name of the bookie would be useful. Here's my card. I'll write my cell phone number on the back. If you get the bookie's name, leave it in my voice mail."

"Let me ask something now," I addressed the two detectives. "Would a person be killed for being slow in paying off a gambling debt?"

O'Brien paused then finally answered my question. "Your friend wasn't killed over a gambling debt. That's no motive to kill. A slow pay gets roughed up a bit to send a message, but you're dealing with businessmen. They want to collect what you corporate types call receivables. Murder doesn't accomplish that."

As the two detectives were leaving my apartment, O'Brien stopped in the doorway and turned to me. "Stein, I think you're full of shit. You know much more than you're letting on. Be careful. Your friend got involved way over his head with some very bad people. If you know things you're not telling us, watch out. Keeping secrets isn't smart. I repeat, they're bad people. Don't mess with them." With that ominous warning, he closed the door.

14

Not waiting for my call, Jane called at six o'clock sharp. I didn't know what to expect. My interactions with her had been limited. Paul mostly met her away from the hotel, during our annual trips to Las Vegas. On those occasions when she picked him up, we exchanged pleasantries. My knowledge of Jane's life since law school came from Paul. She had several bad marriages, worked for years as a dancer in successive strip clubs, and had overcome a drug problem – a Las Vegas soap opera. I didn't know where she was currently employed.

"Steve, you're a real dear." She greeted me with what sounded like genuine affection, but then again, Jane was experienced in creating illusion for the male of the species. I remained silent.

"You can't imagine how much your telephone call meant to me. I always loved Paul. He was the dearest and most important man in my life. I know that's sad, but it's true. He was always there for me. He paid for my drug rehabilitation and for an abortion."

"You're the only one who knew about us." She spoke rapidly, sounding hyper. "You were his best friend and you thought enough of me to call. That means a lot."

"That's what Paul would have wanted. You were special to him."

"He was special to me, too." Jane paused. I could hear her voice momentarily break.

"Can you believe it?" she pressed on. "It's been more than forty years. I first dated Paul in high school. He was so handsome then, and so smart. God we're old."

"I remember well. He dumped Ellen to date you, the prettiest cheerleader on the squad."

"This is so terrible. Why would anyone want to kill Paul?"

"The police at this point don't know. And, I don't either."

"What about the funeral? When is it going to be?"

"This coming Friday. If you want to attend, Phyllis, that's Paul's current wife, would understand. She's special too. You'd like her." If Jane wanted to attend the funeral, I wanted her there. I was sure Phyllis wouldn't mind as long as I didn't tell her the full story about Paul's continuing relationship with his first wife.

"I wish I could," Jane sighed. "The problem is I can't take the time off. I'm the house mom at Big Mama's Saloon. That a strip club in downtown Vegas."

"Oh."

Over the years I've drafted all types of job descriptions, even a light bulb changer at a large hospital. I didn't have the slightest idea what a house mom at a strip club did. Jane came to my rescue without having to ask. .

"I oversee the girls. I see that they're dressed and made up properly. I'm also the stripper police. I look out for drugs and prostitution. And, no glitter, absolutely no glitter. It's a major no-no. We can't have a customer going home and the wife finding glitter on his clothing. Wouldn't be good for business."

"And most important, I'm like a social worker to the girls. Sort of a 'Dear Abby.' I give them advice about everything: their work, their boyfriends, their husbands. We discuss kids, family, anything they want to talk about. You know, I'm the old hand, been there, done that. The most satisfying part of the job is the girls actually like me. They really do. My girls call me, 'Mom'."

"I'd like to attend the funeral, but I don't have a backup, and I need the pay," Jane explained. "As much as I love my job, it's a tough way to make a living. The club pays minimum wage. The rest is tips from the girls. Thank God, it's a classy joint. The girls make good money, as much as a thousand dollars a night. I clear three hundred dollars on a good night." Jane's voice resonated. I sensed pride as she mentioned her earnings and those of her girls.

Strangely, I was disappointed Jane wouldn't be at the funeral. Instinctively, I liked her. Life had thrown her some curveballs since the days in Cambridge. She hadn't become bitter, she'd embraced life. Our brief conversation explained to me why Paul remained connected to her all these years.

"If you change your mind, even at the last moment, I'll arrange a place for you to stay. To keep the cost down, you know. Just give me a little lead time." Why I said that, I wasn't sure. Actually, I did know why. I had an idea, that's not at all like me, although I didn't know whether I'd actually follow through. But if Jane decided to come and I wimped out, several former high school classmates owed me favors.

"Steve, you're a real dear, but really, I can't come. But promise me you'll call Saturday to tell me everything. That'd be so amazing." Her giddy enthusiasm for a moment transported me back forty years in time.

"It's a date," I promised. I decided to go all in and ask her about Paul's February trip to Las Vegas. My gut told me she'd tell me whatever she knew.

"I've a favor to ask. Something has been bothering me that maybe you know something about."

"Just like a man," she answered coyly. Her voice was deep and throaty. Probably she was a cigarette smoker, I guessed. "You set up a date, and always want more. I meant it though when I said you were a dear. Whatever it is, go ahead and ask."

"I learned from Phyllis that Paul visited Vegas for a weekend in February. Paul told her he was taking me to lift my spirits. You see I'm getting divorced after more than thirty years of marriage. It's been tough." I paused for a moment, amazed that I had told her that.

"Not only didn't I go, I didn't know about the trip. What about you?

Did you know about the trip? Did he call you while he was in Vegas, like usual?"

"Yeah. I didn't know he was in Vegas until he called from the Bellagio. I drove over and picked him up late Saturday night. We spent the night together at my apartment. At six in the morning, he left my place. That was the last time I saw him."

"Was he traveling alone?"

"No. He was with a woman named Betsy. Paul introduced her when I picked him up at the hotel. He didn't mention her last name, and I didn't ask. I'm pretty certain he said she was a banker."

"I'm confused," I confessed. "He was traveling with her and sleeping with you?"

"You got it right. It was flattering." Jane laughed. "This Betsy was a good-looking blonde. I'd guess about fifteen years younger than me. But I was the one who got Paul for the night."

She laughed again, apparently still relishing the memory. "I can't swear what happened on Friday or Sunday nights, but Paul told me they were in Vegas to work on an international bank deal. I think it was business only."

Jane's story made no sense. Paul was a litigator, not a business lawyer. He wouldn't know the first thing about an international bank deal. And, if Betsy was Elizabeth Caldwell, negotiating an international bank deal didn't fall within her job description either.

I wasn't certain how much Paul shared with Jane over the years about his work. Keeping my doubts and confusion to myself, I asked whether she remembered anything else Paul might have said about the business deal.

"Paul and Betsy were meeting some bankers. One was Chinese and the other, I think, was an Arab because his name was Muhammad"

"Was that his first or last name?"

"I'm not sure. I don't remember. I know that they selected Las Vegas because the Chinese banker was a big-time gambler who was comped at the Bellagio."

"One final thing," television detectives always have a final question that breaks open the case. "Did Paul act strangely, seem anxious, or concerned about anything?"

"At the time, I didn't pay much attention. We had other things on our minds. But since I got your message, I've been thinking about that. Looking back, he was agitated, mostly about money. He said the deal needed to be successful. He told me his life had become complicated, but he never explained how. Honestly, Steve, that's all I remember."

"If you remember anything else, call me collect. I know calls can be expensive. I'll pick up the tab. Otherwise, I'll call you next Saturday about this same time. I promise."

Jane's final words surprised me. "Steve dear," she said sounding oh so sexy, "promise me you'll still come to Vegas for the yearly visit. I'd like to see you. You'll be divorced by then, so your wife won't be a problem. I promise I'll show you the time of your life."

A better offer I had not received in a long time.

15

In the twenty-four hours since the murder, secret parts of Paul's life had emerged. My conversation with Jane was baffling. Paul and Elizabeth Caldwell meeting with two international bankers made no sense. I had so many questions and so few answers. My instinct told me Paul's trip to Las Vegas with Elizabeth Caldwell was somehow connected to his death. A visit with Ms. Caldwell moved to the top of my to-do list.

Rather than eat Lean Cuisine for one, alone in my apartment, I opted for the short walk to McGinty's to enjoy one of Charley's mouth-watering rib steaks. Like most Saturday nights, The Back Room was nearly empty. Customers were at only three of the tables. Scanning the room for a familiar face, I spotted Warren Prescott sitting alone. Heavyset, balding, and in his early fifties, Warren is one of them, the city's movers and shakers. Second in command and heir apparent at the city's largest commercial bank, he is a mainstay on community and philanthropic boards. I knew him, although not well, from serving together on a committee appointed by the mayor to analyze the finances of the city's school system. Tonight, I didn't want to eat alone, not after the day I had.

As I approached Warren's table, I asked if he wanted a dinner companion.

"Sure, my wife's in Chicago for the weekend. What's your excuse for eating here tonight?"

"Separation after more than thirty years of marriage," I shrugged, feigning nonchalance. These moments still remain difficult. Unaware of my marital problems, Warren probably regretted having agreed to spend the next hour or so having dinner with me. Bitching, whining, and crying are not the bases of scintillating dinner conversation.

"I'm sorry. I didn't know."

"Don't give it another thought." I signaled for a waiter. "Let me order a steak, medium rare, and a drink."

The dinner conversation turned to Paul, a subject that interested Warren. Having read about the murder in the *Chronicle*, he solicited additional details. I told him about the funeral schedule and Phyllis's ordeal last night at the morgue. Over several drinks, I entertained Warren with story after story about my experiences with Paul at law school and in the Army Reserves. Warren laughed frequently. He seemed to enjoy my reminiscences, or perhaps he was just a good sport, happy, with his wife in Chicago, not to be eating alone and willing to tolerate the maudlin memories of a grieving friend, pleased he was not listening to a litany of marital travails.

Warren was eating dessert, two large scoops of vanilla ice cream atop a large piece of homemade apple pie, when I asked about First Mutual Savings and Loan. He seized the opportunity to talk rather than listen.

"Unlike my bank, which is full service and commercial, First Mutual is a thrift. It focuses on mortgages for residential properties of four units and less. In that market, First Mutual is easily Number One in dollar volume in this region."

For some reason, I felt a need to engage Warren. "The Brennan family owns the bank. I think the grandfather, George, founded First Mutual in the early thirties. The grandson Greg owns the bank now. Do you know him?" In those few words, I summarized all I knew about the bank's ownership.

"That's what most people think, but you're dead wrong," Warren corrected me with a trace of too much enthusiasm. "A mutual savings bank is legally owned by the depositors. The Brennan family are just employees, although highly paid ones."

"I'm surprised you didn't know," he continued, arching his right eye brow. "First Mutual is in the process of demutualizing and your firm is handling the transaction. It's a billion dollar deal."

"A large law firm like ours is nothing more than a legal factory." Maybe it was his smug tone or my own discomfort in interacting with someone of his ilk, but I felt the need to justify to Warren why I didn't know our firm was overseeing the demutualizing of First Mutual, whatever that meant. "Have you ever been in a steel plant?" I pointedly asked Warren. He irritated me. Maybe it would have been better to eat alone.

"You would probably never guess," Warren answered, now grinning broadly. "but I was the first one in my family to go to college. My father and all my uncles worked in a U.S. Steel plant in Pittsburgh." Of course, I knew. I had read the Horatio Alger-like bio of his life, run in the *Chronicle* when Warren became COO of the bank.

"Good, then you'll understand. Like a steelworker in the open hearth wouldn't know what's happening in the tolling department, at a large law firm, unless you're management, a labor lawyer like me doesn't know what's going on in the corporate department."

Laughing now, Warren replied with a twinkle in his eyes, "Yeah, Steve, that's why the workers needed the union."

Appreciating the subtlety of Warren's comment, I responded with mock solemnity, "I'll pass your suggestion on to Blackjack. I'm sure he'll appreciate your helpfulness."

"Please, please, anything but that," pleaded Warren, still laughing and feigning horror at the thought. At that moment, I recognized my preoccupation with Paul's death and bias against corporate types made me oversensitive. I had misjudged Warren. For a banker, he had a good sense of humor. I decided I liked Warren after all.

"Getting back to First Mutual, what was the phrase you used? 'Demutualizing'?"

"That's right."

"I'm just a labor lawyer. I confess absolute ignorance. What does demutualizing mean?"

"It is a change of corporate form," Warren lectured, seemingly enjoying his role as teacher. "The thrift is transformed into a traditional stock company. Since the depositors technically own the bank, they're offered the opportunity to continue ownership by buying stock at ten dollars per share."

For the next ten minutes, Warren showed great patience and answered all my questions. He assured me First Mutual stock would be an excellent investment once he learned I was a depositor. Based on similar deals in the last year, he predicted there'd be what he termed "a pop" on the first day of trading of the stock on the NASDAQ of between two and three points. The ten-dollar share would be worth between twelve and thirteen dollars by day's end. Since a well-heeled depositor could buy between fifty- and seventy-five thousand shares, serious money could be made.

"What's the deal to the Brennan family?" I wanted to know. "I don't know Greg well, but call me 'Cynic,' somehow I doubt he's motivated by the best interests of his depositors."

Chuckling appreciatively at my attempt at humor, Warren detailed the advantages of the deal to the Brennan family. "They'll be transformed from highly paid employees into highly paid employees with a valuable ownership interest. I can assure you," he told me, "if you study the fine print of the prospectus your law firm is preparing, you'll discover the Brennans will wind up with millions of shares of stock. If the family ultimately loses control of the bank, they'll have achieved real wealth."

"What's unusual in this deal, an insider explained to me, is that the conversion into a stock company is being done in a single phase. Usually, there's a first phase where the controlling interest of the mutual bank is placed in a mutual holding company and the total conversion into a stock company doesn't occur until a later second phase. Here, they're going directly to the final phase."

Warren answered my next question before it was asked. "My best guess is Greg decided more money could be made by placing First Mutual in play sooner rather than later. The government prohibits the sale of a converted mutual savings bank for three years. So for three years, Greg will use the proceeds from the stock sale to buy other banks. He'll grow First Mutual in the hope of creating a more attractive target for some bigger bank willing to pay a hefty premium for the stock. That's my best guess of what's going on."

"You're a regular banking encyclopedia," I complimented Warren with admiration that was sincere. "I'd trust my money, or should I say my half, in your bank any day."

He laughed. "Flattery gets you everywhere with me, Steve." He was obviously pleased with my praise. "I'll send you a bill for this banking lesson on Monday morning. Does five hundred dollars sound fair?"

This time we both laughed and I bought him an expensive brandy.

16

Warren and I sat engrossed in conversation. I was actually enjoying myself. Just after the waiter brought a third round, Billy Gold entered The Back Room. Noticing me, Billy made a beeline to our table, motivated in part, I am certain, by a desire to learn the latest about Paul's murder.

Oblivious as usual to his surroundings, Billy greeted us loud enough for everyone else to hear. Thank goodness there were just a few other patrons in the room. "Warren, Steve, good to see you. Mind if I join you guys?" Without waiting for the answer, Billy sat down at our table. He wore a black silk shirt and black designer jeans that accentuated his middle-aged paunch. His shirt, open at the neck, revealed his shaggy-haired chest and a diamond encrusted Star of David. Warren grimaced ever so slightly.

As Billy seated himself, Warren drained his brandy, stood up, and announced a bit too eagerly, "Always good to see you, Billy. I was just leaving. It's almost midnight and my wife will be calling from Chicago. Don't want to worry her. I'll leave you two lawyers to solve the problems of the world."

Before Billy could utter a word, Warren left the table and headed toward the door. He paused in the doorway, looked back at me and said, "I enjoyed getting to know you, Steve. Call and we'll do lunch." And then he was gone.

On some other occasion, I would have been tempted to follow Warren's lead, although with far more grace. But this unexpected meeting, I decided, was fortuitous. I had several questions for Billy and had planned to set up a lunch during the week. This unanticipated encounter rendered that lunch unnecessary, turning a lemon into lemonade.

"Who stuck a corn cob up his snooty ass?" Billy glumly asked, watching Warren's hurried departure. Then, lowering his voice, he answered his own question, confiding in a conspiratorial whisper, "I guess the son of a bitch can only tolerate one Jew at a time."

Expressionless, I shrugged my shoulders, not wanting to betray Warren and my imagined burgeoning friendship with the soon-to-be crowned chief officer of the city's largest bank. On the other hand, I didn't want to offend Billy. His cooperation was needed if my investigation was to bear fruit. Understanding the pure enjoyment Billy always derived from talking about his favorite subject, himself, the perfect bromide to lift his spirits was obvious.

"It's been a while, Billy. But I'm reminded of you every time I see John Edwards on TV, running for President." I kept a poker face as I asked, "Who has more money, you or him?"

"Probably a toss-up," Billy answered, a look of self-satisfaction brightening his face. "I'm not into any of his populist bullshit, but Edwards is my man. This country needs a trial lawyer in the White House. I sent him a ten thousand dollar check with a personal note."

I knew it wouldn't be necessary to ask Billy what pearls of wisdom he had imparted to the presidential candidate. "I gave him the name, address, and phone number of a terrific hair stylist in Washington," Billy volunteered in total seriousness. "Told him to mention my name and he'd get the best haircut ever for one hundred bucks. No one should pay four hundred dollars for a haircut. I told Edwards his current stylist is taking advantage of him because he's a successful trial lawyer. Happens all the time. Jealousy, you know."

Billy's revelations left me momentarily speechless. I looked at him, hoping, but not expecting, to detect some hint he was joking; Billy was serious. Before I could recover and respond with a clever quip, Billy remembered why he approached me in the first place.

"Steve, I'm sorry about your loss. You must think me an unconscionable boor the way I've been babbling on. I came over to tell you how sorry I was to hear about your loss." His words were as much of an apology, or introspection, as you could expect from Billy. Putting his arm around my shoulder, he told me with unexpected emotion, "Paul was a great guy, a great friend, one of the best. I liked him. I really did. I'll miss him. If there's anything I can do for Phyllis, let me know. My checkbook's open."

"Let's drink to Paul," I proposed. "I'm buying. What'll you have?"

Billy favors single malt scotch and ordered McCallan straight up. Sipping our drinks, we exchanged stories about Paul's legal and sexual exploits. Then I described to Billy the visit to the funeral home and detailed the funeral schedule. A full fifteen minutes passed without any mention of the police investigation. Billy could no longer tolerate the meandering direction of our conversation.

"Have you talked to the police?" he blurted out. "Do they have any leads?"

Leaning across the table until no more than six inches separated our faces, I spoke softly, barely above a whisper. "The police interviewed me earlier today. I'm probably not supposed to repeat what was said. Confidential police business, you know. But this would be different. You're one of Paul's true friends."

"Yes, I am."

"This Detective O'Brien, he's the head honcho. He did the questioning. Already he doesn't much like me. If he ever found out I told you details of the interview, I'd be in deep shit, which is something I don't need." There was more truth than I cared to admit in what I was telling Billy.

Furtively glancing over my shoulder to dramatically check no one was eavesdropping on our conversation, I whispered, "Can I trust you'll keep what I tell you to yourself?" Actually, the thought of Billy keeping anything to himself is amusing.

Billy's eyes widened, his hands trembled with anticipation. Salivating for the information, he sought to convince me of his commitment to secrecy.

Looking me straight in the eyes while holding his right pointer finger to his lips, Billy uttered a vow of silence. "I won't say a word to anyone. You know me. They could stick bamboo shoots under my fingernails. I still wouldn't tell them nothin'. I swear."

With contrived hesitancy, I described my interview with the two detectives. "Detective O'Brien didn't come out and say it," I equivocated, "but from the thrust of his questions, I'm convinced he connects the murder to gambling debts. Paul owed some people large sums of money and when he couldn't make the payments, he was killed."

I paused, watching and weighing Billy's reaction. He bought my story hook, line, and sinker. Since Billy counted himself a man who knew his way around the streets, I anticipated he might be the source of valuable information. I wasn't disappointed.

Billy nodded. "Yeah, that's my guess. The word on the street," Billy declared, "is that Paul's gambling debts are enormous. Five hundred big ones is what I hear." My surprise and horror when he explained five hundred big ones meant five hundred thousand dollars amused Billy.

"You gotta be kidding" was all I could manage to say.

"No, I'm serious," he explained, pleased he now had my undivided attention. "He started losing and losing and then began doubling down trying to recoup his losses."

"Who's his bookie?" I wondered whether he knew and if he'd tell me.

Without hesitation, he supplied the answer. "Mo Bernstein."

"I can't believe that Paul owed this Mo Bernstein guy five hundred thousand dollars. It's unbelievable." How did he lose so much money? I shook my head with dismay.

Billy stared at me in apparent disbelief. He then began lecturing me on Gambling 101. His tone showed he appreciated the delicious irony that this was a subject where I was the student, and he had assumed the role of teacher.

"Mo Bernstein is small time. Bookies like him don't take on bets the size that Paul was making. Not by themselves."

"What do you mean, 'not by themselves'?"

"Bookies don't gamble. They're what you might call risk averse. They set odds, the line, to balance the money bet on both sides. No matter who wins, they get the vigorish. That's their cut, their profit. Small-time bookies like Mo balance their book by laying off their bets with the Syndicate. The Syndicate keeps the money balanced." Billy grinned when I told him this Syndicate acted like an insurance company in laying off the risks of natural disasters. When pressed to elaborate about the details of this syndicate organization, Billy suddenly became vague. I assumed from his discomfort that the Syndicate was part of organized crime.

"There's no way bookies would have extended Paul five hundred thousand dollar-credit," Billy insisted, and then added, "Maybe for a good customer like Paul, one hundred big ones, but no more."

"But you said the word on the street is that Paul owed five hundred thousand dollars. I'm confused."

My confession of ignorance was real and seemed to please Billy. He asked with the kind of mixture of disdain and pity that is directed at the slowest student in the class, "Didn't you ever hear of loan sharks?" Recognizing the question was rhetorical, I remained silent.

"Paul obviously borrowed the money from loan sharks, money lenders," he explained, with a trace of impatience. "Let me make it simple. They're bad people. If you borrow money from them, it's hard to ever get their claws out of you. Their interest rates make credit cards look reasonable."

"Can you give me a name?"

The question upset Billy. Suddenly pale, a pained look on his face, Billy began rubbing the Star of David that dangled from his neck.

"At best, it would be an informed guess." His voice and body language betrayed him. He was lying. "If I did know, I wouldn't tell you," he added. "Those guys find out you're even talking about them and it's bad for your health. I suggest you don't go there. Close it down. I'm telling you this as a friend."

Rather than continue further in an area Billy was declaring off-limits, I transitioned to a less threatening subject. Did he have connections at the Bellagio hotel in Las Vegas, particularly in reservations? Curious and ever the gossip, Billy wheedled to learn more about my sudden need for reservations. "I'm not certain yet," I replied with a sheepish grin, "but I might be planning a trip there soon with a friend." And then, slapping him on the back, I winked, "I strongly suggest that you don't go there." I added laughing, "Close it down. But you can order another scotch on me."

"You're in luck. My friend Shecky Levine—the one who used to work at Caesars Palace—he's been at the Bellagio for about two years. He can do magic, especially for a friend of Billy's." Recently divorced for the third time, he seemed to enjoy the idea of helping me cope with my first. He promised to email Shecky, first thing Monday morning, asking as a personal favor that I be extended every courtesy. He'd send me Shecky's phone number and email address. "Like I've said many times," Billy concluded with his own friendly wink, "when you get thrown off the horse, you gotta pick yourself up and get right back in the saddle." I realized that was almost to the word what he had told Paul after his divorce from Marti.

I bought two more rounds of drinks before I left Billy and The Back Room and unsteadily weaved my way back to my apartment, pleased with my night's work and myself.

17

I peeked through the slight opening of the blackout drapes that hid the bedroom window in my eighth-floor apartment. The rainy overcast Sunday morning mirrored my dark mood. Four Tylenol had proven unequal to the challenge posed by the excruciating pain throbbing through my head. Further sleep definitely wasn't an option. Maybe a couple hours of mindless reading would prove an antidote to my colossal hangover. I could hope. I brewed a carafe of my favorite Starbucks coffee, toasted a frozen pumpernickel bagel, and picked up the Sunday *Chronicle* lying on the doormat outside in the apartment hallway.

Before I could pull out my first read, the sports section, I noticed Paul's picture positioned below the fold on the front page. My mood darkened further. The banner headline proclaimed, "Gambling and Drugs Suspected in Attorney's Death." The front page story was authored by P.J. Ettinger, the *Chronicle*'s star investigative reporter. As often is the case, the story's substance bore little resemblance to the attention-grabbing headline. P.J. traced Paul's matrimonial history, described his bitter divorce from Babs, and recounted some of Paul's major legal victories. Only the article's concluding paragraph focused on "Paul's darker side," large gambling debts financed by loan sharks and speculated, based on unnamed sources, Paul's involvement in a drug deal gone awry in an effort to raise money to pay off gambling debts. Normally I would have paid the story little heed, but I know P.J. Ettinger personally; his authorship lent the report credibility.

A former army special ops captain, P.J. prides himself on his toughness, marching to the beat of his own drum, and telling a story like it is, or at least as he sees it. Nearly six feet tall, he's still slim, with a bushy mustache and shoulder-length dirty blonde hair worn in a ponytail. P.J. moves fearlessly anywhere in the city, dressed in his signature combat boots and olive green combat jacket. His nose for news is legendary, although at times he's a loose cannon. I've known P.J. for a long time. In his early years at the newspaper, P.J. was an active member of the negotiating committee of the Newspaper Guild, the union that bargains for the *Chronicle*'s editorial employees. That's how I first met P.J., across the bargaining table. I've represented the *Chronicle* in its dealings with the Guild for the last thirty years. P.J. was too free a spirit to walk lockstep with the Guild. I wasn't surprised that before too long, P.J. became disenchanted with the wrangling of Guild politics that he categorized as "all bullshit."

More recently, a little over a month ago, P.J. took on Judge Sebastian Campo, one of the county's best known and least qualified judges. Lucille Bracha, an attractive thirty-year-old high school teacher, was charged with rape when school authorities discovered she was having an affair with a sixteen-year-old male student. The case, tried in Judge Campo's courtroom, was a media circus. With a sensitivity matched only by his intellect, Judge Campo, during the trial, commented from the bench that he couldn't understand all the fuss. As he so bluntly put it, the affair with Bracha made the sixteen-year-old boy the envy of his classmates. Matters got worse when, following Campo's controversial jury instructions, the jury acquitted Bracha of all charges because of the consensual nature of the affair. The acquittal outraged the public and embarrassed the legal community. Judge Campo panicked. In a blatant and predictably unsuccessful effort at post-trial damage control, he instructed members of the jury not to discuss their deliberations with the press.

P.J. knows a good story when he sees one. Never one to back down from an opportunity to expose governmental incompetency while challenging authority at the same time, P.J. ignored Campo's edict. He wrote a story critical of the judge, liberally quoting from interviews he conducted with several of the jurors. They blamed their acquittal of Lucille Bracha on Judge Campo and his jury instructions. The judge escalated the dispute, threatening, without legal basis, to hold the *Chronicle* and P.J. in contempt. The fight was one the judge could not win. The *Chronicle* on a daily basis skewered the judge on its news and editorial pages. Judge Campo scheduled a contempt hearing. Only a clandestine meeting in chambers brokered by Blackjack, with a firm partner expert in first amendment issues, convinced Judge Campo to drop his proposed contempt citation and avoid further embarrassment to himself and the judiciary.

The matter should have ended there, but not surprisingly it didn't. As P.J. left the courthouse, a Channel 2 television news reporter, microphone in hand, confronted the veteran newspaperman apparently still spoiling for a fight. The vignette was classic P.J. Channel 2 played and replayed the brief interview, and it was picked up and aired nationally by *NBC Nightly News*.

"Mr. Ettinger, what was behind Judge Campo's attempt to hold you in contempt?" The reporter stuck a microphone in P.J.'s face.

"The problem," P.J. responded without a moment's hesitation and slyly smiling squarely at the camera, "is the decision of the voters in this county to continually elect a judge whose intellect is a few French fries short of a Happy Meal and whose only qualification for his job is an electable name."

You would have thought P.J. insulted Mother Theresa. All hell broke loose. With that flippant remark, P.J. crossed an invisible line. The judges on the local bench, most of whom privately agreed with P.J.'s observations, circled the wagons in a public defense of one of their own. They demanded the *Chronicle*'s publisher fire, or at least discipline, P.J. I was summoned to the newspaper to negotiate an acceptable accommodation with the Guild hierarchy and P.J.

"P.J., you've done it this time. Stop smiling. This is serious. You went too far," I lectured the pony-tailed newsman grinning across the conference table at me in the *Chronicle*'s labor relations conference room. Larry Minkster, the Guild's mild-mannered executive director, sitting next to him, had on his best game face.

"The local judges are yelling for your scalp. You've violated the *Chronicle*'s Code of Ethics. You've embarrassed the newspaper. How do you expect to ever go in the courthouse again?"

"It's all bullshit. All the judges, or at least the three with half a brain, know Campo is an idiot. Isn't truth a defense?"

"Unfortunately, no. But you've done some good work and the Publisher is fond of you. So we're not talking discharge."

"Tell the Publisher I'm fond of him, too. So to make his life easier when he's drinking with the Chief Judge at The Back Room, I'll take a written warning. Slap me on the wrist, tell me I've been a bad boy, and don't do it again." P.J.'s blue eyes twinkled. "I could live with that."

"Get serious, this is a big deal. The judges are a blood-thirsty mob. They want your blood. We need at least a ninety-day suspension."

My proposal didn't go over well. Minkster made a face and started to speak. Before he could say a word, P.J. tapped him gently on the arm, a signal for him to remain silent. P.J. slowly shook his head, and still grinning, replied, "No, you guys get serious, make it a one-day suspension."

"One month."

"Two days," P.J. countered. I could sense he was enjoying himself.

"Two weeks. The judges are watching."

"A three-day suspension. That's as far as I'll go. Otherwise we can arbitrate."

"I don't know. What do you think?" I looked over at Mike Rowan, the *Chronicle*'s director of labor relations. Mike, a former college linebacker, six feet four inches and close to two hundred fifty pounds, is a bear of a man. Weightlifting in the *Chronicle*'s employee gym several times a week, he's remained in shape despite recently celebrating his forty-fifth birthday. His intimidating physical presence exudes authority.

Mike thought a moment and looked directly at P.J. "One week, five working days. That's the bottom line. Do we have a deal?"

"Deal." P.J. stood and extended his hand to Mike.

18

Paul involved in an illicit drug deal? Unimaginable. Not the Paul I knew. But given P.J.'s reputation for credibility, the story troubled me. Unlike the run-of-the-mill *Chronicle* reporter, P.J. is not a hack or cheap-shot artist. I hadn't figured out what to believe when the phone rang. Phyllis interrupted my musings.

"We need to sue the bastards." Phyllis was so irate she hadn't bothered to introduce herself or say hello. She had read P.J.'s article and was steaming. "We need to teach those bastards at the *Chronicle* a lesson."

"We won't do anything of the kind. No lawsuits."

"But Steve," Phyllis tried to interject.

"That's final," I said firmly, not sharing with her how much the article had also upset me. "The *Chronicle*'s a client of the firm. I've represented the newspaper for years. It would be a conflict to sue them."

The potential legal conflict didn't interest Phyllis. She was indignant. Always the good tactician and wanting swift action, preferably revenge, she seamlessly changed course. "Can you imagine how upset Marti and the girls will be? You have to do something for their sake," she pleaded. "We know it's a lie." Phyllis was right. The girls and Marti would be upset.

"I've known the writer, P.J. Ettinger, for years. I'll talk to him. If you read the article carefully, there are no hard facts. Unnamed sources speculate about a drug deal. That's all there is. It's bullshit that Ettinger even mentioned the drug angle without substantiating evidence. He should be ashamed, and I'll tell him so. Maybe I can get him to undo the speculation in a later story." But I knew it was already too late. The damage had been done. Readers remember the titillating allegations of a story, not the later clarifications.

Unable to think of anything that would not further inflame the issue, I transparently changed the subject. "Are the living accommodations working out?"

"Better than I imagined. Peter's friend, it turns out, is quite the cook. The beef Wellington he made last night was like eating at a restaurant," she enthused. "And Peter, he's really happy. What about you, Steve? How's the eulogy coming?"

"I've written a rough draft. I'm fine-tuning now." I lied without the slightest shame, promising myself to start the task that afternoon. Hopefully, by then I'd be rid of my hangover.

After the conversation with Phyllis, I drank a third cup of coffee, gulped down two more Tylenol and, physically and mentally exhausted, curled up on the living room couch for a nap. Immediately I fell asleep and slept soundly. Two hours later, I awoke, refreshed, ready to begin writing Paul's eulogy. First, however, I dialed the phone number Detective O'Brien had given me. I'd give him the name of Paul's bookie. Then, in gratitude, I convinced myself the detective would tell me whether the police had any leads; particularly, if there was any evidence of Paul's involvement in an illicit drug deal.

My call went directly into the detective's voice mail. Without thinking, I left Detective O'Brien a message.

"Detective O'Brien, Steve Stein calling. Wanted to let you know I've completed your assignment. Paul's bookie is Mo Bernstein. when you get a chance. I was hoping for some info on this morning's story in the *Chronicle* linking Paul's death to a drug deal. Paul's family is most upset. Anything you'd share on the subject would be appreciated."

Immediately, I regretted leaving the message. I was delusional. Two chances existed that Detective O'Brien would be responsive: slim and none. There was a far better chance of winning the lottery. Or, maybe I'd learn something meaningful from P.J. Time would tell. In the meantime, a eulogy needed to be written. Writing ordinarily comes easily, but a sense of dread attached itself to this undertaking. With every painful word, my thoughts focused on the finality of Paul's death. The task proved painstakingly slow and required the balance of the afternoon.

It wasn't until late afternoon that I'd finished a first draft. I was debating the relative merits of ordering a Chipotle bean burrito versus a sub sandwich when John unexpectedly called from Chicago. He wanted me to alert Phyllis of his plans to attend the visitation and funeral. And he hoped to have dinner with me when he arrived in town late Wednesday afternoon.

"Does dinner fit into your schedule? It'd be special. I'd like to hear stories about Dad, especially when he was my age." Pleased that the belated blossoming father-son relationship appeared to have survived Paul's death, I told John to call when he arrived at the airport. By then, I'd have arranged a dinner reservation. Sounding genuinely appreciative, John thanked me. He had one additional question.

"Are you the executor of Dad's will?" John's unexpected inquiry, although logical under the circumstances, took me by surprise.

"Yes, I guess I am." I've remained executor through the countless revisions to Paul's will occasioned by his successive marriages and divorces. After revising his will once again after marrying Phyllis, Paul joked that the only constant in his will was my role as executor.

"Am I named in the will?" John asked. "Will there be a formal reading like you see in the movies?" John's tone sounded earnest. He wasn't pushy, but his questioning bothered me. Maybe money was what John was all about. I was having difficulty getting a read on him.

"Honestly, John, I don't know the specifics of what's in your dad's will. I'm not a trusts and estates attorney. Someone else at the firm drafted it. Years ago, Paul asked me to serve as the executor and I agreed. But that's been it. We never discussed content. Never. As far as a formal reading of the will, I think you're right, that's movie stuff. Beneficiaries get notified. As a son, I'm sure you're entitled to a copy of the will. I'll check this out for you during the week."

"That would be great. While you're at it, could you check whether Dad added me as a beneficiary to his life insurance policy like he promised? I think I mentioned that before."

"You did. You mentioned insurance when you were talking about your dad's premonition about death, or at least concern of something bad happening. I'll check it out for you. But this premonition, I haven't been able to shake that phrase out of my mind."

"I'm certain he had a premonition," John insisted. "He was worried."

"Yeah, you mentioned your dad was worried. But you were vague about what was bothering him. Think hard. Can you remember anything, anything at all that your dad said, that might give us a clue?"

"I've been thinking a lot about that. He was dealing with someone involved in a white-collar crime. I'm pretty sure the guy was a broker who peddled fraudulent investments to some powerful people. I think Dad worried there was someone out to get him because of this connection."

John's description of this mysterious client confused me as I tried hard to remember our earlier conversation. "I'm puzzled. I thought you told me the guy was a banker."

"No, no," John replied, his voice rising. "Dad said the man was a broker. I'm sure of it. Banker . . . No, I couldn't have told you he was a banker. If I did, I must have been upset and somehow misspoke. He was a broker with an Italian last name. I remember that clearly."

"Anything else?"

"Well, maybe drugs were involved."

"What makes you say that? You never mentioned drugs before."

"No, I didn't," John admitted, without argument. "But replaying my conversations with Dad, over in my mind, I realize now he hinted several times that this broker guy had a cocaine problem."

I didn't ask John to explain himself further, wondering whether he'd read the Sunday *Chronicle* online. Instead, I revisited his travel plans, the ostensible reason he had given for his telephone call. "Have you discussed your plans with your mom? When you come to town on Wednesday, will you be staying with her?"

"I spoke with her earlier today. I'll stay at her house, but she won't come to the funeral. It's better that way. She's still bitter."

"You're right. Babs at the funeral might create a problem." Knowing her presence wouldn't be missed, I added, "it's probably best for everyone."

Abruptly ending the conversation, I announced, "Unless I hear otherwise, I'll expect your call from the airport Wednesday afternoon."

19

My alarm, set for 7:00 a.m., was to wake me Monday morning. Actually, though, I woke up a half hour before the alarm went off. No way would I chance being late for my nine o'clock with Blackjack. I knew P.J.'s article in the Sunday *Chronicle* would displease the man and, a day later, he'd still be in a foul mood. Old school, Blackjack is averse to all forms of publicity. He believes quality lawyering combined with connections brings clients through the door. In more than one diatribe to the partnership, Blackjack blasted marketing as the evil empire transforming the legal profession "into nothing more than a bunch of plumbers." Ten years ago, for competitive reasons, he relented and permitted others on the firm's managing committee to hire a marketing director and establish a marketing department, a group he continues to ridicule as being useless as "an udder on a bull."

Leaving my downtown apartment for the ten-minute walk to the office, I took a deep breath. The early spring morning air was brisk and the ground still damp from the previous day's downpour. Government workers were already entering their cubicles. At the Starbucks across from the Union National Bank Building, I ordered a double espresso to clear my mind and picked up the morning's *Chronicle*. Spreading the newspaper on an empty table near the door, I scoured its pages for a follow-up story by P.J., muttering a silent prayer of thanks when I found none.

By 8:50 a.m., ten minutes early, I paced nervously outside Blackjack's corner office on the fifty-eighth floor. Attached to his office are a wood-paneled conference room and an associate-sized office for his personal secretary, Miss Maryanne Brodsky. She was there already. A heavy-set woman who wears her hair in a bun and favors two-piece woolen suits, the unsmiling Miss Brodsky zealously guards access to Blackjack's office. She's the gatekeeper, although I'm not sure what firm lawyer would be so foolhardy as to enter the executive partner's lair uninvited.

"Mr. Townsend will be pleased you are on time." Miss Brodsky's high-pitched nasal voice made me wince. She picked up the phone and announced, "Mr. Stein is here," listened for a moment, and then pointed to one of two chairs across from her desk. "Mr. Stein, have a seat; Mr. Townsend will be with you shortly."

Miss Brodsky busied herself with typing, and spoke not one additional word to me. The executive secretary to Mr. John Townsend did not fraternize with the hired help. At exactly 9:00 a.m. sharp, the phone rang; Miss Brodsky picked up the receiver, listened, and nodded. "Mr. Townsend is ready to see you now," she announced. She immediately resumed her paperwork.

Blackjack was sitting in a high back, navy blue leather desk chair behind a large Victorian mahogany pedestal desk with a navy blue insert leather top. A medieval oil painting entitled *The Banker* hung on the wall to the right of the desk, over a matching blue three-person leather couch. The painting portrayed a banker stylishly dressed in the clothing of the fifteenth century with a trimmed black mustache and goatee, and a large hooked bulbous nose. A multi-colored skullcap perched on his head, the banker held three gold pieces in his hand. The picture just as easily could have been called *Shylock*. I stood awkwardly in front of the desk waiting for Blackjack to acknowledge my presence. Dressed impeccably in a three-piece gray, pin-striped suit, he was twirling the chain of a gold pocket watch that dangled across his middle while reading the front section of the Sunday *Chronicle*. After what seemed an eternity, he looked up, an intense scowl on his face and spoke.

"This story about your friend is as bad, today, as when I first read it yesterday. I gotta tell you Steve, your ability at damage control is exceeded only by your uncanny ability to protect the image of the firm and your best friend."

I remained silent, knowing rebuttal on my part would only aggravate Blackjack further.

"Have you spoken to the police beyond that first meeting Friday evening?"

"The police interviewed me Saturday afternoon," I answered trying to control my nervousness.

"So what can you tell me about their investigation?"

I'd rehearsed my answer all morning, repeating my observations in my mind; that mind now failed me; it was blank. Yes, I'm a sixty-year-old partner at a national law firm and yes, Blackjack's demeanor intimidates me like I'm still a first-year associate. Finally I was able to string a few nouns and verbs together in coherent sentences.

"The lead investigator, a Detective O'Brien, is playing the investigation close to his vest. He's pretty hard to read and not one to share information. He knows Paul was a heavy gambler. He asked, and I gave him the name of Paul's bookie; figured that was prudent. I didn't tell him much beyond that, and absolutely nothing about the firm or its business. Absolutely nothing."

"What about this writer, P.J. Ettinger? Do you know him?" Blackjack was carefully watching my eyes.

"I've known P.J. for years. He's one of the *Chronicle*'s few competent reporters. That's what concerns me. He's solid, not the kind who makes up something out of whole cloth. He doesn't engage in flights of fancy. There's got to be a disconnect. Paul would never be involved in a drug deal. I don't believe it."

Silent at first, Blackjack finally responded.

"Paul was one helluva lawyer. That's what I believe," he mused, "but he was a confirmed gambler. Shit, you never know what those guys will do, especially when they start losing."

Without warning, Blackjack changed the subject.

"I got a twofer assignment for you."

"First, get your ass over to the *Chronicle* right away. Randall Anders wrote an editorial piece for Wednesday's paper criticizing our client Bert Joseph, the city's largest developer, for not spending enough money on low-income housing. When Bert learned of the embarrassing column, he called me, said he'd pull his advertising at the *Chronicle* for a year if Anders's negative piece ran. Hell, I couldn't let that happen. The paper needs the revenue to pay our fees. I spoke to the publisher and explained the realities of life; the *Chronicle* couldn't afford the hit. He agreed the column was left-wing social babble and killed the column."

"I guess the Writer's Guild, or whatever the damn writers' union is called, filed a complaint. They're meeting this afternoon. I promised the publisher you'd be there to deal with the union."

"When you're finished with that, get a hold of Ettinger and see what you can find out. I don't like publicity."

Blackjack finally paused and looked me in the eye. "You understand your assignment?"

"I take care of the union problem and then speak to Ettinger," I repeated, hoping this would end the meeting.

"I don't want another story like the one in Sunday's paper. If that happens, I'll be most unhappy, and I'm not pleasant when I'm unhappy." As if needed to hear that. At this point, Blackjack dialed his secretary and instructed her to send in his 9:30 a.m. appointment.

Turning to me, he concluded the conversation with a nod. "Thanks for the fill in, Steve." Then, as I hastily started for the door, he added ominously before I could leave, "Don't fuck up."

The *Chronicle*'s offices are also a ten-minute walk from the Union National Bank Building. I left shortly before the 11:00 a.m. scheduled meeting with the Newspaper Guild, I ran the gauntlet of clustered office workers gathered just outside its doors, enjoying the beautiful spring morning while satisfying their addictive cravings for nicotine. Dozens and dozens of brilliant yellow daffodils filled the manicured flower beds that bordered the cement plaza fronting the building. I resisted my temptation to snatch a daffodil to bring as a peace offering to the Newspaper Guild.

Once, at the *Chronicle* building, I flashed my specially issued identification card at the security guard on duty and proceeded to the third floor labor conference room where union-company meetings are held. The *Chronicle*'s Mike Rowan and Deputy Editor Miriam Goodstein were waiting for me. Miriam runs the editorial department on a day-to-day basis, allowing her boss, *Chronicle* Editor Ed Charles, to focus on editorial policy and community involvement. Miriam is petite, barely over five feet in her stocking feet. Beneath her good looks, Miriam is one tough journalist. On more than one occasion, I've heard Ed remark in admiration of his deputy, "You don't want to mess with that hellion. She may be small, but she's mighty."

When I walked into the conference room, Mike and Miriam were engaged in conversation. Mike looked up and greeted me.

"Well, hello Mr. Stein."

He looked over at the deputy editor. "I told you, Miriam, when Jack Townsend tells the Publisher a partner from his firm will be here at eleven o'clock, book on it." Pointing to a table at the far end of the conference room, he added, "Help yourself to a cup of coffee and a pastry."

"Yesterday, Miriam killed a column critical of Bert Joseph that Randall Anders wrote for Wednesday's paper. In her inimitable, sensitive supervisory style, she told Anders the column was a piece of shit." Mike offered this abbreviated version of what I might expect to hear when the Guild committee arrived, while I filled a Styrofoam cup with black coffee to wash down my blueberry Danish.

"The column was ridiculous and poorly written," explained Miriam. "Bert Joseph is one of the city's most successful developers. His specialty is in mixed-use projects and high-priced urban condos. Anders criticized him for ignoring low-cost housing in the city; it made no sense to me, so I killed it." No mention of Blackjack or the publisher.

"Anders didn't like my decision. He went crying to the Guild's Larry Minkster, spewing First Amendment bullshit. The paper, Anders claimed, was selling him and the First Amendment out because Bert Joseph is buying an advertising supplement to publicize the opening of a new downtown mall. Never one to miss a chance to create controversy, Minkster has rallied the staff in support of Anders. He requested this meeting to beat us up. I'm not good at dealing with their b.s. That's why you're here."

"It's good to feel needed." Actually, I enjoy the give and take of meetings with the Guild.

"I'll bet you ten bucks and lay odds that Minkster and his Guild pals can't name a single amendment other than the First," Mike chimed in. He never tried to mask his disdain for the Guild leader. Mike dislikes Minkster and the Guild because they are ideologues, never willing to compromise. He prefers the pragmatic leadership of the Teamsters Union which equates every problem to money.

Five minutes later, Minkster, Anders, Marty Abrams, the Guild President and obit writer, and two grievance committee members, Joanne Rivers, a feature writer, and Timothy Jones, a sports writer, entered the conference room. The juxtaposition of Minkster and Anders was striking, like Mutt and Jeff. Minkster, whom I've known for years, is a short pudgy man, balding with black horn-rimmed glasses and a gray goatee. I never met Anders before. He was maybe a few years past thirty but looked like he could still play college basketball: slim, well-built, perhaps six feet eight inches with reddish blonde hair.

After perfunctory introductions, Miriam, Mike, and I seated ourselves on the side of the long conference table closest to the door while Minkster, Anders, and the Guild committee lay claim to the opposite side, their backs to windows overlooking the newspaper's parking lot. This seating wasn't happenstance. Management and union committees religiously position themselves on the same side of the table at every meeting. One time, Mike and I upset the Pressmen's Union president by arriving early and occupying the window side of the conference table. The Pressmen president refused to start the meeting until we relocated to "our" side of the table.

"The *Chronicle* ought to be ashamed. It's a sad day in American journalism when a great institution like the *Chronicle* kowtows to an advertiser by killing a critical column." Never raising his voice, Minkster adopted the demeanor of a parent let down by his wayward child, trying to explain rationally the basis of his disappointment.

"I killed Anders's column because it was based on sophomoric platitudes, and for no other reason." Miriam's voice was equally calm, only the tenseness in her jaw suggested she was angry and ready to explode at any moment. She didn't appreciate the challenge to her authority.

"Goddamn it, Miriam," interrupted Anders. "Where is the freedom of the press? You've violated my First Amendments rights."

"They wouldn't know about the First Amendment. They worship the almighty dollar. They'd sell anything or anybody for a few pieces of gold." Joanne River's tone was as mean spirited as her words. I wasn't sure whether her veiled reference to Judas was a jab directed at me or at the Jewish ownership of the *Chronicle*.

"I don't know what law schools you each attended," I said, surveying the Guild side of the table. "But let me tell you what Harvard Law School taught me about the First Amendment. Mr. Anders, Marty, none of you have a First Amendment right to print anything in the *Chronicle*. All the First Amendment rights at the *Chronicle* belong to the owners of the newspaper, the Levinsohn family, who own its printing presses, and, by extension, to the Publisher and his representative, Miriam."

With the exception of Minkster, who peered at me from behind his horn rimmed glasses with what I interpreted as benign bemusement, Anders and the remaining members of the Guild committee glared at me. If looks could do injury, I would have been grievously wounded. Despite them, or perhaps to spite them, I continued my legal lecture. "Now, Mr. Anders, I don't mean to intimate that you don't have rights guaranteed by the First Amendment. You do. You have the absolute right to: resign employment with the *Chronicle* and pay to have several hundred copies of your rejected column printed at Kinko's, and then stand in front of Mr. Joseph's mall, handing out those copies to all the passersby. That's your First Amendment right." I paused for dramatic effect and flashed a grin to let the committee know how much I was enjoying myself. "And, personally, I hope you exercise that right."

Miriam beamed while Mike bit his lip.

After another ten minutes of bickering, Mike signaled the meeting to end. There was no contract violation, he repeated. If the Guild wanted to pursue arbitration of its grievance, he invited them to do so. "If your committee wants to stay and discuss things further, the conference room is yours for the next hour," he told Minkster. He then rose from the table and left the room; Miriam and I followed.

We adjourned to Mike's office, adjacent to the conference room, where the three of us chatted for fifteen minutes.

"You were fantastic," Miriam complimented me. "The imagery of Anders handing bills outside Joseph's mall was beautiful. Anders is such a pompous ass."

"Randy could barely control himself. He wanted to pummel you," Mike smiled, obviously enjoying the thought. "I loved it. Changing the subject, Paul Martin's murder was a shocker. Wasn't he your best friend?"

"He sure was. We were best friends since high school. I wanted to speak with P.J. while I'm here. I can't believe Paul was involved in drugs like P.J. suggested in his Sunday article." Turning to Miriam, I asked, "Do you know whether he's around?"

"I saw him in the office earlier this morning. By now, I'm sure he's having lunch, no doubt a beer at the Headliner across the street. I'm not supposed to know, but I'd bet dollars to doughnuts, he'll have more than one beer before he's finished. Still, he's our best investigative reporter. I could use a few more P.J.'s."

"Careful what you wish for," I quipped. "A few more P.J.'s would certainly help our legal fees."

"Why don't you to talk to Tony? If there's anyone who can get off-the-record information about gambling, drugs, and the mob, it's Tony," Mike suggested. "He's always liked you." Anthony Piscatelli runs the Teamsters Union at the newspaper. The mob's historical influence within the unions representing the drivers, at most large city newspapers, the *Chronicle* included, is a well-known secret.

"Thanks, that's a good idea. This morning's meeting worked. I'll be surprised if the Guild doesn't drop the grievance. I gotta get going now. See you later." Leaving Mike's office and the Chronicle Building, I hurriedly crossed the street and headed straight to the Headliner Café.

The Headliner, a reporter hangout, is a dingy bar with noteworthy *Chronicle* front pages decorating its otherwise cheerless gray walls. Inside the storefront, an ancient wooden bar and stools, four wooden booths along the wall, and a dozen tables fill a single darkened room. Despite the recent municipal law prohibiting public smoking, even in bars, the stale smell of forty years of cigarette smoking permeates the air.

P.J., dressed in his familiar olive green fatigue jacket, sat in the wooden booth farthest from the door, animatedly talking to two men, one in his twenties, the other middle aged. I recognized them as *Chronicle* reporters but didn't know their names. Miriam was right: P.J. was drinking from a large, now half-filled, mug of draft beer; a few uneaten French fries remained on his plate.

Engaged in discussion, P.J. didn't notice me until I stood almost next to him at the foot of the wooden booth.

"Steve Stein, what the hell are you doing in this place? You lost?"

"Actually I'm looking for you."

"Guys, let me introduce you to the *Chronicle*'s celebrated labor attorney, Steve Stein. If you ever fuck up, he's not a bad guy to know. This young tiger here," he tilted his head toward the younger of his two companions "is the *Chronicle*'s future Pulitzer prize-winning photographer, Frank Pierce. And Sam Brown here is a copy editor."

"Would you mind if I stole P.J. from you?" I asked P.J.'s two companions. "I'd like to speak with him privately."

Without waiting for Frank or Sam to respond, P.J. stood, drained his draft, belched, and gestured me to follow. He headed toward a table in the back of the room, mumbling so that only I could hear, "This should be interesting."

He stopped for a moment, and looking back, bellowed to Sam and Frank. "If I'm not back in the office in an hour, you know I've been canned."

No sooner had we seated ourselves at a table in the farthest corner of the room, then a frail-looking, gray-haired waitress limped toward us. Instantly I felt sorry for her, unable to imagine how she could eke out a living waiting tables in this place. She should have been collecting rather than still paying Social Security. She welcomed P.J., flashing a smile of recognition with crooked nicotine-stained teeth.

"P.J. what can I do for you and your friend?"

"Mary, my love, this is the *Chronicle*'s lawyer. For me, make it one Miller draft." Turning toward me, he continued, "Steve, if you haven't had lunch, I'd recommend a brew and the hamburger platter. It's the house specialty."

"I'll follow my man's recommendation; he seems to be a regular. Make it medium without cheese." Ordering, I tried to block from my mind all thoughts about the kitchen or the cook. They weren't pretty.

P.J. and I exchanged meaningless small talk until Mary served our beers. Once Mary left, P.J. shrugged his shoulders slightly and chuckled.

"So, Mr. Stein, you were unhappy with the article I wrote about your best friend."

"That's why you're so respected and good at what you do. You read people well. If any other reporter wrote the article, another reporter, I'd have been upset, but I wouldn't have believed a single word of it. But, you're not a cheap-shot artist. Knowing Paul has three daughters and a wife, you wouldn't have written the story without solid facts."

"Those same respected psychic powers tell me you're blowing hot air up my ass." P.J. leaned back, took a long sip from his mug of beer, and waited for me to continue.

"Paul was certainly not perfect. He womanized his whole life. He gambled too much. But I can't believe he'd get involved in a drug deal. And your article, P.J., your allegation of a drug deal in the last paragraph of your article was more speculation than fact. And then to write a headline—'Gambling and Drugs Suspected in Attorney's Death.' In my book, that's unfair to Paul's family."

"Bullshit!" He smashed his fist on the table.

P.J.'s face turned crimson. "You know perfectly well I wrote the story, not the headline. Someone on the copy desk read the story and decided to sensationalize it. Too bad; it wasn't intended. In battle, we called that collateral damage."

P.J. leaned across the table until our faces were not more than twelve inches apart. I could smell his beer breath. He spoke slowly, accentuating for my benefit each word. "I'm not saying, yet, your friend was selling drugs, but I am saying his death was connected to drug dealers. That's from an impeccable source."

"I don't suppose you'd share the source." Immediately I regretted my words, knowing P.J.'s reaction.

"Give me a break," he snorted. "You know better than to ask."

"I'm sorry," I paused, needing to defuse the situation. "But how can you be so sure? I've been told Paul had huge gambling debts and owed money to loan sharks. Maybe the mob killed him."

P.J. guffawed. "You may be one good lawyer, but you're incredibly naïve. The air's too thin at the top of the Union National Bank Building and made you lightheaded. It's affected your powers of reasoning. Dead men don't earn legal fees. Your friend owed a lot of money. He was considered a good credit risk. He was earning vast sums of money. Now he's dead and uncollectible. Those you would call the mob are unhappy about Paul's death. In its world, the killer has assumed Paul's debt. If I was the killer, I'd fear those people a whole lot more than the police."

"You mean the mob's trying to find Paul's killer?" That seemed strange to me.

"You're a quick learn. Look, Steve, I've been feeding you information. How about some reciprocity?" I looked at P.J. to see if he was serious; he was.

"Go ahead, ask." I wasn't quite sure what the reporter had in mind.

"Tell me about John Martin, Paul's son?"

I decided to answer, but cautiously. "John's the only child from Paul's marriage with Babs Brown. If you remember, she was the hostess of *Coffee Klatch* on Channel 7 for many years. The marriage ended in a nasty divorce. Paul and John's relationship was one of its victims. Using your phrase, collateral damage I'd call it. For years, father and son were estranged, rarely speaking. They began seeing each other about six months ago. John lives in Chicago, but I've been in contact with him. He's coming to the funeral."

"Six months ago. What a coincidence. That's the same time frame when John entered a rehab center for his cocaine problem. Did you know that?" I felt P.J.'s eyes watching my reaction to his revelation.

"No, I didn't," I answered truthfully, trying to mask my surprise. Looking up, I saw Mary limping toward our table carrying my hamburger platter. Surprisingly, coated with enough ketchup, the hamburger was edible. P.J. shared my French fries as we finished our beers. We agreed to also share information on an off-the-record basis.

The grandfather clock chimed two o'clock as I entered my office. Within five minutes, I was speaking to Tony Piscatelli. He's run Newspaper Drivers Union Local 567, a local of the Teamsters Union, at the *Chronicle*, since I was a young associate at the firm. I spoke guardedly. No way would I talk freely on Tony's phone, not knowing which government agency might be listening. Tony agreed to see me at Teamsters headquarters within the hour.

The Teamsters own a six-story brick building twelve blocks south of the Union National Bank Building. It houses three separate local unions and the regional Joint Teamsters Council as well as the administrative offices of three Pension Funds and two Health and Welfare Funds. I parked, as I always do, in a corner of the parking lot away from all other vehicles. While not superstitious, I am cautious, very cautious. I still remember when, ten years ago, Stan Black, a Teamsters business agent with underworld connections, was blown to bits in this same parking; a bomb, triggered by the start of his car engine, exploded.

Ushered into Tony's office, I found him sitting behind his desk, wearing an open-necked yellow polo shirt, undoubtedly selected to highlight his physique and tan. Tony stays in remarkable shape and doesn't much look like most seventy-six year-old men. I know his exact age because six years ago, I attended a Jewish National Fund dinner honoring Tony on his seventieth birthday. Every labor leader, judge, and politician in the city attended as well as quite a few bankers and financial types who make their livings by investing Teamsters pension money. That night, those attendees donated enough dollars to eventually plant an entire Jewish National Fund forest, in Israel, in Tony's honor.

Slightly over six feet, with a perpetual suntan, Tony still has the body of a weight lifter, his bulging biceps are tooled by the hour every other day that he spends lifting weights in the gym. A product of a rough Italian-Eastern European neighborhood, he rose to his current position on a combination of muscle and brains, and a rumored connection with organized crime. Tales of the Teamsters leader's fearlessness and toughness abound at the *Chronicle*.

My favorite Tony story occurred twenty years ago when Ted Stone, Mike Rowan's retired predecessor, ran labor relations at the *Chronicle*. Tony had agreed not to challenge the discharge of a driver fired for theft. Convinced he was the victim of a union sellout, the disgruntled driver showed up on the loading dock, waving a handgun, and threatening to kill Piscatelli, who was inside the building meeting with Ted. Hearing the commotion, Tony hurried to the dock to confront the gun-waving teamster. He disarmed him with a single blow to the jaw. Kicking the prone body off the dock onto the ground below, Tony ordered the gaping onlookers "to get the motherfucker out of my sight before I give him a real beating."

I sat in one of two plush brown leather chairs facing Tony's desk. A picture of James P. Hoffa, the current International president, hung on the wall above Tony, smiling down at me. A dozen or so photographs of a grinning Tony embracing various local, state, and national politicians including one shaking hands with President Ronald Reagan decorated the wall.

"Tell me, Steve, to what do I owe this unexpected pleasure? I'm intrigued." His curiosity was justified. Tony and I enjoyed a friendly working relationship, but I'd never before asked to see him on personal business. I wasn't certain what I hoped to accomplish. I'm normally reticent to ask a favor from anyone, let alone someone like Tony.

"My best friend and law partner, Paul Martin, was murdered on Friday." I felt quite uncomfortable but continued.

"It turns out Paul owed a huge gambling debt on the street. I'm naïve about these things, but I've talked to P.J. Ettinger, the reporter at the *Chronicle*, and he assures me those people wouldn't have killed Paul. He thinks they're probably now after the murderers to cover Paul's debts."

Now I came to the hard part. I didn't know quite how to phrase it. "I was hoping, I guess," I gulped and then blurted out my request. "you might check with your sources to see if they'd tell you who killed Paul and why."

As soon as I said this, I realized how crazy I sounded and the danger in even asking Tony for this kind of assistance. The thought crossed my mind that I was playing the supplicant in a scene straight out of *The Godfather*. What if Godfather Tony granted my request, but the cost was some unknown future favor? I felt a sinking feeling in my stomach.

Luckily, Tony found my proposal hilarious. Struggling I could see to maintain his composure, he spoke with tears in his eyes. "And if I told you who killed your best friend, what Mr. Fix-it, – I think that's what they call you – would you do about it? Buy a gun and kill the murderers?" . . .a muffled guffaw . . . "Arrange a hit? Let me share a secret. You're not the type. You don't have the stomach for it. Steve, I gotta tell you, for your own good, you are not messing with people who play by the rules."

Tony was right. If I knew who killed Paul, what would I do with the information? Tell the police? Would knowing help me and Phyllis better deal with Paul's death? Tony's voice jarred me from my internal debate.

"Why do you always park in the farthest corner of our parking lot away from the other cars?"

Tony's question took me by surprise. My face reddened. I wasn't aware that anyone, let alone the Teamster leader, noticed my choice of parking spots.

"Don't look so surprised. I notice everything." Tony beamed, delighted in my discomfiture. "That's why I'm still around after all these years. Let me answer my own question. You're scared shitless when you come here. You remember the car bomb in our parking lot that blew Stan Black to eternity and think you'll be safer if you park away from all the other cars. Do I get it?"

"Yes," I stammered, "but..."

"But, nothing. Those are the type of people that killed your friend. They blow people to bits after breakfast and then eat lunch with a hearty appetite." Tony stopped, letting his words sink in, and then continued. "I never thought I'd hear myself say this. I tell you this as a friend, Steve, 'Leave your friend's murder to the police.' I'll ask a few questions and see what I find out. But be careful. Sometimes secrets best remain secret. Poking around in this kind of business could prove dangerous to your health."

PART THREE
ENTANGLEMENTS

22

Billable hours fuel the large law firms. These firms, known as "Big Law," pay young associates exorbitant salaries and compensate equity partners equally well. Such extravagance requires the continued flow of billable hours – time spent working on clients' legal affairs – at high hourly rates. How can "Big Law" afford to pay an associate, two years out of law school, an annual salary exceeding one hundred seventy-five thousand dollars, you might ask? Mathematics. It's all mathematics based on billable hours. The newest associate bills twenty-two hundred hours at an hourly rate of two hundred and fifty dollars, adding more than a half million dollars to the firm's coffers—fifty thousand dollars more to be exact. After paying the overpriced associate salary and another hundred thousand dollars to cover overhead, the equity partners divide the balance. Leverage is the key, at eight associates to every partner. Yes, billable hours fuel our law firm.

In the aftermath of Paul's death, my productivity was becoming a problem. Here it was, four thirty in the afternoon, and I had billed less than two hours. Incredible. Even more incredible, I no longer cared. The facts surrounding Paul's death were pieces of a complex jigsaw puzzle that needed to be put together. Work could wait, as could the flashing green light on my phone. The written messages my secretary stacked so neatly on my desk would remain there. Speaking to Elizabeth Caldwell topped my agenda.

"Elizabeth," I politely introduced myself. "This is Steve Stein. I was hoping to see you in person later today or early tomorrow morning."

"That's not necessary. No need to waste your time. I know I haven't sent you the work I promised. Don't worry; I will. As soon as I find an appropriate matter, I'll send it to you. You can tell that to Blackjack. That should get him off your case."

She spoke rapidly, never asking why I was calling. Obviously, I didn't top her agenda.

"Let me explain. This call isn't work related. We need to meet personally to discuss Paul Martin."

A hush followed on the other end of the phone. I imagined a distraught look on Elizabeth's face as she was deciding how to respond to this bombshell.

"There's . . . there's frankly nothing to talk about. I . . . I honestly don't know him," Ms. Caldwell stuttered. She recovered, although not convincingly. "Maybe I met him a few times at parties. There's honestly nothing to talk about, honestly." Mentally, I noted her use of the word honestly, twice in one sentence. Over the years, I've observed that people who use words like honestly, candidly, truthfully are hiding something.

"What about the dinner with Paul at Morton's? Dinner doesn't count?"

"I've no idea what you're talking about. Paul and I never dined together at Morton's or any other place. So let's just end this conversation."

I decided it was time to end Elizabeth's façade of innocence.

"Then, of course, there was the February trip with Paul to Las Vegas. I'm curious. Did you enjoy the Bellagio? I've never stayed there. Do you think I'd like the accommodations?"

Elizabeth didn't respond, although I could hear her breathing heavily into the receiver. I looked at my watch and counted off ten seconds before continuing.

"Really Elizabeth, you've produced enough b.s. to make the grass grow green. Do you want to meet tonight or first thing in the morning? Those are your only options."

"I won't let you bully me. We've nothing to talk about. . Do you hear me?" Elizabeth's voice grew louder and higher. I said nothing.

"O.K., O.K., I admit it. Are you satisfied? I confess. I had an affair with Paul. There was one weekend together at the Bellagio in Las Vegas, and then he broke it off. He was in love with his wife. What's her name?"

"Phyllis."

"Yeah, Phyllis. He was in love with his wife, Phyllis, so he broke it off. That's the whole story. I've no intention of meeting with you. What are you going to do? Tell the grieving widow her husband had an affair. You're not that big an asshole."

Information obtained in a telephone conversation is hard to evaluate. Without observing facial expressions and body language, it's difficult to determine truthfulness. But I could tell Elizabeth was trying too hard, way too hard. I again enlisted silence as an ally. Glancing at my watch, I allowed ten more seconds to pass before responding to her outburst.

"Elizabeth, you're lying again. You and Paul had separate rooms at the Bellagio. You didn't sleep with him. He slept with someone else. Phyllis knows about you, Morton's, and Las Vegas." I treated Elizabeth with a large dose of the truth, just not the whole unvarnished truth. She needed to be convinced that any claim of a relationship with Paul gave her no leverage and meeting with me was the most attractive (or the least objectionable) of her available alternatives. So I pulled out my trump card.

"This entire conversation bores me, Elizabeth. I'm looking right now at a business card with the phone number of Detective O'Brien. He's investigating Paul's death. Since you've nothing to hide, here's what I propose to do. I'm going to count slowly to five. If I reach five and you haven't agreed to meet tonight, I'll hang up, call Detective O'Brien, and give him the lowdown on Morton's and the Bellagio. From what I can tell, he's a real sweetheart, an understanding man. One . . . two . . . three . . . ." Elizabeth, like others I've met over the years, needed a little push to hurdle the initial barrier that separated us from a possible friendship.

"Stop! Stop! You win," Elizabeth screamed into the phone. "I'll meet with you." She paused to catch her breath and then continued. "Six. Can we meet at six? I have a dinner date on the east side at eight. I can't be late. My boyfriend would never understand."

"Fine. It's a date. I'll meet you tomorrow at The Rusty Nail at six o'clock. That's the bar off the lobby of the Downtown Marriott. I'll get a table and we'll talk." I repeated as ominously as I could, "Six o'clock sharp. Don't be late." With that final warning, I pressed the disconnect button on my phone.

23

Enough time remained before the short walk to The Rusty Nail, to call Shecky Levine, Billy's contact at the Bellagio, maybe even enough to talk to my partners, Marla Taylor, the trust and estates lawyer probating Paul's will, and George Rushing, the head of the firm's litigation practice. Fearing protracted telephone tag, I first phoned Shecky. Lady Luck smiled, and the Bellagio telephone operator connected me directly to Mr. Levine.

"Hello, Mr. Levine," I formally introduced myself hoping to establish my bonafides.

"Steve, you don't mind if I call you Steve, do you?" Shecky interrupted before I finished my first sentence. He spoke with a thick Bronx accent; his cadence was pure New York City.

"Of course not."

"Good. Steve, you're a friend of Billy and that makes us friends. No more Mr. Levine bullcrap. All my friends call me Shecky. Mr. Levine was my father and he's been dead for twenty years. You with me on that?"

"Yes, Shecky," I replied, admiring how Billy's friend had seized control of the conversation. Shecky had no intention of allowing me to speak.

"Billy told me you're not a gambler, but hey, no one's perfect." He chortled at his own humor. "The Bellagio will provide you with a suite, meals, shows, the works; no cost to you. I promised Billy we'd extend you every courtesy."

"I'm overwhelmed," I stammered, "I really am."

Shecky wasn't finished bestowing largesse. "Billy told me you're getting divorced." Shecky laughed again. He was a man who enjoyed his own humor. "What a downer. Hell, I never made it past five years in any of my marriages. Not to worry. Billy says we gotta get you back in the saddle. That's not going to be a problem, Steve. I'll fix you up with some of the finest ass in Vegas; really hot stuff. They'll give you whatever you want. The pussy, though, that's not on the house. You got to pay for it, but it'll be money well spent. That's a promise. Only the best for a friend of Billy."

"Thanks, but those types of arrangements won't be necessary," I replied with unintended swagger. "I have my own lady friend in Vegas and she's promised to show me a great time." I verbalized my plan to take Jane up on her suggestive offer, but without waiting until January. Just the thought of spending a night with Jane excited me. Of course, Jane hadn't been informed, let alone agreed, to these plans that I just confided to a total stranger. Shecky and I scheduled the Las Vegas visit for the July 4th weekend.

"There's one other thing, Shecky, you could do to help. Two friends, Paul Martin and Elizabeth Caldwell, stayed at your hotel for a weekend in February; in separate rooms, I understand. They met with a Chinese banker and an Arab banker named Muhammad. Any chance you could get me the names of these bankers?"

"This Paul Martin," Shecky inquired, "wouldn't happen to be the friend Billy said was murdered?"

"Yes," I answered. "Does that make a difference?"

Apparently it did. "I'd love to help you, Steve, I really would, but Nevada has privacy laws. You just can't go rummaging through the casino's reservation computer for anyone, even if he's a friend like you, Steve. Someone could get into a lot of trouble. Gaming commission, licenses, privacy laws are a bitch."

"You forget, Shecky, I'm a lawyer. I understand the problem. Perhaps if you can't do it for me," I suggested, "you'd consider doing it for a great American like Benjamin Franklin."

"Ten," he countered without hesitation, "but only because I'm fond of Americana, a collector actually. Benjamin Franklins are a special favorite."

"That's a lot of Americana, but you got a deal." While more expensive than expected, the information was important.

"For each banker," Shecky added.

"There's a lot of Billy in you," I told him. The cost of the information was escalating. "I couldn't afford not being your friend."

For cash, payable in advance, Shecky promised to obtain the coveted information from the Bellagio reservation system. The conditions of our deal were simple: a plain white envelope containing twenty Benjamin Franklins was to be delivered in a FedEx package to Shecky tomorrow morning. Upon receipt, he'd call with the information. Another important piece of the puzzle would be in place: the identity of the bankers whom Paul and Elizabeth met with in February.

Both an internal elevator and stairwell connect the firm's ten floors. I make a point of using the stairs. At my age, every bit of exercise helps. George Rushing's office is located on the fifty-second floor, near accounting.

I knocked on the open office door as I entered. Hunched over his computer, George was fully absorbed in the screen. Not surprisingly, as I moved closer, I identified a Yahoo finance page on the screen. A wealthy man, George spends part of each day following his, or more accurately, his wife's substantial portfolio. Once, at a firm party, Blackjack—as only he can—pointing to George, succinctly characterized the secret of George's financial success.

"I tell each group of young associates joining the firm the key to success is to marry well and invest her money wisely. George listened and has done both."

George coordinates the firm's litigation practice. Litigation at a large law firm like ours is far less exciting than what is portrayed on television; George spends little time in the courtroom. Ten years ago, the Federal Government built a new courthouse. It wouldn't surprise me if George never has been inside. Motion practice, discovery, and preparation for trials eventually settled constitute most of the litigation department's billable hours. By contrast, Paul reveled in courtroom combat, handling more than a half dozen trials annually. The cases that would not settle were assigned to him as lead trial counsel.

George, stylishly dressed in a tailored, navy blue pinstriped three-piece Italian silk suit, looked up from his computer screen. He swiveled in his chair to face me. In his early fifties, George was well-maintained with a perpetual tan.

As I stood in front of his desk, I admiringly asked, "What's the secret of your tan?"

"A condo in the Caymans," he replied. "What can I do for you, Steve?" George's tone was affable but businesslike. We weren't friends; our respective paths seldom crossed. But, over the years, we'd never butted heads. I was confident he'd furnish straight answers.

"Was Paul working on any white-collar crime cases, like a broker charged with selling fraudulent securities?"

"Sure, the firm represents David Giacomo. You must not read the newspaper you represent," George chided. "For months, his saga has been front-page fodder. What specifically do you want to know?"

"Give me the condensed version of his problems with special emphasis on Paul's role."

"David Giacomo's a former Merrill Lynch broker. Bluntly, he's a crook who's in deep, deep shit now. The Feds charged him with every type of security fraud imaginable. The day after the story broke, Merrill fired him, and he was arrested two days later. I shouldn't say this about a client, but he's a scam artist and not a particularly pleasant one. Very arrogant. What he did was nothing more elaborate than a Ponzi scheme. But he thought big. He peddled his wares to some of the most prominent and well-to-do citizens of the city, especially ethnics like himself, with last names ending in a vowel."

"What kind of money are we talking about?" I wanted to know the magnitude of the scam.

"We're talking big bucks, perhaps thirty million, maybe even more. Not much has been recovered. From what I've seen and heard, there are some very upset people around: some mobbed-up people invested. Tony Piscatelli, who runs the Teamsters at the *Chronicle*, lost three hundred thousand. If I were Giacomo, I'd worry as much about the Mob as the government; they don't worry about due process."

"So where did Paul fit in?" I thought I could guess, but I wanted to hear George explain Paul's role.

"Unless Giacomo comes up with the missing money, or comes up with satisfactory restitution, which he doesn't show interest in doing," George explained, "the government won't plea bargain. Without a plea, Giacomo faces thirty years in the Federal slammer where there's no parole."

"When a trial appeared inevitable, we involved Paul. He didn't know much about securities fraud, but he was our best trial lawyer. I've always said, you can teach a lawyer the law, but you can't teach courtroom presence. It's a gift of God. That's where Paul fit in. But he's gone now."

"Was Paul handling other white-collar crime cases, maybe one involving a bank?"

"Same case." George answered without a moment's hesitation. "Giacomo founded what's called a de novo bank. That's business jargon for a new bank. The bank attracted a large number of investors. Everybody wanted to own a piece. They thought there was real money to be made and didn't want to be left out. The bank was the linchpin of Giacomo's schemes and now its stock is worthless. That's where Tony P. invested his three hundred grand."

A gold pocket watch hung from George's vest pocket. He opened and examined the watch with exaggerated care.

"Steve, I don't want to be rude, but your three minutes needs to be up. The wife and I are hosting a dinner party tonight. If I'm late, there will be hell to pay – can't afford that. If you have more questions, we can set a time tomorrow to meet again."

"George, you've been super, like I knew you'd be; so understanding of the needs of a grieving friend," I assured him. "One final question: I promise it'll be the last. How do you see Paul's death as impacting the Giacomo case?"

"It'll create some logistical problems, though nothing I can't handle. I'll need to select another trial lawyer and familiarize him or her with thousands of pages of documents. That'll take considerable time. The trial was scheduled to begin in three weeks. The court will be unhappy, but we'll be asking for an eight-month postponement to prepare our new first chair trial counsel. My best guess is the judge will grant a four-month postponement, maybe six months."

"What about Giacomo? Where does he fit in with all this?"

George smiled. "So much for your promises. Here's one of mine. This will be my last answer. " To emphasize his determination to end the conversation, George rose from his chair and picked up his umbrella from behind his desk.

"Giacomo is elated. He'll pay a bigger legal bill, but will now postpone incarceration for another six months. For him, Paul's tragedy is fortuitous, probably the best thing that could happen. If you have anything else, see me tomorrow. I have to run."

"Nothing else. You've been most helpful." I abruptly turned and left the office before George did.

After stopping to cash a two thousand dollar personal check in Accounting, I placed twenty neatly stacked one hundred dollar bills in a plain white envelope on which I printed "Shecky Levine" and "Personal and Confidential" in small block letters. Mary McAllister, my secretary, would overnight a Federal Express letter package to Shecky, care of the Bellagio Hotel in Las Vegas.

Two flights of stairs later, I stood outside of Marla Taylor's office located in a section of the fifty-sixth floor reserved for trust and estates lawyers. Marla joined the firm, from the University of Michigan Law School, as its third female associate, at the same time as Paul and I. Her original ambition was to become a deal-making corporate lawyer. That dream was transformed into a nightmare by the old boy network that ran the firm's corporate department. They denied her admission to their club. The corporate partners flooded Marla with no-win assignments, followed by biased performance appraisals impugning her legal ability. In lockstep with the corporate department, firm management questioned Marla's continued tenure. Marla, strong-willed and stubborn, unlike two earlier female associates, refused to surrender to the prevailing sexism. She doggedly persevered and became the firm's first female partner.

Marla found her path to success as the protégé of Walter B. Church III. Wally, as everyone fondly called the pipe-smoking, bow tie-wearing genteel blueblood, headed the trusts and estates department; not one ounce of prejudice in his blood, despite his august lineage. Offended by his colleagues' loutish behavior, Wally placed Marla under his protective wing, becoming her guardian angel.

Wally managed the affairs of the city's old money. He introduced Marla to his elite clientele. It turned out that Marla was a natural with them — bright, witty, and charming. With Wally's blessing, she was making house calls to dowagers, enjoying afternoon tea at their mansions. She, as advisor, companion, and friend, discussed with the widows their ever-changing plans on how to divide, give away, or in some cases manage, their dead husbands' fortunes. Marla sits on the board of directors of three of the firm's largest local clients. She's even had tea with Blackjack's wife. The new generation of business lawyers pays her homage. Life at the firm can be full of delicious ironies.

Dressed in an elegant chocolate brown two-piece suit, which I'm sure was selected by her Saks Fifth Avenue personal shopper, Marla got up and greeted me with a hug. After thirty-five years, I remain one of her favorites.

"I was wondering when you'd stop by; we've got a lot of things to discuss and get in order." Marla was reseated behind her desk. It was remarkable how little she'd aged. A milk-cream complexion, her dark brown hair was cut stylishly short but without a hint of gray. I was too late: she had divorced and remarried two years earlier.

"I don't think I can handle it right now. I'm still numb from the shock of Paul's death. Could we postpone the executor thing until after the funeral?" I gave her my best hangdog look. "You got my word that I'll be a quick study."

"When's the funeral?"

"Friday."

"There's nothing, as far as you're concerned, that can't wait until next Monday. I'll start some of the paperwork."

"There's something else I need to ask."

She smiled. "Ask away, Steve."

"Was Paul's son, John, included in the will?"

Marla stopped smiling. She frowned. "Why do you ask?"

"I've been in contact with John," I saw no reason not to be completely candid with Marla. "He's coming in early for the funeral to have dinner with me Wednesday night. Apparently within the last half-year, father and son reconciled. John tells me Paul spoke of including him together with Marti's three girls as beneficiaries to a large insurance trust. I promised John I'd check it out. Can you tell me anything?"

"Unbelievable!"

"What does that mean?" The forcefulness of Marla's tone surprised me.

"You're not the first person today to ask that question."

"Who was the first?"

"Barbara Brown called earlier today and posed the identical question. Interesting, isn't it?"

"So what did you tell her?" I wondered whether Babs was freelancing or John had asked her to inquire. In either case, I didn't like it.

"I told her I could not and would not share that type of information with her. She wasn't a beneficiary in the will or any of its ancillary trusts." Swiveling in her chair, Marla reached down and picked up a file folder from the floor. She pulled out a yellow legal pad from the file and placed it on her desk.

"Let me read you several of Barbara's choicer comments. I took notes." Marla put on reading glasses to read from the pad. "'Lady, don't you know who I am?' 'You better watch your back Missy, I still know some important people in this town.' And, then there is my personal favorite: 'My boyfriend plays golf with Blackjack. We'll see to it that he throws your ass right out of his law firm. That's a promise.'"

The years had not changed Babs.

Laughing, I responded, "At our age, Marla, we should be thankful for the few constants in life. Babs is still the same sweet lovable bitch. You got to save that yellow pad." Then after an additional moment's reflection, "I didn't know Blackjack played golf. He never plays at the outing."

"He doesn't," Marla shot back. "She's full of shit."

"Are you permitted to tell me whether Paul made changes to his trust like John thinks he did?" I needed to decide how much weight to attach to John's story.

"No problem. As the executor of Paul's estate, you're entitled to the information. You have a right and need to know. Several months ago, Paul approached me to adjust his insurance trust. He'd begun to visit John regularly in Chicago and, if anything happened, he wanted his son to share his insurance monies equally with Phyllis and his three daughters."

"What kind of money are we talking about? John mentioned seven-hundred fifty thousand dollars."

"A million dollars each," Marla paused for effect. "Not too shabby. John is one lucky young man. Even though Paul was in a rush, he didn't complete and execute the necessary papers until April 2. That date sticks in my mind because I remember Paul bantering how he wouldn't have signed a day earlier because he's superstitious and never signs important papers on April Fools' Day. Think about that, if I'd completed the paperwork two weeks later, John would be receiving fifty thousand dollars instead of the million."

"Yes," I mused, "John is one lucky young man."

24

The Rusty Nail, the bar adjacent to the Marriott's first floor lobby, was nearly empty. At a long semicircular glass and stainless steel bar that constituted one end of the large dimly lit room, a gray-haired gentleman in his seventies sat on a bar stool chatting to two fiftyish women wearing clingy black dresses. Behind the bar, a young bartender with fashionably cropped blonde hair dressed in a tuxedo shirt and black bow tie stood wiping glasses. Four shelves of multi-colored bottles of trendy flavored vodkas and gins, as well as expensive high-end bourbons and blended and single malt scotch whiskies, lined the mirrored wall behind the bar.

Two groups of customers sat at tables in front of the bar; the tables that lined the walls at first glance appeared empty. I scoped the entire room. Elizabeth, wearing a charcoal black pants suit, sat alone at one of the tables along the wall. I walked over and sat down across from her.

For the first five minutes, we engaged in small talk while waiting for the cocktail waitress to bring our drinks. Elizabeth drank chardonnay; I drank my usual Ketel One and cranberry. Elizabeth was uncomfortable. The uncontrolled twitching of her right foot and continued tapping of the table with her perfectly manicured fingernails betrayed her nervousness.

"I'm frightened." Her voice was throaty and she spoke softly. "I'm in way over my head and need someone I can trust. I don't know what to do.

You threatened to go to the police if I didn't meet with you. So I'm meeting you. But if I tell you things, I'm sure you'll tell the police. And, if my boyfriend knew I was meeting with you, he'd kill me. No matter what, I'm in big trouble." While she talked, her jittery fingers shred a tissue clasped in her right hand. Her eyes were watering as she fought back tears.

"Give me a dollar," I instructed Elizabeth. Absorbed in thought, she sat stonefaced, gazing into her glass of chardonnay while her fingers continued to fiddle with the tissue. She acted as if she didn't hear me. "Open your purse and give me a dollar, now," I repeated louder.

We'd been conversing in hushed voices. My sudden strident tone startled Elizabeth. She fumbled through her purse. Finally. Success. She found a wrinkled dollar bill and placed it on the table. I picked up the dollar and put it in my wallet, at the same time handing her one of my business cards.

"What was that about?" Elizabeth stared at me wide-eyed with rapt attention. Her green eyes captivated me.

"You just hired me as your lawyer," I announced. "That dollar is my retainer fee. Since you've paid, there's a binding employment relationship. I'm your lawyer now. Anything and everything you tell me falls within the attorney-client privilege. No matter what you say, I'm not legally permitted to tell the police and they can't force me to tell them."

Elizabeth furrowed her brow, apparently trying to make sense of what I'd said. She was unaware, of course, that my cryptic description of attorney-client privilege was a bit exaggerated. Something must have clicked. Her face suddenly visibly brightened. For the first time she flashed a grin, even if just for a moment.

"Okay, Steve Stein, I trust you." Looking straight at me, she said, "I do. Call me Betsy."

"O.K. Betsy, let's start at the beginning. Tell me how you met Paul."

Elizabeth's chest heaved. She took a deep breath, but said nothing. She stared at me soulfully, her green eyes growing large. I waited without saying a word. My patience was rewarded when Elizabeth took a second deep breath, a swallow of chardonnay, and began speaking.

"I met John Martin six months ago in a rehabilitation center. The facility's located in Chicago; connected with Betty Ford. Paul arranged and paid for John's treatment." Elizabeth paused, took another deep breath and, this time, a gulp of chardonnay.

"I had a cocaine problem. First Mutual intervened and sent me for treatment. I finished treatment in December and have been clean since then." She looked directly at me. "I'm clean now, I really am. It's important that you believe me." As she made her plea in a low sultry voice, Elizabeth placed her hand on mine and gently squeezed. "You do believe me, don't you, Steve?"

The thought of having sex with Elizabeth was tempting, but I pushed the thought out of my mind. I pulled my hand away. "Elizabeth, I mean Betsy, I'm your lawyer. Of course, I believe you. How did you first meet Paul?"

"I first saw him on visitor's day with John in a visitor's lounge. It was right after Halloween. He was so handsome."

I gave Elizabeth a stern look. She blushed and continued.

"I knew about Paul. At the center, in group therapy sessions, John discussed his relationship with him, personal stuff. He told us about everything from enormous gambling debts to juice lenders."

"Juice lenders?"

"That's exactly the term he used. I hadn't heard it before either, so I asked what it meant. John told me it was mob money lenders."

She sighed again with a look of resignation. "Money lending is something I know and worry about. It's how I financed my drug habit. When I completed rehab, I was free of my habit but remained trapped. I was on the hook to those people for big money. Not as much as Paul, but a lot of money." Elizabeth reached out and placed her hand again on my arm that was resting on the table. Without a word, I gently but firmly repositioned her hand from my arm to the table and waited for her to continue. I said not a word, refusing her sympathy. She flashed an unhappy look and resumed her story.

"I approached Paul and John. I asked John to introduce me to his father, which he did. My forwardness embarrassed John. But that's me." I swear Elizabeth winked at me.

"I waited. Later that day, after Paul hugged John good-bye, I intercepted him in the reception area as he was leaving. I told him we shared a common predicament, large debts to loan sharks. I had a solution for the problem, but needed his help. When he wanted to know more, I clammed up. You have to string men along, especially good-looking ones, little by little. I told him I'd fill in the details, in December, after I returned home from rehab." Elizabeth's voice initially so shaky was now calm, her tenseness gone. She spoke with a measured sultry rhythm that hinted of Southern roots. Elizabeth seized this opportunity to tell her story. All I had to do was listen.

"Your friend was more adventuresome than you, Steve. Paul handed me a business card and told me to call after I completed rehab. I was instructed to phone at the office, using my title at the bank if his secretary answered."

"After returning home, in December, I dined with Paul at Morton's. He said it was one of his favorite restaurants. For the first time, we talked. I explained my plan. Paul didn't agree immediately, but he was intrigued."

Elizabeth interrupted the flow of her story to ask, "How'd you learn about Morton's? Did someone see us?"

"Not important. Tell me about this plan of yours. I'm curious."

"You're my lawyer and can't tell the police. Right?"

"That's how it works," I assured her.

"First Mutual is in the process of demutualizing."

"Yes, I know. The bank's planning to sell stock to its depositors. They're the actual owners of the bank since it is a mutual savings bank," I flaunted my one little piece of knowledge with pride. Maybe I was her lawyer, but I still found myself laboring to impress this good-looking woman. Thank God for Warren's lecture on mutual savings banks.

"That's right. Each depositor will have the opportunity to purchase up to seventy-five thousand shares at ten dollars per share as part of the bank going public. The investment bankers assured Greg Brennan there'd be an immediate bump when the stock started trading, two and half dollars, maybe three. I'm a depositor, and as it turned out, so was Paul."

"There has to be more to the story than that," I responded. "Even if Paul could get his hands on let's say three quarters of a million dollars, he'd only make around two hundred thousand. The problem, Betsy, is that Paul needed more money than that. Much more."

"So did I," Elizabeth whispered.

She stopped speaking and started fiddling again with the tattered tissue.

"I don't know if I should tell you more." Elizabeth verged again on tears. "You'll blame me. And, there's my boyfriend, if he finds out I talked to you, God only knows what he'll do."

I needed Elizabeth to finish. "You owe it to Paul. You owe it to yourself," I urged. "You'll feel less alone when you've shared with me what happened."

Elizabeth finally detailed the plot she hatched with Paul. She exploited her position as head of human resources, which oversaw the information technology department, to create four fictitious accounts in names designated by the mob. When the stock sale to depositors would begin, these four accounts combined with Paul's and Elizabeth's legitimate accounts would support the purchase of four hundred fifty thousand shares of First Mutual's stock. If as expected, when trading began on NASDAQ, the stock bumped up at least to the projected two dollars and fifty cents, the moneylenders will earn a cool million, wiping out Paul and Elizabeth's combined seven hundred thousand dollars debt. Any profit beyond a million dollars would be split equally between Paul and Elizabeth.

"Why did you need Paul?" As I saw it, Paul was superfluous, adding nothing of value to the scheme.

"No. No," Elizabeth responded with animation. "The plan would have gone nowhere without Paul. Paul gave the plan credibility. Our creditors considered me just another cokehead. The stock buy would cost four and half million dollars and we needed to borrow that money from them. I wasn't trustworthy. Hell, I wouldn't have bankrolled me. I needed someone of Paul's stature to sell the deal. Paul never said whom, but I know he met with people high up in the mob to get the deal approved. He may have been a gambler, but everyone respected him."

"Where does the First Mutual deal stand now?" I asked, not wanting but needing to know. It didn't take a Clarence Darrow to know Elizabeth had just confessed to a serious crime and implicated Paul, except that he couldn't be prosecuted because he was dead. To make matters worse, if that was possible, the firm represents First Mutual in the stock offering. The thought of explaining this mess to Blackjack sent shivers up my spine.

"The depositors have submitted their money to escrow and the bank is selling the maximum fifty-five million shares. That means we'll be purchasing the full four hundred fifty thousand shares to sell when the stock begins trading on the exchange on June 1," Elizabeth explained. "Paul's estate will receive the value of the full seventy-five thousand shares registered in his name. That means the mob won't get enough money from the deal to wipe out our debts. I'm praying they'll at least get their investment back. If not, I don't know what I'll do. Paul's death makes this a nightmare." Elizabeth became misty-eyed again and her lower lip was quivering.

"What about your February trip to Vegas with Paul? How does that fit in?" Given Elizabeth's barely controlled sexual energies and knowing the sexual history of my friend Paul, the answer seemed obvious. But I wanted to hear it directly from Elizabeth.

Her answer was involved and tortuous. "I have this boyfriend. We've had an on-again, off-again relationship for some time. I know he's not good for me. He has a bad temper and I have bruises to prove it. He's the one who introduced me to what he called 'white candy,' which led to my cocaine addiction." Elizabeth explained that in rehab, she promised herself and her counselors to end the relationship. The separation only lasted one month.

"David showed up in January on my condo steps. He stood there, bootless, snow up to his ankles in ten degree temperature crying. He was so sorry for everything he'd done. He was frightened. I knew the government had been trying to send him to prison for decades. He told me he loved and needed me."

I couldn't believe what I was hearing. I remember shaking my head in disbelief. Elizabeth's boyfriend was David Giacomo. I was learning much more than I had bargained for. Suddenly I was hearing her take on his fraud.

"You see it was actually David's master scheme to establish a new bank. He tried hard, to make it a success, but the bank failed and his investors lost everything. Now everyone, the government, the investors, are saying it was a scam. But it wasn't. David wanted the bank to succeed. It was his hook. He planned to use the bank to launder money for a Hong Kong bank with ties to terrorist organizations. That's where it's hidden, Steve. That's why we were in Las Vegas."

"I'm not following you at all," "What's hidden where, and why were you and Paul in Las Vegas?"

"David's using his international connections to hide thirty million dollars in secret accounts in this Hong Kong bank. No one will ever find the money. The FBI is constantly monitoring him, so when he needed money to live on and pay his legal bills, he sent me to Vegas to pick up that money. He couldn't go himself because the conditions of his bail don't allow him to leave the city.

"How did Paul get involved?" I hoped against hope that Paul was not involved in Giacomo's fraud.

"David learned about my business deal with Paul at First Mutual." Elizabeth looked away from me, down at her hands. "I know it was stupid. Telling him was a big mistake. As usual, I didn't use good judgment and paid for it. It was the first time since we got back together that he lost his temper. David was pissed off because it was too late to set him up with an account at the bank. He pushed me against a wall, and slapped me a couple times with the back of his hand."

She paused, sighed, and added with what sounded like a mixture of sadness and resignation, "I'm trapped, Steve, and I can't get out. I hate the son of a bitch. I really do."

"Betsy, I'll try to help but I need to understand the Vegas connection. How did Paul fit in?"

"I was picking up one million dollars in Vegas. David was concerned that his so-called friends might scam me. That's why he needed Paul. He believed they wouldn't mess with him. At first, Paul refused to go. That's when David threatened to expose him. I begged Paul not to get involved. I was certain David was bluffing. Paul didn't want to chance it. He said he had a family to protect. After about a week, he agreed to go."

I decided to push further to probe the extent of Elizabeth's relationship with Paul. David sounded like a possessive lover who would not have taken kindly to Elizabeth sleeping with another man.

"Did you sleep with Paul? I need to know." I watched, weighing Elizabeth's reaction.

She stared at me wide-eyed. "Never," Elizabeth declared, her voice rising. "I never slept with him." Her eyes misted. By now I was concerned that this beautiful woman could turn on and off tears at will. "I tried. God, I wanted him, but he refused. He told me it wouldn't be right for him or me. I was too special to be a one-night stand. I believed him until we got to Vegas and he spends a night with this Jane. When he saw I was upset, he told me she was his first wife from back in law school. It's not as if she wasn't attractive. But she was old, probably about sixty. Look at me, I'm fifteen years younger. Aren't I good looking, Steve?" she looked straight at me, waiting for an answer.

"He wasn't lying. Jane was his wife back at Harvard Law School. I knew them both." Maybe my validation of Paul's relationship with Jane would assuage a wound that even on its retelling seemed to upset Elizabeth's fragile ego.

I wasn't sure what more to say. "Any man would be lucky to have you, Betsy," was my lame effort to lift her spirits.

"I did something shameless the next afternoon." The tears appeared once more in her eyes. "Paul and I were in separate rooms on the same floor. At 5:00 p.m., he phoned to suggest drinks at the bar before our dinner with the bankers. I told him to stop by my room. When Paul knocked, I called through the door, saying he should come in the room while I finished putting on my makeup. Paul found me stark naked, spread-eagled across the king-sized bed. 'I'm yours,' I whispered, begging him to come inside of me."

My heart pounding, I listened spellbound to Elizabeth's graphic account, trying to visualize the scene. Her vivid tale exceeded the boundaries of my life experience. Good-looking women never have thrown themselves at me.

The story troubled me. Had I asked the wrong question? Just minutes ago, she denied categorically sleeping with Paul. Reading my thoughts, Elizabeth responded.

"No, I didn't pull a President Clinton on you." She winked. The retelling of this story for some reason seemed to raise her spirits, at least momentarily. "We never had intercourse or sex of any kind. A white hotel terrycloth robe was lying on a chair next to the bed. Paul first covered me, then leaned over, kissed me on the cheek, and whispered, 'Betsy you're too good for this. Now finish putting on your makeup.' Neither of us ever mentioned the incident again."

I checked my watch. No more than fifteen minutes remained to get the information I needed.

"Do you remember the names of the two men you met in Vegas?"

"Sure. The Hong Kong banker was Chen Chao. Everyone called him Chaz. The other man was connected with a Saudi Arabian banker. He went by the name of Joseph, but I think his real name was Youssef Muhammad."

Wondering how Elizabeth and Paul could have transported one million dollars out of Vegas, I asked "Was the trip a success?" One million dollars is ten thousand hundred dollar bills. I remembered, with regret, now that I had learned the names of the two bankers, the thickness of the twenty Benjamin Franklins I'd Fedexed to Shecky. In today's world of code orange airport security, carry-on luggage is thoroughly examined. Had Paul brashly checked the money through airline baggage, still x-rayed, randomly opened, and so often lost? I imagined Paul struggling to describe the item lost. How do you fill out airline paperwork for lost baggage when the item is a suitcase filled with one million dollars?

"Yes," Elizabeth replied. "After dinner we adjourned to Chaz's suite. He verified the transfer of the million dollars to Joseph. I'm not exactly sure how it's done, but for a twenty-five percent service charge, Joseph's people transferred the money to David."

"Betsy, that's your get-out-of-jail free card." Assuming the role of her lawyer, I explained that if she helped the authorities recover the hidden thirty million dollars and exposed a terrorist money laundering operation, her crimes would be forgiven. She might even get a new identity and life in the Federal Witness Protection Program. One of my more endearing traits is a willingness to pontificate on subjects I know little about – in this case, criminal law. It didn't require a Phi Beta Kappa key, though, to realize how badly the government wanted to recover the missing money and imprison Giacomo. I saw my plan as a lifesaver that Elizabeth would gratefully embrace. I was wrong. She was a bundle of extraordinary contradictions.

The proposition unnerved Elizabeth. She wanted to be rid of David, but he terrified her. Apparently Rasputin-like, Giacomo controlled her mind. "I'll think about it," was the extent of her commitment. It was hard to blame her. Giacomo was a sociopath.

Her continual nervous peeks at her watch made it a good bet that Elizabeth was moments from leaving for her date with Giacomo. I had one final question. "Was David Giacomo involved in Paul's murder?"

She shook her head for emphasis. "I don't know. I wish I did, but I don't. I never would have thought he could kill. But the pressure is changing him. The government is squeezing him and he is getting desperate."

She rose to leave. I reached out and squeezed her hand gently in mine. "Betsy," I urged plaintively, "please think about what we've been talking about. I want to help."

"I know you do."

Elizabeth was a woman who looked quite sad. She turned and walked out of the lounge

25

Emotionally exhausted, I sat, staring vacantly at the spot across from me where Elizabeth had been sitting. The discovery of so many disturbing aspects of Paul's life left me nonplussed, uncertain what to do next. A tonic for the stress was needed, so I ordered another Ketel One and cranberry. Thirty minutes of drinking alone and only one additional drink later, I paid the bar bill and left. The nighttime air was crisp. A refreshing spring breeze carried the scent of the flowers, now in full bloom, which bordered the plaza in front of the hotel. Absorbed by the replaying in my mind of the conversation with Elizabeth, I was oblivious to the light rain that had begun to fall. By the time I reached my apartment lobby, I was drenched.

After toweling down, I Googled Chen Chao and Youssef Muhammad. Chen Chao is the scion of the Chen family, one of the richest families in Hong Kong. His father, the legendary Chen Chung, controls the Bank of Hong Kong and through an interlocking network, more than two dozen smaller banks. Chen Chung trades on influence. Early on, he established a working accommodation with Mainland China and its Communist rulers, often serving as their financial proxy. Well known in Vegas in his own right, the eldest son, Chen Chao, or Chaz, is a gambler and a playboy. He favors baccarat and tall, buxom blondes and generally loses to both. The Chen family reputation was far from stellar: Internet blogs reported involvement in insider trading, money laundering, and the financing of Middle Eastern terrorist organizations

The three Muhammad brothers were outright frightening. The oldest, Youssef Muhammad, a Saudi Arabian businessman, married to one of the Saudi king's many daughters, is a central figure in Saudi finance. He serves as a director of the Saudi National Bank, which, through its support of multiple Arab charities, I learned, finances terrorism throughout the Middle East. The middle brother, Ahmed Muhammad, migrated to Gaza and is a leader in Hamas, the terrorist organization that controls the Gaza strip. Suspected of directing several suicide bombings in Israel, over the last two years, he is in hiding, hunted by the Israeli army. The last sighting of the third and youngest brother, Ibrahim, was in Afghanistan, among the staff of Osama Bin Laden.

After completing the research, I picked sparingly at the pizza I'd microwaved for dinner. The puzzle was missing some vital pieces but it did not portend a pretty picture. The vibes were dark and dangerous. Paul met Elizabeth through John at a rehab center. Elizabeth, in turn, involved Paul in serious criminal activity. During their trip to Las Vegas, Paul and Elizabeth met a dangerous cast of international businessmen. Paul's subsequent murder cost the mob's moneymen substantially more money than I initially realized. The mob's seven hundred fifty thousand dollar-investment in Paul's purchase of shares of First Mutual stock was now beyond the mob's reach. Maybe Tony was right. Maybe poking around could prove dangerous to my well-being. Maybe Paul's murder investigation should be left to the police.

My new client was also a source of concern. Elizabeth's victimless criminal scheme gnawed at my conscience. More disturbing was her involvement with David Giacomo. My gut told me he was the evil genius, in the middle of everything, who had created an entangled web of crime and deceit that had snared Elizabeth and Paul. To further complicate my life, the firm represented both Giacomo and First Mutual, and now, through me, Elizabeth. My temples throbbed contemplating these conflicts of interest. Blackjack would be most unhappy. And that would have repercussions.

I swallowed two Tylenol and climbed into bed trying to remember the lyrics of the song sung in that musical by the little freckled, red-headed girl, Annie—"Tomorrow."

26

Tomorrow came all too quickly. Two puffy white clouds floated lazily in a deep blue sky. Rays of the brightly shining early morning sun reflected off the puddles left by the previous night's rain. Suburban commuters, their long lines of cars filling the downtown streets, were arriving at work. With the moves of an NFL running back, I zigged and zagged around the puddles to the Starbucks to get my morning caffeine fix.

Armed with a mug of coffee and a blueberry scone, I bought the morning's *Chronicle*. The banner headline grabbed my attention. "Hit-Skip Driver Kills Two, Police Suspect Foul Play." A sudden overpowering nausea rose from the pit of my stomach as I read the first paragraph of P.J.'s most recent attention grabber.

"A hit-skip driver rammed into a forty-five year old banker and twenty-year-old valet last night outside of Michael's Restaurant, killing both instantly. A late model black Crown Victoria plowed into Elizabeth Caldwell, Director of Human Resources at First Mutual Savings, and parking valet, Julio Hernandez, as Caldwell climbed into the driver's seat of companion David Giacomo's Mercedes Benz. The car sped away without stopping."

"David Giacomo, an investment broker charged with multiple counts of fraud, is scheduled to stand trial next month. Among his alleged victims are persons with suspected mob connections. Anonymous police sources, who are not authorized to discuss the investigation, speculate the hit-skip driver may have been a disgruntled investor or a hired killer who thought Giacomo would be driving. Giacomo told police Caldwell was driving because he had been drinking heavily at dinner. At the last moment, he handed Caldwell the car keys when the valet brought the car."

The news stunned me: Elizabeth dead only hours after leaving The Rusty Nail. The sad expression on her face when she left to meet Giacomo lingered in my memory. I didn't believe for a moment Elizabeth had been the victim of an attack intended for David Giacomo. That story was far too convenient. Paranoia consumed me. Had Giacomo learned about my meeting with Elizabeth? Had he discovered she was planning to betray him? I was convinced that I was responsible for Elizabeth's death. Was I also in the crosshairs of the killer?

The short walk to the Union National Bank Building and the elevator ride to my fifty-fourth floor office passed in a blur. My mind was spinning. First, my lifelong friend is found murdered, execution-style, in a parking lot. A hit-skip driver then kills Elizabeth, a client of less than twenty-four hours, standing outside a restaurant. I had just begun to leaf through my accumulated phone messages when my secretary Mary entered my office.

"Mr. Stein, I didn't see you come in. Three policemen are in the fifty-sixth floor reception area waiting to see you. They arrived here ten minutes ago."

"Bring them into my office, please."

Mary returned five minutes later, accompanied by Detectives O'Brien and Mancini and a third man I didn't recognize. To my surprise, Detective O'Brien's wardrobe proved more extensive than I had imagined: he was wearing a rumpled black suit. Detective Mancini, in contrast to his partner, looked debonair in a light brown sports jacket, pleated beige slacks, and cordovan tasseled loafers. The third member of the trio resembled a banker, dressed in a well-tailored navy pinstriped suit, starched white shirt with French cuffs and a conservative red club tie with a small American flag in his lapel. In his mid-thirties, he was about six feet tall, muscular with a square chin and short cropped black hair. Handsome, he reminded me of Denzel Washington. Mary seated the three men in the chairs facing my desk. She offered them coffee. They politely refused. She then left my office, closing the door behind her.

"We meet again, Mr. Stein." O'Brien addressed me as the door closed. "You already know Detective Mancini, and this gentleman here," he said pointing to the banker look-alike, "is Agent Andrew Duncan, FBI."

My antennae immediately went up. What, I wondered, was this FBI agent doing sitting across from me in my office? The FBI doesn't investigate a murder like Paul's unless there's a federal angle to the case. But I had a greater concern. Providing false information to the FBI is a crime. I lecture clients that when an FBI agent comes knocking, they can respectfully refuse to answer questions; or, alternatively, they can tell the FBI agent to go to hell (a non-criminal but not advisable tactic), but never, ever lie to the agent. Lying morphs the visit into a serious federal crime. The interview is used by the FBI as a formidable tool, often knowing the answers before questions are asked. If the interviewee lies, the agent owns him.

Ignoring the bromide that an attorney representing himself has a fool for a client, I tried to keep a straight face, hoping anxiety wasn't written all over my face, and allowed the interview to proceed. If the questioning became problematic, I'd halt the interview. I promised myself that under no circumstance would I lie.

"Nice to meet you, Mr. Stein." Andrew Duncan flashed a broad toothy smile, revealing movie star-perfect white teeth.

Allowing for no further small talk, Detective O'Brien pulled out a small notepad and ballpoint pen from his suit pocket. He cleared his throat and ceremoniously opened the pad in anticipation of recording notes

"Do you know Elizabeth Caldwell?" O'Brien straight away established eye contact. His interview technique, now familiar, was more a nuisance than unsettling. Did he have a technique B? I wondered.

"Yes." I stared unblinkingly back at the detective.

"Are you aware she was killed last night?"

"Yes. The story was in this morning's *Chronicle*. I was shocked."

"When did you last see Ms. Caldwell?"

"Last night. That's what makes her death all the more unsettling." I watched O'Brien's eyes as I responded to his questioning with quick, crisp answers. The detective involuntarily blinked in what I interpreted to be surprise. I was certain he didn't know I was with Elizabeth last night.

"We found your business card in Ms. Caldwell's purse at the crime scene," O'Brien countered, struggling to regain his rhythm.

"That means she didn't change her purse before her date with David Giacomo," I explained matter-of-factly.

"Mr. Stein, would you be so kind as to share with us the circumstances of your meeting last night with Ms. Caldwell?" Agent Duncan interjected. His voice was deep. Each word was enunciated with precision and authority. "The more detail, the better."

"Elizabeth met me in The Rusty Nail at the Downtown Marriott at about six p.m. She hired me to be her lawyer. We discussed her legal problems for more than an hour. She had to leave for a scheduled dinner with her friend, David Giacomo. She never mentioned the restaurant's name, but from what I read in the *Chronicle*, it must have been Michael's. At the beginning of our meeting, when she hired me, I gave Elizabeth my business card. She placed it in her purse." I glanced at my audience. Dissatisfaction with my non-informative answer was written all over their faces. I was not providing details.

"Anything else you guys want to know?" I asked cheerfully.

A scowl darkened Agent Duncan's face. "Is that all you're going to tell us?" he grumbled.

"About the content of my legal discussions, yes, I think so. There's this ethical consideration called attorney-client privilege that I must honor. I'm sure you understand my predicament. At the beginning of our meeting, Ms. Caldwell made her desire in that regard crystal clear."

"She's dead," O'Brien pointed out, gripping tightly the arms of the chair as his face reddened and knuckles whitened.

"I'm not an expert, but I don't think her death makes any difference. But, I promise, I'll consult one of my partners expert in matters of attorney-client privilege. And Detective O'Brien, you'll be the first one I'll call, if I have a change of heart. Promise." Antagonizing the detective was childish, perhaps even foolish. But O'Brien enjoyed pushing my button, and pulling his chain in response gave me a perverse pleasure.

"Since I know you're a patriotic American, Mr. Stein, your government is going to lay its cards out on the table and ask for your help." Agent Duncan must have recognized the need to change tactics. He spoke with passion. He had a theatrical flair to go with his good looks.

"After the September 11, 2001 terrorist attacks, the FBI implemented surveillance programs under the USA Patriot Act as part of the Department of Homeland Security. Suffice it to say, we've been monitoring a particular Saudi Arabian businessman with family and business ties to terrorist organizations. Your client, Elizabeth Caldwell, first appeared on our radar screen in February when she met this gentleman in Las Vegas accompanied by a Paul Martin."

Jolted and unnerved by this revelation, my eyes riveted on Agent Duncan. He held my absolute attention. I realized when he walked into my office with the two local detectives, he'd already connected Paul with Elizabeth. What else did he know? This worrisome thought reinforced my fears of the FBI. If I falsified information to hide the connection between Paul and Elizabeth, I'd be in serious trouble. I wanted the interview over.

"Since 9/11, we at the FBI have made strides in information sharing with local officials, but we have a long way to go. I only learned today Mr. Martin was murdered on Friday and the local investigating team,

Detectives O'Brien and Mancini, weren't aware of the connection between Elizabeth Caldwell and Paul Martin."

"Today, I've learned a few things from them. First, you're Mr. Martin's law partner and best friend since high school. Second, your law firm represents Ms. Caldwell's boyfriend who is—how shall I say it delicately—a soon-to-be convicted felon. And finally, five minutes ago, we learned you claim to be Ms. Caldwell's attorney." Agent Duncan flashed his perfect white teeth and paused for dramatic effect. "Certainly food for thought, Mr. Stein, don't you think?"

I smiled backed and ignored his question as rhetorical and responded laconically, hoping to camouflage the panic I felt. "Go on, I'm listening."

"David Giacomo swindled thirty million dollars, most of which is still missing. We believe some of that money is finding its way into the coffers of terrorist organizations. Ms. Caldwell and your friend, Paul Martin, were facilitators, involved in money laundering activity. They're dead now, so they don't need protection. It is your country that needs protection. We want Giacomo badly and we want to nip any terrorist activity in the bud. I am asking you as a patriotic American to help the FBI in the global war against terror. Quite frankly, your nonsense about privileged communication with a dead person troubles me. Your stubbornness comes close to aiding and abetting our enemies. I'm concerned."

Somewhere in the middle of his speech, Agent Duncan ceased acting. He became apple pie and the American flag, incapable of seeing gray, only black and white. Instinctively I knew crossing Agent Duncan, backed by the full resources of the United States government, could prove perilous. I sensed that following the rules was not his forte.

"At this juncture, I'm not prepared to share the details of my conversation with my client. I'll discuss the issue with my own legal counsel here at the firm and will let you know my ultimate views more definitively down the line. But honestly, Agent Duncan," I insisted, feeling that I needed to express my own bona fides, "you misjudge what I know. I do want to help. I really do."

"I'm disappointed in you, Mr. Stein," I could hear the considerable exasperation in Agent Duncan's voice.

Addressing Detectives O'Brien and Mancini, I sought to refocus the direction of the interview. It was going badly, and I knew it.

"The idea that the hit-skip driver was attempting to kill Giacomo and killed Ms. Caldwell by accident is a fairy tale," I told them. "Giacomo was responsible for Elizabeth's death. I'm certain of it. I can feel it in my gut."

"Detective Mancini and I appreciate your candor. I'm recording your suspicions right here in my notepad. Do you happen to have any hard evidence to support this gut feeling?" O'Brien asked. "Or should I record it as the product of clairvoyance?"

"Only that Ms. Caldwell was a battered woman. Giacomo beat her and she was terrified of him. I'm certain he was involved in her death."

"When Ms. Caldwell left this – what shall I call it – legal consultation with you at The Rusty Nail, at what time did you say she left?" O'Brien's sarcasm was a none-too-subtle effort to focus Agent Duncan's ire back on me. The frown on the agent's face told me that O'Brien's effort was unnecessary. A bull's-eye decorated my back.

"I never said and you never asked, Detective. My best guess, she left five or ten minutes after seven o'clock. Ms. Caldwell told me she had dinner plans with Giacomo at seven thirty. She didn't want to be late."

"Did Giacomo know Ms. Caldwell was meeting with you?"

"I don't think so. From her general comments about Giacomo, I don't believe she wanted him to know she was meeting with a lawyer. That's why she was concerned about being on time for dinner."

Detective O'Brien had apparently heard enough. He stood up and closed his notepad, signaling the meeting had concluded. Then placing his two hands on my desk, he leaned forward and growled, "How long were you sleeping with her?"

Something snapped. To my surprise, I directly confronted O'Brien's bullying tactics. I stood up and went nose to nose. I replied in cold fury. "Let me make one thing perfectly clear, Detective O'Brien. Outside of a pitch some months ago for First Mutual's human resource work, I had never met Ms.Caldwell, alone or with other people. And another thing: I don't sleep with clients or with their employees, however attractive. I never slept with Ms. Caldwell. I never dated Ms. Caldwell. And, until last night at The Rusty Nail, I was never alone with her. Write that down on your notepad."

I walked over, opened the door to my office, and gestured for the officers to leave. "It's been a pleasure, gentlemen. If I can be of further assistance, I'm certain you'll let me know."

The two detectives left. Trailing behind them, Agent Duncan stopped by the door, shook my hand, and slipped me his business card. "The card lists all my numbers including my cell. I know your firm. I respect Blackjack; give him my best. Talk to your people and call me. We need your help, and I know you're a patriotic American." He flashed a final photogenic smile and was gone.

27

Agent Duncan's visit was trouble with a capital T. The FBI knew of Paul and Elizabeth meeting with Youssef Muhammad and Chen Chao in Las Vegas, linking the trip to Giacomo, money laundering, and payment of legal fees from tainted proceeds. And to make a bad situation worse, if that was at all possible, the key players were connected to terrorism. People go to jail for less, far less. And Agent Duncan's veiled reference to Blackjack was potentially career threatening.

I raced to Blackjack's office on the fifty-eighty floor. Miss Maryanne Brodsky sat at her desk, as usual, gatekeeping outside Blackjack's office, surrounded by stacks of billing statements. I stood near her desk panting, trying to catch my breath. Ignoring my presence, she continued peering through her bifocals at the pages and pages of numbers detailing hours worked and corresponding fees. I lost patience with her gamesmanship. "Tell Mr. Townsend I need to see him right away," I demanded. "It's urgent firm business."

"That, Mr. Stein, is impossible," she did not look up from her work. "Mr. Townsend left the country this morning and won't be back until Thursday at noon. He's turned off his Blackberry. His instructions to me were clear. He doesn't want to be disturbed under any circumstances. You certainly are no exception. I'll give you a slot at three thirty, Thursday afternoon, if you want. That's the best I can do."

"Shit," I mumbled as I turned and returned to my office light-headed. I sat and gazed into space, trying to decide what to do next. I was stymied. No satisfactory plan came to mind. The phone rang. To my surprise, the caller was P.J. Ettinger. After confirming I knew about Elizabeth's death, with little finesse, P.J. probed straight to the jugular. "Your business card was found in Caldwell's purse. Why?"

"How the hell did you already find that out?" I was mystified. My three visitors wouldn't have shared that type of detail with the media, not at such a preliminary stage of the investigation.

"I told you my sources are first rate."

P.J. did have a network of informers. His assistance might produce dividends in discovering who killed Paul as long as his involvement couldn't be traced to me.

"I'll supply you information, P.J., but on deep background. I need your promise not to print or mention my name. I'm already skating on thin ice with the authorities, let alone with Blackjack. Without assurance of anonymity, I can't talk." I knew if P.J. agreed to my terms, he'd go to jail before betraying me.

"You've got my word, cross my heart," P.J. promised. "Now what can you tell me?"

"I met Elizabeth last night at The Rusty Nail. That's when I gave her my business card after she hired me to be her attorney. I can't share with you much of what we discussed because of attorney-client privilege. She left me about seven o'clock for a dinner date with David Giacomo."

"Did she say anything about that asshole that you can tell me? He's one bad dude. It'd be a real pleasure to nail the arrogant little prick." P.J.'s passion heartened me. The public spotlight needed to be focused on Giacomo.

"He frightened Elizabeth. He physically and mentally abused her. There's no question he killed her. This concocted story about the murderer being after him is pure bullshit."

"You have evidence?" P.J. quizzed me. "Anything I can sink my teeth into?"

"No," I admitted. "It's just a gut feeling. There's a hit-skip driver hiding out there whom Giacomo paid. You're the one with a network of sources. You gotta find him."

The thought of a man like Giacomo murdering Elizabeth and escaping detection infuriated me. I had no confidence that any investigation headed by Detective O'Brien would be successful. The police needed help. Who better than P.J. and I? On an impulse, I decided to reveal Paul and Elizabeth's relationship.

"We're not having this conversation. You never heard what you're about to hear. You with me on this?"

"I already gave you my word."

"O.K. Earlier this morning, O'Brien, Mancini, and an FBI agent interviewed me about Elizabeth's death. They have linked Elizabeth and Paul."

"Paul and Elizabeth," P.J. mulled over the thought. "So what's the connection?"

"Check out the Bellagio hotel in Vegas in early February. They stayed in separate rooms, so they both should have registered. That's all I can tell you right now. I've probably talked too much." Maybe I had. Almost immediately I had misgivings about the wisdom of sharing the information with P.J., let alone on a telephone. Agent Duncan was a particular concern. He couldn't have tapped my phone already, I assured myself.

P.J. must have sensed my anxiety. He asked clairvoyantly, "Who is the FBI agent? Can you tell me that?"

"An Agent Duncan. Andrew Duncan. Ever heard of him?"

"He's sharp. Not someone to mess with," he told me, to my chagrin. "He's in line to become Agent-in-Charge in the city if he doesn't get a major assignment in Washington first. Don't fall for his shtick. Sometimes he'll play the country bumpkin, sometimes the right-wing zealot. It's mostly a charade. But watch out. He believes in his mission and he'll do whatever is necessary to win."

This was not the description I wanted to hear. "If you're trying to frighten me, P.J., you're doing a good job."

"A little fear can be a good thing. You need to be careful," he cautioned. "We're a team now. Don't underestimate the man. And, remember Steve, never lie to the FBI. For what it's worth," he continued without waiting for a reply, "I've learned your friend Paul met with two Latino drug dealers, Paco Rodríguez and Juan Rodríguez, at least once prior to last Friday."

"What else can you tell me?"

"Nothing really. I haven't been able to confirm Paul was meeting with the Rodríguez brothers when he was killed. And I don't know the nature of Paul's dealings with them."

For the first time since Friday, when P.J. hung up, I felt positive. Aside from the fragment of intriguing information about the Rodríguez brothers, I realized I still had no leads as to who killed Paul or any evidence to tie David Giacomo to Elizabeth's murder. Agent Duncan loomed as a formidable threat. But, somehow I didn't feel quite as alone.

28

Over the next fifteen minutes, I spoke first with Phyllis and then with Shecky Levine. Phyllis had read the morning's *Chronicle*. Elizabeth's death stunned her, as did her reported relationship with the notorious David Giacomo.

"How could Paul be involved with a woman like that?" she demanded to know.

"He wasn't."

"Say again?"

"Phyllis, I've positively confirmed there was nothing going on between Elizabeth and Paul. It was all business."

"What kind of business?"

"I'm really not at liberty to share that with you right now."

That was not the answer she wanted. "Steve, you have a problem with communication." Phyllis raised her voice as she spoke. "Friends communicate. They don't keep secrets." She hung up. The rebuke stung, even though I knew I was serving as Paul's surrogate for Phyllis's hurt and frustration. She was right, I was keeping secrets. But I had no choice. That's what I told myself.

Shecky proved even more problematic He'd received and was returning the package of Benjamins.

"I'm returning the package unopened. Never opened it. Wouldn't.

Couldn't." Shecky spoke rapidly, making no effort to hide his concern. "It wouldn't be healthy for me to give you the info. I couldn't get a friend like you in trouble. Wouldn't do that to you. If anyone even found out what I was planning to do, getting fired would be the least of my problems. You gotta promise you'll never tell anybody about sending the package." He was frightened. "I'll owe you, big time."

"What package?" I responded without hesitation.

"You're a prince." I could hear Shecky sigh with relief. "You and your lady friend will have the time of your lives. That's a promise. Won't cost you a penny. I'll even spring for the airfare."

Shecky's second thoughts had saved me two thousand dollars since his help was no longer needed. I had already identified the two men Paul and Elizabeth were meeting at the Bellagio. But for someone like Shecky to return two thousand dollars and to insist on erasing all memory of our conversation brought home the dangerousness of what I was getting into. It was scary. Just as I was in the process of trying to logically evaluate my sudden second doubts, a curly-haired man with a bushy brown mustache entered my office, closing the door quietly behind him. Surprised, I stared at the short, stocky figure clad in blue designer jeans and a brown turtleneck. He was smiling at me. Where had I seen his familiar looking face? Recognition sent a chill down my spine. David Giacomo was standing in my office.

Wordlessly, Giacomo plopped down on my couch and placed his alligator boot-clad feet carelessly on my coffee table. He pulled a ruby-and-diamond-encrusted silver case from his jean pocket, removed a cigarette, and lit up. Inhaling deeply, he blew rings of smoke in my general direction.

Glaring at me, he hissed in a hoarse, raspy voice, "What did she tell you?"

"In case you're unaware," I pointed out in calm, even tones, "it's against state law to smoke in offices."

"Indict me. That should be the worst of my problems. Now what did Elizabeth tell you?"

Giacomo's brazen presence was puzzling. Elizabeth's probable killer lounged in my office, defiantly thumbing his nose at me. His bravado astonished me. I could feel my heart pounding. Giacomo knew I'd met with Elizabeth. The police wouldn't have let that slip out. Had Elizabeth told him? How much did he know? My head was spinning but I knew it was important to maintain a calm exterior.

"What are you talking about?" I stammered. Calm down Steve, I kept telling myself. Don't panic.

Giacomo eyed me coolly, all the while puffing on his cigarette.

"Stop bullshitting. You met with Betsy last night. What did she tell you?"

That was the second time he asked that question. I breathed easier, now certain Giacomo was trying to learn how much of his business I knew.

"You're the man with the answers. Why don't you tell me?"

"No problem if that's how you want to play it." Pausing to slowly drag on his cigarette, when I didn't respond, he continued. "As she told you, Betsy and I had dinner last night at Michaels. During dinner, she goes to the ladies' room and leaves her purse on the table. I need a pen so I open her purse. You can imagine my surprise when I find your business card. I put two and two together and, buddy, it doesn't add up to three."

"Betsy calls and says she's running a half hour late. Heavy traffic. When she does arrive, she's all hyper. Her mind's somewhere else. I'm the sensitive type. I ask, 'Is something bothering you?' 'No,' she tells me. 'It was a hard day at the bank.' Bullshit. She was with you."

"I place your business card back in the purse and pretend nothing's wrong. Five minutes later, I go to the men's room. When I come back, I scream at her. I tell her, 'I got a call on my cell and my source tells me before dinner you met with a lawyer from my law firm, a Steve Stein.' When I mention your name, she turns pale. Like she's seen a ghost. She's a trooper, denies everything. I grab and rummage through her purse until I find your business card. I throw the card on the table and warn the bitch that if she doesn't come clean, I'll beat the crap out of her."

"Yeah, she told me you're good at that, a regular Mike Tyson." My anger rising, I looked at Giacomo's smug smile and remembered Elizabeth's tale of abuse and her fear of him. I haven't been in a fight since I was a teenager. I wasn't good at it then, but involuntarily my hand tightened into a fist.

"Cool it, big guy," Giacomo looked me up and down. "I don't want to hurt you. But if you take a swing at me, I just might. I can press over two hundred pounds. You don't want to mess with me."

Giacomo was right. His barrel chest and muscular arms were an invitation to the hospital that I sensibly declined. But I promised myself right then and there to bring the bastard down. I wasn't sure exactly how or when, but I vowed I would.

Picking up his train of thought as if there hadn't been an interruption, Giacomo continued matter-of-factly. "With a little bit of pressure, she folded." He laughed apparently enjoying reliving the memory. "Owned up to meeting with you at The Rusty Nail before dinner. And don't get so goddamned high and mighty with me. You played the bitch. First, you frightened her. You threatened to tell the police about her dinner at Morton's with Paul Martin. And then you bullshit her with that routine where you take a dollar and tell her she's hired you as her lawyer so you can't tell the police anything she tells you. So what does the bitch do? She's a real mental giant. She lays out the scam she concocted with Paul to use the First Mutual IPO to pay off the loan sharks. She swears on her mother's life that's all she's told you."

"Was the lying bitch telling the truth?" Giacomo asked himself rhetorically. He looked straight at me. "Hell, you were there. What do you think?"

Giacomo provocatively dropped his cigarette butt on my carpet and, with the heel of his boot, crushed it. Silence followed as Giacomo lit up another cigarette from the silver case and resumed blowing ringlets of smoke in my direction, as he waited for me to answer his question. I noticed that the diamonds on the case were in the shape of the white Swiss cross set against a background of rubies.

"So, you're the silent type," Giacomo commented when he realized no answer was forthcoming. "For a lawyer that's an unusual trait."

"O.K., if the cat's got your tongue, I'll tell you what I think." Giacomo flashed a derisive smile. "Betsy blabbed a whole lot more. She was good in bed, but she suffered from diarrhea of the mouth."

"So, you killed her."

Giacomo looked at me in mock horror. "Don't you read the *Chronicle*? Your brand new client was at the wrong place at the wrong time. She was the unfortunate victim of a hit-skip murder intended for me. Greater love hath no woman." He snorted in appreciation of the cleverness of his own repartee.

"And you've come to share your sorrow with me. Is that the drill?"

The self-satisfied gloating expression on Giacomo's face infuriated me. Any remaining semblance of civility vanished. I wanted him gone. Actually I wanted him dead, preferably a lingering, painful death. "Get your fucking boots off my table and get the hell out of my office." No longer was I Mr. Cool. I was shouting.

My anger amused him. He laughed and mimicked my tirade. Finally he stopped and grew serious.

"The situation here is complicated, full of what I'd call ironies. Think for a moment, Mr. Stein. To begin with, this law firm represents me and that makes you one of my lawyers."

Observing I was about to interrupt, Giacomo cut me off. "Keep your fuckin' mouth shut and listen. You wanted to know the drill. That's the fuckin' drill."

"I'm not going to prison. That means I got to disappear before trial. I'm going to need your help to pull that off. Mr. Stein, you're about to become my new 'Paul.' It'll be easy enough. You'll run a few errands for me. That's all, I promise."

I looked at Giacomo with disbelief.

"Why, you might ask, would you do that for me? I'm guessing I'm not exactly your favorite person." He smirked. You could tell he felt in control. "Let me play lawyer and explain. First, there's the reputation of your friend Paul; you don't want his wife and kids, and the public, to know he was a crook. Defrauding a bank your firm represents and money laundering, hell, those are serious felonies. Second, your firm certainly doesn't want the authorities to know your buddy Paul went to Vegas to get my ill-gotten funds to pay its legal fees. I assure you my legal fees were paid from those monies, and your friend Paul knew that. And I'm a persuasive and successful liar. A professional you might say. I'll bet the prosecutor might even work a deal if I gave him a big firm like yours on a platter."

"I saved the best for last. I'm not a nice man. Sometimes unlucky things happen to people who cross me. You could be crossing a street, and suddenly get run over by a car, or maybe you're the victim of a random shooting in a parking lot. Shit happens. It'd be a shame if it happened to you."

"You arranged Paul's murder, too?"

"No," he shook his head. "I don't off useful people and Paul was useful. If he was alive, we wouldn't be having this conversation. I wouldn't need a little shit like you. He was under my control. I owned him. For whatever its worth, I heard Paul was killed by a couple of Latino candy sellers. That's my best guess."

"Give me your answer, Stein. If you help me, within the week, I'll be out of your life forever." He took a long drag, and blew the smoke at me.

"You gotta be a raving lunatic to think I'd help you."

"Don't be compulsive. Not a good trait for a lawyer. Think about it. If you don't cooperate, I'll make a trip to the prosecutor and I promise your firm will never be the same. Help me, and within the week, I'm out of the country forever, to a place where even if they find me, they can't touch me. You'll be rid of me forever. I'll contact you tomorrow afternoon for an answer."

"Now, gotta see my lawyer, George Rushing. The pompous prick is a trifle formal for my tastes, but not a bad guy. Smart guy. He's using Paul's death as an excuse to postpone my trial. What do they say? Every cloud has its silver lining. Paul's death certainly has."

With that piece of wisdom, Giacomo rose slowly from my couch, stretched, and dropped another still smoldering cigarette butt on my carpet. With the heel of his alligator boot, he ceremoniously ground the butt into the carpet. He opened the door of my office, saluted, and for good measure, he slammed shut the door behind him, and vanished.

29

I stared at the charred remnants of the cigarette butts ground into the carpet. Giacomo had stripped away my protective cocoon. A week ago, full of myself, I had been contentedly ensconced on my own ivy-covered pedestal in the rarified air of the world of Big Firm law. I boasted to my corporate counterparts at McGinty's about the excitement of my practice. I dealt with real people with real problems. Now I realized the superficiality of these problems. I feared I was now dealing with life and death problems. Since Paul's death, my life had become a B-grade movie.

Giacomo hadn't made the slightest effort to deny killing Elizabeth. His claim that he wasn't involved in Paul's murder didn't ring true. He was a loose cannon and I was in his crosshairs. The more I considered Giacomo's threats, the more alarmed I became. Bank fraud and money laundering were titillating tabloid fare as was the connection between a beautiful bank executive and a married partner at the bank's law firm. Publicizing Paul's crimes on the front page of the *Chronicle* would devastate Phyllis and the girls. And my livelihood might be at stake. Sanctions and lawsuits have destroyed larger law firms than ours.

My imagination ran amok. What if, in an effort to cut a deal with the prosecutor, Giacomo spun a tale of how the law firm assisted him in money laundering to secure payment of its legal fees? Undoubtedly, the government would be able to trace the funds Paul secured for Giacomo to money used to pay the firm's fees. A big corporate law firm or accounting firm is a choice target, an unfortunate lesson learned by Arthur Andersen. If Blackjack needed a scapegoat, as Paul's best friend, I'd top the list.

So much of my conversation with Giacomo was already a blur. I desperately tried to recreate Giacomo's words. What was that he said? "Sometimes unlucky things happen to people who cross me." Yes, he used that expression. I was certain of that. And, he mentioned a hit-skip driver running over someone crossing a street and a victim of a random shooting. I was frightened.

Responses to fear differ depending on the individual. Self-preservation is the primary instinct. It triggers the gazelle to utilize its speed and agility to elude the predator lion. The tortoise withdraws into its protective shell. Fear induces some people to perform superhuman feats, while paralyzing others into inaction. I fall into the second category. My mind closed down and refused to process. For what seemed like forever, but was probably not even fifteen minutes, I couldn't concentrate or sort out my thoughts. Finally, I opted for a change of scenery. Without a word to anyone, I abruptly left the office.

For the next half hour, I wandered the downtown streets, going nowhere. I was unable to enjoy the beautiful spring morning. An uncomfortable nervousness settled in my stomach. Usually I can quickly analyze a problem and formulate a responsive plan of attack. Now, paralysis enveloped me. Finally I sat down on a bench and watched passersby. I played a mental game in which I tried to guess the occupations of each passerby. The familiar musical ring of my cell phone interrupted my mental meandering.

Looking down at the phone, I saw Mike Rowan of the *Chronicle* was calling.

"Where are you?" he demanded. "Mary says you just left the office without telling her where you were going."

"I'm handling some personal business. What do you need?"

"We suspended a driver this morning in contemplation of discharge. The discharge hearing is this afternoon at one. Tony and the grievant will be in the third floor labor conference room. If there's an arbitration hearing you'll be handling it so I want you there this afternoon."

Checking my watch, it was 12:15 p.m. "No problem," I replied. "What's the discharge about?"

"You'll have to wait until you get here to find out. I don't want to spoil the story. It's wild. We're calling it *A Funny Thing Happened on the Way to the Office.*" Mike laughed aloud, enjoying his own humor. "See you at one."

"One it is," I repeated as the line disconnected.

I arrived at the labor conference room shortly before one. Mike was waiting together with Ed Maroni, the *Chronicle's* director of delivery and Joe Santamaria, the general foreman. Slightly under six feet tall, olive-skinned with curly black hair and a mustache to match, Ed is a sharp dresser. He was wearing an Italian blue silk suit and a white-on-white shirt with French cuffs. The general foreman was the same height as his boss but with the beginning of a paunch hanging over his jeans. A redhead, he, too, had a bushy mustache. Seeing me walk through the conference room door, Mike flashed a smile of welcome.

"Hey guys," I loudly announced. "Do I get a preview?"

"The suspended driver is Tim Flannagan," Mike answered. "He and Tony are in the men's room. They'll be back in a moment." Just then, I heard Tony's booming voice from behind.

"Steve, good to see ya. Mike never mentioned you'd be here." Tony entered the conference room in the company of a short, balding, middle-aged man with wire-framed glasses. "Tim, meet Steve Stein. He's the *Chronicle's* super lawyer," Tony nodded at me. "Steve, this is Tim Flannagan, your client's latest victim. He drives for the *Chronicle*."

We shook hands and sat facing each other around the long conference table. Tony and Tim sat on one side of the table; Mike, Ed, Joe, and I, on the other side. Mike asked Ed to relate the morning's events.

"At about eight this morning, Joe and I were driving downtown to the headquarters building from the Production Technology Center." The Production Technology Center, called PTC by everyone, was built five years ago on a southeastern suburb interstate highway. The *Chronicle* is printed at PTC on three modern printing presses and then loaded on trucks that deliver the daily newspaper. The editorial, business, and advertising departments continue to be based at the downtown headquarters building.

"We're traveling west on Main, at the intersection with 97th Street, when I notice one of our blue-and-white trucks with its flashing lights on, parked in a driving lane facing east. I don't see a driver in the cab, so I'm worried. I figure maybe the driver's in distress, maybe the victim of a robbery. Main and 97th isn't a good area. I pull over to the curb and Joe jumps out of the car and runs across the street. No one's in the cab and he can't see in the back of the truck because the partition is up. Joe goes around the truck and opens the side door. Then I see Joe running to the back of the truck, waving his arms, and yelling. 'Ed, get over here. You're not going to believe this.'"

"I get out of the car, cross the street, and go to the truck. I look into the back of the truck. Tim is standing there, pulling up his pants, with this scantily clad woman on her knees. Joe kicks the lady out of the truck and tells her to get lost. She's screaming, creating a scene. Holding three-inch high heel shoes in one hand, she's yelling she hasn't been paid. Tim owes her twenty bucks. After Joe shoos the woman away, he suspends Tim on the spot and tells him there'll be a discharge hearing at headquarters later in the day. Tim didn't have a cent on him so we gave him cab fare and called for a garage man to pick up and drive Tim's truck back to PTC. I still haven't figured out how Tim was planning to come up with the twenty bucks if he didn't have any money on him."

"You want to add anything or tell us your side of the story, Tim?" Mike asked.

"She's my sister."

"Say again." I could see Mike was biting his lower lip to keep from laughing. I winked at Tony and he rolled his eyes but kept a straight face.

"Really, she's my sister," Tim doggedly insisted. "She flagged me down because she needed some money. She has a sick child."

Mike frowned and shook his head. "Tim, you're fired."

"For what reason?" Tony, his face turning crimson, bellowed "The man was trying to help his sister for heaven's sake." Tony always put on a good show.

"There's a sign 'No Unauthorized Passengers Allowed' inside every one of our trucks," Mike pointed out. "I'm terminating Mr. Flannagan for having an unauthorized passenger in his truck."

"That rule has no applicability in this case," Tony argued. "Since the truck wasn't moving, the lady couldn't have been a passenger. There was no violation. I ask, no, I demand you reinstate Tim," Tony continued. "Be reasonable. You don't have passengers on a truck that isn't moving. My six-year-old granddaughter knows that." Tony ended with a flourish, obviously pleased with his imaginative argument and oratory. Flannagan nodded his head in agreement. Sometimes life as a labor lawyer is stranger than fiction.

"Let's agree to disagree on this one." From the tone of Mike's voice, I could tell he didn't want to spend any more time on the matter. "We'll see you at the arbitration hearing."

On that note, the discharge hearing ended. Tony escorted Tim from the conference room whispering to him as they left. Moments later Tony reappeared at the doorway. "Guys," he looked over at them. "Would you mind if I meet alone with Steve for about five minutes? It's personal. Nothing to do with the *Chronicle*."

"We'll leave you guys the conference room," Mike answered. Then to me, he added, "Stick your head in my office before you leave, Steve." Mike, Joe, and Ed left the room. Tony closed the door behind him.

"I kept my word." Tony settled into the chair at the head of the long conference table. "I checked with some people in the neighborhood about your friend Paul. Here's the skinny. He was meeting with two punk drug dealers who hadn't paid their taxes. That's dangerous shit."

"I didn't know the IRS went after drug dealers."

Tony shot me a look of disbelief. "Don't you watch *The Sopranos* like the rest of the world?" He chuckled, enjoying my confusion. Without waiting for a response, he explained, "You work in Tony Soprano's territory; you better give him his share. It's like a tax, Steve, the cost of doing business. These punks didn't show respect. They ruffled feathers you don't want to ruffle. They disrespected. That's not healthy."

"Can you give me names?" I wanted to compare Tony's information with what P.J. had told me. "I know they're Latinos."

"You never cease to amaze me. I didn't realize you had connections on the street. Yeah, they're Latinos. I probably shouldn't tell you their names, but I will. Juan and Paco Rodríguez. They're small-time cocaine dealers. My friends tell me they swear they didn't kill Paul. My friends believe them."

"Can we be sure?"

"Of course not. People lie all the time. But I don't think the Rodríguezes have the cojones to lie to these people. If they offed your friend, it would only cost them money." He paused and looked me in the eye. "Steve, there are far worse things."

"Can you tell me anything else?"

"The Rodríguezes were sitting with Paul, in his car, in the Wal-Mart parking lot. A guy wearing a black ski mask comes, climbs in the car, and pointing a gun tells the Rodríguezes to scram or he'll blow them away. They got no dog in the fight, so they jump out, and leave the parking lot as fast as they can."

"Why were they in Paul's car in the first place?"

"Let that go. You're getting in over your head. Remember what curiosity did to the cat. I didn't ask and you don't want to know. My friends are looking for the murderer. He owes them a lot of money for popping your friend. If I hear anything, I'll let you know."

Tony's information didn't identify Paul's killer and raised more questions than it answered. Was drug dealing involved? Why had a masked gunman sought out Paul? My morning meeting with David Giacomo was still very much on my mind. He was connected with Paul's death. I just knew it. "Thanks for the help Tony, but I'll still show your boy no mercy. I look forward to cross-examining Tim about his sister."

Tony ignored my comment. "Be careful, my friend. I don't want to have to train another company lawyer. Besides, I like you." Coming from Tony, this was high praise.

As promised, I stopped by Mike's office. He, Joe, and Ed were still discussing Tim's alibi and Tony's defense.

"I can't believe Tony seriously arguing the woman wasn't a passenger because the truck was parked. That's crazy. What do you think?" Mike wanted me to confirm, what he already knew, that the Teamsters had no case.

"The Teamsters will pull the case before hearing and Tim will resign. That's my prediction."

Leaving the *Chronicle*, I headed toward the Union National Bank building, a fifteen-minute walk. On a whim, I stopped at my apartment building, three blocks from my office. Some quiet time, away from the office, would provide needed white space to decide how best to respond to Giacomo. I took the elevator to my eighth-floor apartment. Nothing looked out of order until I unlocked the door and walked into the living room. Couches, chairs, and tables were overturned. Two table lamps were lying on the floor. My heart sank. My beloved Sony television had been smashed by a baseball bat; its large screen reduced to a mass of jagged glass.

I stood stunned, surveying the mess. The door slammed closed behind me. Peering first into the dining room and then the kitchen, I saw more of the same. Chairs and tables were overturned. In the kitchen, pots and pans were strewn everywhere. Broken dishes and glassware littered the floor. Returning to the living room, I noticed a single sheet of white paper taped to the base of the broken television. Individual capital letters cut from *Chronicle* headlines haphazardly were pasted on the paper. The message sent a chill up my spine:

BE CAREFUL

SHIT HAPPENS

PART FOUR
ESCAPE

The living room, dining room, and kitchen were in shambles. A narrow hallway connected the living room to the master bedroom. From the hallway, I could see the mattress tossed from its bed frame and at least one of the nightstand lamps smashed on the floor. Goose feathers from slashed bed pillows covered everything. A second bedroom to the right of the master bedroom served as my home office. This room was also demolished. Desk drawers and work papers cluttered the floor. In the middle of this chaos, Agent Duncan reclined comfortably on the convertible sofa that abutted one wall. Wearing a starched white shirt and red suspenders, he sat holding an open bottle of Amstel Light in one hand. His navy pinstriped suit jacket was neatly hung on the back of the desk chair.

I stood speechless at the doorway. Oblivious to my presence, he intently gazed at a small television screen positioned atop a bookshelf. I coughed loudly. Agent Duncan casually looked up from his television program. "Either you're a messy housekeeper or you threw one helluva party." Tipping the bottle of beer in my direction, he saluted me.

"What the hell are you doing in my apartment?" I asked, unable to decide whether the condition of my apartment or the uninvited FBI agent was the bigger surprise.

"Drinking a beer and watching *As the World Turns*. It's my favorite soap. I try to never miss it."

"You broke into my apartment."

"No a young man working for David Giacomo broke into your apartment. He left the door unlocked. I came in when he left." He shook his head and winked. "The help you hire today just doesn't give the same attention to detail as in the old days."

I was confused. How did the FBI agent know David Giacomo was responsible for trashing my apartment?

Agent Duncan picked up the remote and clicked off the television while I stared at him. "You seem upset. Don't worry, my wife records the show for me. I'll catch it tonight. We need to talk. No, change that, you need to talk. Mr. Giacomo expended considerable effort to send you a not-too-subtle message. Care to tell me why?"

Of course, I wanted to, but should I? Conflicting thoughts and impulses flooded my mind.

"How do you know this was Giacomo's doing?" was my feeble response.

"David Giacomo left the garage connected to your law offices this morning in his rented BMW. Two blocks later, he picked up a young man waiting for him dropped him off at your apartment building, and drove off. The punk broke into your apartment, performed his handiwork, and departed, not bothering to relock your front door."

"You didn't arrest him? What kind of officer are you?"

My righteous indignation served as further amusement for Agent Duncan. "Why would I do that? Remember, I'm FBI. Breaking into and trashing your apartment, while no doubt an inconvenience to you and creating a mess, isn't a federal crime. Besides, making an arrest would blow our surveillance. Believe me, Mr. Stein, I know who is responsible and can have him picked him up when and if it serves my purposes. Right now it doesn't."

Taking another swig of beer, Agent Duncan shook his head and looked slowly around the room. "The kid sure did a job on your apartment. I'd be pissed if I was you." He coolly turned and faced me. "So do we talk?"

"I don't know. This may sound strange, Agent Duncan, but decision making never has been a problem before. It's how I make my living, solving clients' problems. Now I'm stuck. I'm confused. I'm having trouble processing. Things are moving too fast."

"Sit down on the couch," Agent Duncan motioned for me to sit next to him. "You need help. You really do, and only I can help you. You're going to have to trust me. Maybe a beer would calm your nerves. There's more Amstel in the fridge. Take one."

The agent's offer brought a reluctant smile to my face. "I know. You may have forgotten, but this is my apartment." The faintest smile appeared on Agent Duncan's lips. I finally laughed, breaking the ice. "O.K., Agent Duncan, I'll accept your hospitality. You're quite the host."

Returning to the kitchen, I found most of the food from my refrigerator splattered on the floor. The intruder apparently was a beer man. Two six packs of Amstel remained untouched except two bottles were missing. Agent Duncan was drinking one and I assumed my uninvited guest purloined the other one. From the kitchen, I heard Agent Duncan bellow, "Yeah, he must have been a beer drinker. While you're at it, bring me another."

Returning, I handed the agent his beer and sat down next to him. I opened mine and took a long drink. "Agent Duncan, you're a wise man. Beer does sharpen your mind or at least loosens your lips. Let me tell you why I've been hesitant to share anything with you. It's your reputation. Not yours personally, but the FBI's. You Feds have a reputation for giving snowballs to Eskimos in the wintertime."

Agent Duncan thought for a moment. "As an educated man, you know the government has many secrets." He spoke slowly, choosing his words carefully. "There are many things I'd like to share with you, but I can't. Instead, let me tell you a fairy tale. You do like fairy tales, don't you Mr. Stein?"

"I'm all ears."

Agent Duncan leaned back on the couch. His gaze narrowed on my face. "Once upon a time," he began in his best bedtime story voice, "a handsome knight lived in a kingdom far, far away. The knight was one of the best jousters in the kingdom and won most of the tournaments. This handsome knight, our hero, was a favorite of the ladies. He changed damsels more frequently than he did steeds. He had one major failing. He gambled too much."

"A dice game similar to craps was played throughout the kingdom. The knights enjoyed playing this game. Our heroic knight loved the excitement of playing and betting large sums of money. Unfortunately, he lost more often than he won and didn't have the funds to cover his losses."

I listened, intrigued with the story's meaning.

"As in most of these stories," Agent Duncan continued, "there is a woman. A beautiful damsel lived in the kingdom, although she didn't see herself as beautiful. She spent large sums of money, buying magical potions and spells guaranteed to make her feel beautiful. None of the spells and potions worked. She always focused on her imperfections. The damsel soon had large debts that she couldn't pay."

"Both the beautiful damsel and the handsome knight borrowed large sums of money from unsavory characters known as usurers. The usurers lent money and charged large sums of interest. You wouldn't believe this Steve, but in those days, if knights and damsels failed to repay their debts, these usurers arranged to have limbs cut off."

"The damsel possessed brains as well as beauty. Knowing of the handsome knight's enormous debts, she developed a plan. The king was holding his annual jousting tournament at his castle. All the knights in the realm traveled from the farthest corners of the kingdom to participate; the winner would fly a special banner from his lance for the next year. Each year, the king's subjects flocked to the tournament to be entertained and to bet money on their favorite knight."

"The damsel suggested they arrange with the usurers to bet heavily against the knight in the final joust. When he lost, they would be relieved of their debts and wind up with some additional money. Of course, this arrangement was a grievous affront to the king and a crime. Still, the handsome knight agreed and threw the tournament."

"So what do you think, Steve, do you think our handsome knight and beautiful damsel live happily ever after?"

"My guess would be 'No.' But somehow, I'm confident you're about to tell me."

"I will, but first get me another beer."

Sipping his third beer, Agent Duncan continued the tale. "The beautiful damsel fell in love with an evil knight. And, as beautiful damsels often do, she talked too much. She confided to the evil knight that the final joust had been fixed. With this knowledge, the evil knight threatened to expose the handsome knight unless he revealed secret information about the fortifications of the king's castle. The evil knight had arranged to sell this information to the king's bitter enemy."

My mind was spinning. Somehow Agent Duncan knew the details about Elizabeth and Paul's relationship, including the sale of the First Mutual stock. He had been playing possum in my office during Detective O'Brien's interview. P.J. was right. Underestimating the agent would be a fatal mistake.

Agent Duncan noticed that I was staring at him. "Ah, Steve, you probably want to know what happened next. The handsome knight was remorseful. And, he was a patriot who loved his king deeply. He secretly approached Sir Andrew, the king's special minister, and confessed everything. He became Sir Andrew's special informer. In return, the king, through Sir Andrew, promised to pardon the handsome knight and the beautiful damsel. But, they didn't live happily ever after. The evil knight killed the beautiful damsel and the handsome knight was mysteriously murdered by an unknown enemy."

This fairy tale that Agent Duncan spun impacted me just as I suppose he intended; I dramatically changed my thinking. The FBI knew about Paul and Elizabeth's First Mutual caper. Paul no longer needed protection. His dealings in Las Vegas were as a government informer. There also was no need to divulge Elizabeth's confidences protected by attorney-client privilege. Agent Duncan knew everything.

Agent Duncan and I spoke frankly. I recounted my confrontation with David Giacomo, describing his threats and blackmailing effort to secure my assistance in what I thought was a plan to flee the country.

Agent Duncan shrugged, unimpressed. "He's been planning his escape for a while," he confided. "Are you familiar with the name Chen Chung?"

"Sure, about two years ago, *Business Week* profiled him. He's a billionaire Hong Kong banker." I conveniently didn't mention that I read the article yesterday, when I Googled the Chens.

"That's right. Giacomo set up secret accounts in Chen banks around the world. That's where he's hid the missing thirty million dollars. Chen Chung allowed Giacomo to create secret accounts, but refused to let Giacomo withdraw money directly. He feared how American regulators might respond if they ever discovered a direct connection. Giacomo relied on intermediaries to obtain his money. For their efforts, they took a cut of the proceeds."

"That must have pissed him off."

"Probably did. But beggars and thieves hiding thirty million dollars in today's world can't be choosy." Agent Duncan paused, took another swig of beer, and smiled, enjoying his own wit. "Anyway, Number One son, Chen Chao, decides to freelance to make some spare change by serving as an intermediary without his father's knowledge."

"You're talking about Chaz," I interjected. "He's a notorious gambler and womanizer in Vegas." There was no particular reason to volunteer that I was privy to this information other than an infantile compulsion to show Agent Duncan that I, too, knew more that I could tell him.

My childishness amused Agent Duncan. He smiled again. "Yes, that's the one. Did you know that in Chinese Chao means excellent? I'd translate it as lucky sperm club. Quite a disappointment to his father, I'd imagine. Anyway, I'll assume Ms. Caldwell shared with you the highlights of her Vegas trip with Paul, at least those things she knew about. She didn't know anything about Paul's dealings with the government or the electronic surveillance device he planted. With the evidence Paul helped gather, we went to Chao's old man and made him an offer he couldn't refuse. The government agreed not to prosecute his son, in return for turning over to us all remaining Giacomo money hidden in his banks together with a full accounting."

"Does Giacomo know his money is gone?"

"Not yet. He'll know soon enough as soon as he tries to tap into the funds. But here's the rub: there's five million dollars left to recover. The Chens are transferring twenty-two million dollars into an FBI account. Giacomo has spent or hid another three million or so in this country, including the money from the Vegas transaction. The Chens swear the final five million is in a Middle Eastern money pipeline controlled by Youssef Muhammad. I'm sure Elizabeth mentioned Youssef."

"His name vaguely rings a bell." I still did not want to reveal the full extent of my knowledge.

"Terrorist elements are helping Giacomo. I want you to cooperate with him and do as he asks. You'd be the mole we need to identify the bad guys and keep the money away from the terrorists. Like I told you, I want you to be a patriot."

Agent Duncan's words hit a responsive chord, changing my calculus. Up until now, fear was the impetus driving me to do Giacomo's bidding: I feared Giacomo would expose Paul's criminality. I feared charges of money laundering levied against the firm and Blackjack blaming me for allowing that to happen. And, I feared David Giacomo. He'd killed once and might do so again. Most of these fears had vanished. Now, my primary concern focused on personal safety. Maybe Agent Duncan was right; it did come down to patriotism. But I'm a sixty-year-old big firm lawyer, I told myself, not a hero.

At that moment my cell phone rang. Looking down at the screen, I didn't recognize the phone number.

"What kind of jerk-off lawyer doesn't tell his secretary where he is?"

"Who the hell is this?" I did not recognize the belligerent voice.

"David Giacomo. I called your secretary. The poor woman has no idea where you are. That's not proper etiquette for any successful professional, my friend, whether a lawyer or stockbroker. Where the hell are you?"

"First, you're not my friend," I snapped. "Second, I'm standing in my apartment, which has been trashed. And, third how did you get my cell phone number?"

"My, my, we are a bit testy this afternoon. If you don't want people to know your cell phone number, I suggest you stop writing the number on the back of your business card, which somehow found its way into Betsy's purse. What can I say? I'm clairvoyant. I wrote the number down, thinking it might prove useful someday. I was right. As for your apartment being trashed, that's too bad. We live in a violent society. Shit happens."

I cursed him under my breath. "O.K., you got a hold of me. If you're following up on this morning's conversation, I haven't made up my mind. I'll tell you this, though, trashing my apartment isn't a big plus in your column." I loathed the man, his voice, his tone, everything about him.

"Certain unsettling news I've received today changes everything," Giacomo informed me. I thought I heard a slight tremor in his voice. "I'm moving the schedule up. I've got no time for your dawdling. Take my word counselor, I'm desperate. You don't want to cross me. It wouldn't be a pretty picture."

Giacomo hesitated for a moment and then spoke slowly, emphasizing each phrase with chilling precision. "Listen carefully. I'll say this once, counselor, and once only. You'll meet me at The Rusty Nail at six o'clock tonight. That should be a familiar rendezvous point. Be there, my friend, or I promise you'll regret it. Got that? Six o'clock. Rusty Nail. Good-bye." The phone disconnected.

"So, what did he want?"

Hearing half of the conversation, Agent Duncan knew Giacomo was the unwelcome caller, but the substance of our conversation eluded him.

"Giacomo got 'unsettling news' today and moved his schedule up. Probably learned you got most of his money. The son of a bitch told me – no he threatened – if I didn't meet him at six tonight at The Rusty Nail, I'd regret it. He called himself 'desperate'."

Agent Duncan's eyes widened. "You've an important decision to make. I'd like to help in any way I can. In the end, though, it's up to you." Agent Duncan spoke earnestly. I could sense he was no longer acting.

Giacomo's threat presented a dilemma with no apparent solution. On the one hand, if I didn't show up at The Rusty Nail, Giacomo might blame me for his inability to flee the country and come after me in one final, violent, desperate act of vengeance. On the other hand, if I showed up, I'd become an accomplice in Giacomo's scheme and placed in harm's way.

"I don't know what to do," I admitted to Agent Duncan after a prolonged silence. "I can get injured or killed either way. He's a mad man."

"You'll be safe at The Rusty Nail. I promise." Agent Duncan assured me. "First, he'd never do anything crazy in a public place – too many witnesses around. Second, my undercover agents will be there."

"Yeah, but what happens if I have to leave with him?"

"If you decide to work with us, I have a geophysical locating device to attach to your key chain that will allow us to trace your every move. It's no bigger than a half dollar." Duncan pulled out a metallic coin-like disk from his pocket and handed it to me.

I held it in my hand. The device was the size of a half dollar and twice as thick, but light, with the Statute of Liberty embossed on its face. I've seen larger, more ostentatious trinkets on key chains. I noticed a small yellow button on the outstretched arm of Lady Liberty. I pressed the button. Nothing happened.

"What's the yellow button for?" I continued to press the button. Nothing was happening. "I thought maybe there'd be some sort of siren."

"You're close. It's a distress alarm, a silent one. When the button is pressed, a signal is sent out. The tailing agents know you're in trouble and will come to your assistance within minutes." Agent Duncan thought for a moment and added, "At least that's the way it's supposed to work."

"If I don't agree to become the government's canary, what protection can I expect?"

Agent Duncan glanced at me and shrugged his shoulders. "A most interesting metaphor." He didn't try to answer my question.

"One, unfortunately, that may be all too apropos," I countered. "In my early years, I represented a coal mine in Kentucky. Whenever the miners feared a gas leak, they sent a canary in a cage down the mine shaft to determine whether it was safe to go down. Never heard of a canary that survived trouble in the mine. You didn't answer my question."

"Honestly, no protection. The Bureau can't provide you personal protection. Agents will continue to discreetly tail Giacomo. Of course, if he should assault you, they'd intervene. Should Giacomo use a hired third party, as you seem to think he did in Ms. Caldwell's murder, we wouldn't be there to help. I don't think you can put much faith in the local police either. This may come as a surprise to you, but I recently checked and learned you're not on Detective O'Brien's Christmas card list." The agent thought for a moment and then suggested, "You could drop out of sight until Giacomo is convicted and incarcerated."

"That wouldn't work. It could be years before he'd be jailed. I can't just give up my law practice. Besides, the man's crazy. Imprisonment might make him even more determined to arrange my demise."

I faced a genuine legal conundrum, a puzzle without an apparent solution. Joining Agent Duncan to entrap Giacomo was potentially life threatening. The alternative of refusing Giacomo's entreaties was equally bleak. The last time I enlisted in government service was in law school, when I joined the army reserves to avoid being drafted. That military service seemed safer than Agent Duncan's proposed enlistment in the service of the FBI. But maybe, I thought, a soon-to-be divorced sixty year old needs some excitement in his life. My close friends keep suggesting I find a new interest or hobby. I made up my mind. "Agent Duncan," I announced, "you've enlisted a patriot."

My pronouncement seemed to energize Agent Duncan. He lifted his beer bottle. "To Citizen Stein," he toasted, "and to justice throughout the land." I lifted my bottle in response to his toast and tapped his bottle. I declared with total conviction, "L'Chayim, To Life."

A gent Duncan, that is, Andrew (never Andy) as he instructed me to call him, and I strategized about my upcoming encounter with David Giacomo at The Rusty Nail. Two agents, he assured me, positioned in the lounge before my arrival, would monitor the rendezvous. He first activated and then connected the geophysical locating device to my key chain. Much could not be planned, he admitted, and would be improvised, depending on Giacomo, but Andrew pledged that he and the other agents would trail close behind at all times. And he reminded me to press the device's yellow button if I encountered a problem. In a matter of minutes, the agents would rush to my rescue, or so he claimed.

"I sure am putting a lot of faith in someone I first met today," I confided to Andrew. "I know nothing about you except you're an FBI agent and P.J. speaks highly of you."

Perhaps it was the three bottles of beer, or maybe he wanted to allay my anxieties, but Andrew shared the Reader's Digest version of his life. Much to my surprise, he transformed into a real person.

"I was born in the District of Columbia in 1972. I was five when my father abandoned the family. My mother died from a heroin overdose before my eighth birthday. You better grab some tissues, the story is a real heart breaker." Andrew joked, but I saw him tear up. "My grandparents raised me. The old man was a retired master sergeant. Nana worked as a clerk in a department store. They were tough old birds with high expectations. They cared and wouldn't let me run wild like my friends. Nana expected good grades while Sarge expected me to star in every sport I tried."

"So how did you join the Bureau?"

"Sarge wanted me to be a military officer, maybe even a general like Colin Powell. If I'd gotten admitted to West Point, he'd have died and happily gone to heaven, right then and there. But I didn't. The appointment was all arranged, or so we thought, but somebody knew somebody, and my appointment went to someone else. I don't think Sarge ever got over the disappointment. Instead, I went to Howard University and then Washington College of Law, which is part of American University."

"Did you ever practice law?"

"Never," Andrew answered, too quickly I thought and with too much emphasis. "I never wanted to practice law. Truth is, present company excepted, I generally don't like lawyers. After graduation, I joined the Bureau, which made Sarge happy. The FBI wasn't the army and I couldn't be a general as he hoped, but I was fighting crime and serving my country. He liked that. Sarge died five years ago, and a day doesn't go by that I don't miss him."

Andrew looked uncomfortable. I knew the type. Admitting vulnerability embarrassed him. "What else do you want to know? I'm a married workaholic with two wonderful children, Andrew Junior and Deidre, and a beautiful wife Roberta whom I never see." Andrew was silent for a moment. "But of more importance to you, I'm an award-winning marksman with citations and a shelf of trophies to prove it." He then brought our conversation to an abrupt end. "I do need to go now. Logistics need to be arranged before you show up at The Rusty Nail."

"I'm helping you. You gotta help me," I pleaded. "Paul Martin was my best friend since high school. His murder has been tough to take. You've no idea how angry and frustrated I am. Do you know who killed him? Is there anything at all you can tell me?"

Andrew hesitated before answering. "Fair enough. You're sticking your neck out for me. I'll level with you. The Bureau was unhappy when Paul was killed. He was a valuable asset. Your friend was meeting with two drug dealers when he was killed."

"I already know that," I interrupted. "He was meeting with Juan and Paco Rodríguez. They dealt cocaine. But did they kill Paul? That's what I need to know."

The expression on Andrew's face changed. He looked surprised.

"I'm impressed. I really am. I don't suppose you'd tell me the source of your information."

I shook my head. "I can't do that."

He smiled. "I didn't think you would."

"But did they kill him?" I asked again, impatiently.

"No, I don't think so, I really don't," Andrew finally answered. "An informer whom I trust claims the Rodríguez brothers fled the scene before the murder."

"That's a strange choice of words," I responded, feigning bewilderment. "What do you mean fled the scene? Fled from what?"

Choosing each word with care, Andrew explained himself and confirmed what Tony told me earlier. "Paul was meeting the brothers in his automobile, when an unidentified armed person wearing a ski mask, probably the murderer, entered Paul's car. The Rodríguez brothers say they fled."

"Maybe a few Benjamin Franklins might jog their collective memories. I'd gladly supply the money," I volunteered looking over at Andrew. "But not to worry. I'll put off speaking with them until I've completed my current assignment." So much for the two thousand dollars Shecky was returning. "If your informer is correct, the Rodríguezes are the obvious sources to identify the killer. Do O'Brien and Mancini know about them?"

"I guess not." Perhaps Andrew did not care for the locals any more than I did. "But if my information is correct," he continued, "it doesn't make any difference. No one will be speaking with them, at least not in this world."

"What the hell does that mean?" I did not like the sound of that.

"The word on the street is they're dead; killed, execution-style."

I muttered a curse. My mind was abuzz. "What do you mean killed, execution-style? Maybe the Rodríguezes knew who killed Paul. Maybe Paul's murderer found out they could identify him and killed them, too. You need to tell me more," I begged.

"This conversation is over," Andrew announced in a tone that left no doubt that further information wouldn't be forthcoming. And, despite continued pleading and even whining, Andrew became all business. He reiterated the instructions for the evening. To my surprise, before leaving, he asked for the keys to my apartment and promised to have the mess cleaned up.

I thanked Andrew and asked him to wish me luck. I still remember his response.

"We make our own luck, my friend," Then he stopped for a brief moment and looked squarely at me. "Sarge's favorite sport was baseball. He worshipped Jackie Robinson and admired Branch Rickey, the white general manager of the Brooklyn Dodgers, who brought Robinson to the big leagues. 'Andrew, we make our own luck,' he used to tell me when I asked him to wish me luck before a game or a test. Branch Rickey got it right when he said, 'Luck is the residue of design.' He got the championships to prove it. Sarge was right, Steve. We won't fail."

We shook hands and embraced before Andrew left the apartment.

33

I examined the damage to my apartment one final time before leaving and locking the door behind me with a spare set of keys. Once outside, the beautiful spring afternoon offered a needed change of pace. I took a deep breath and checked my watch. It was almost four o'clock, two hours until I was due at The Rusty Nail. I headed for my office, using my cell phone to check for voice mail messages left on my office phone.

Five messages. The last, received ten minutes earlier, was from P.J. He left his cell phone number and asked that I call back immediately.

"P.J."

"Stein, where the hell are you? I've important information. We need to meet right away."

"I'm walking toward my office as we speak. We can meet there in fifteen minutes."

"No, not a good idea. I can't be seen there. It would be bad for my image. You never know. Someday I might decide to run for Guild office. We need someplace neutral." There was a momentary silence. "There's a Starbucks nearby, isn't there?"

"Yes, two blocks away."

"Good. Meet me there in ten minutes."

In less than five minutes, I arrived at the Starbucks. P.J. wasn't there yet. Only three people were inside. Two attractive thirty-something women in jogging outfits sat at a table along the wall, sipping their coffee drinks and munching pastries. A young man, probably a college student, occupied a corner table, bent over his computer surrounded by books.

Ordering a small coffee, I sat down at a table in the far corner of the room that would provide privacy. Several minutes later, P.J., dressed in his trademark green army field jacket, strode into the shop. He nodded at me as he walked up to the counter and ordered a drink from the barista. Drink in hand, he nonchalantly strolled over and sat down next to me.

"Double espressos, love 'em. You're old school," he commented dryly, looking at my black coffee. "Apparently, you're not the type to spend four bucks for a cup of coffee whose name you can't pronounce."

"Why so anxious to meet? What's up?" I asked, ignoring P.J.'s social commentary on my caffeine habits.

"I thought you'd want to hear the progress I've made in our investigation in this short time." He emphasized the word "our." "If I do pat myself on the back, I'm good, or maybe better than good, I'm just damn lucky."

"What did you find out?" It was hard to believe P.J. made progress in a matter of hours while the police remained stymied. But then, again, I doubted that Detective O'Brien, for all his bluster, could organize a two-car funeral.

"With the Bellagio hotel lead you gave me, connecting Elizabeth Caldwell to your friend, Paul, was easy. The question was what brought them together. Sex was my initial guess. Caldwell was an attractive woman and your buddy was a skirt chaser. But I asked myself whether there was something more. That's when I hit the jackpot.

Bobby Briggs, an old army buddy, called this morning to tell me he was in town. We had lunch. I hadn't seen Bobby for more than a year. Bobby's a sad story. He was a good old boy from a wealthy New Orleans family. After graduating from Louisiana State University, he enlisted. All gung-ho, he also joined Special Forces. I first met him when he was assigned to my platoon. We faced a lot of shit together."

I saw no connection between P.J.'s army buddy and Paul or

Elizabeth. Knowing what awaited me in less than two hours, I grew impatient. I forced myself to say nothing, certain P.J. would tie together this disjointed narrative.

Perhaps, noticing my edginess, or maybe like many vets preferring not to open up old wounds, P.J. never explained the details of exactly what happened to Bobby. "Suffice it to say," he continued, "Bobby was severely wounded on a secret mission. He lost his right leg from the knee down." P.J. looked down at the table, pain etched on his face. "Bobby never fully recovered. Became addicted to morphine, and was never the same. Since then, he's had an addiction problem – booze, heroin, cocaine, you name it. His family stands by him and has paid for rehab at least half a dozen times. There's always a relapse."

"When I mentioned to Bobby I was working on a story about the murders of two people, Elizabeth Caldwell and Paul Martin, Bobby almost fell out of his chair. He was shocked. 'I knew Elizabeth,' he told me, 'and I heard lots about Paul Martin.'"

"How'd he know Elizabeth?" I automatically assumed he'd heard about Paul from her. How wrong I was.

"About six months ago, Bobby signed himself into rehab at a facility connected with Betty Ford on the Gold Coast in Chicago called Hazelden, really first rate. Elizabeth was a patient and so was John Martin. Group therapy was a major component of the program. John spent considerable time at those sessions talking about his father, and often in none-too-attractive terms."

"What do you mean by 'none-too-attractive-terms'? What did he say?"

"John blamed his father for his addiction. He told the group he was abandoned by his father and raised by a doting mother. According to Bobby, John was extremely bitter, even though he told the group his father was paying for the rehab. Bobby distinctly remembers John calling it 'guilt money'."

"Did Bobby know whether Paul ever met Elizabeth at the rehab center?" I couldn't reveal the information Elizabeth shared with me as her attorney.

"I asked, but he didn't know. He remembers Elizabeth, and he recalls Paul visiting John several times but doesn't know whether Paul met or visited Elizabeth."

"What do you make of this?" I wanted P.J.'s take on this information. "It's not inconsistent with John's story. He admits negative feelings toward his father but claims they reconciled over the last six months."

P.J. laughed. "You're the one who was Paul's best friend. Did Paul ever mention reconciliation?"

To my surprise, I found myself defending John. "Paul was preoccupied.. I attributed that to his work. You're right, though, he never mentioned John's entering rehab and kept his visits with John a secret. But, on the other hand, John's claim that, as part of the budding new relationship, Paul promised to add him as a beneficiary to his insurance trust turned out to be true. As executor, I've confirmed those changes were made. Over all, John's story seems true."

"What kind of money are we talking about? Maybe John set Paul up."

P.J.'s question shook me up. First, I felt guilty sharing private, personal information with a newsman, information Marla adamantly refused to tell Babs. Second, the amount of money was significant. Although I hated to admit it, people have killed and been killed for far less. Adding John as an equal beneficiary proved Paul believed he had reconciled with his son. That was only half the equation. Maybe P.J. was correct. Maybe John was a good actor and the reconciliation was a charade, designed to secure the change in the trust. I remained silent trying to sort out these thoughts.

My obvious reluctance to share the amount of money involved angered P.J. "You proposed, just this morning, we work together to find Paul's killer. I'm here, sharing information with you, and I don't see reciprocity. That's bullshit." He stuck his face six inches from mine. I could smell alcohol on his breath. "I promised you I'd be discreet. I'd never publicize information that could be traced to you without first receiving and verifying the information from another source. I assure you I can break the story without you. I've been a successful reporter long before I met you, Mr. Stein."

Before I could respond to this outburst, P.J. stood up from the table like a diva and started to leave.

"P.J., please, please sit down." I didn't want our relationship to end. "Working with a newsman is new to me. You've got to understand sharing confidential information runs counter to all my legal training. My clients' business always has been something to keep confidential. I do want to work with you on the case. I really do."

"Fine," P.J. said, sitting back down. "Now answer my question. Show me you have faith in me or we're finished. I keep my promises."

An immediate decision was required. "One million dollars," I blurted out. I sighed feeling relief. Sharing the information with P.J. was my symbolic crossing of the Rubicon; so much for the cautious, conservative big law firm attorney. I'd made my second life-altering commitment in a matter of hours. There'd be no going back. I felt good about the decisions, at least momentarily.

P.J. whistled. "Wow! That's a lot of scratch."

"Did you learn anything else?" I asked.

"Yeah, let me finish the story. Bobby's been living in Chicago. No surprise, but this most recent rehab didn't take. His rehabs never have. Bobby admitted that he began using again shortly after he checked out of rehab. Like most junkies, he's in total denial. He claims he only uses on special occasions and his problem is under control. Of course, he and I both know that's bullshit."

"Bobby starts hunting around Chicago for a reliable source for drugs. Whom does he contact?" Not knowing whether the question was rhetorical, I remained silent, although I anticipated an answer.

"Our soon-to-be millionaire, John Martin, Bobby's friend from rehab. But there's more. The story strikes even closer to home. John's street connections are good. He still owes his dealers a sizeable sum of money. To keep them at bay, John serves as a shill for his old dealers, setting them up with friends looking for drugs. He's a go-between, taking the money and delivering the drugs. They give John a commission, which comes off his tab. The dealers, my friend, are none other than Juan and Paco Rodríguez."

Now it was my turn to whistle. "Juan and Paco Rodríguez," I repeated. "John must have introduced them to his father."

"Yeah, and maybe he arranged for them to kill Paul. Think about it: He hates his old man, but otherwise pretends to manipulate a guilt-ridden father into changing his trust. Then he promises to pay the Rodríguezes what he owes them, or maybe offers them a piece of his inheritance, if they'll off his old man. All the pieces are there." P.J. spoke rapidly as he spun his theory. He beamed having, at least in his own mind, solved Paul's murder.

"I've been pushing my sources hard to locate Juan or Paco, so far without any luck. They've vanished without a trace. But I'll find them. All in all, though, not bad for one day's work." He looked over expectantly, waiting for my reaction, no doubt hoping for a buy into his theory and expecting an "at-a-boy".

"Not to burst your bubble, but your theory has a major flaw." P.J. frowned at me. My response wasn't what he expected.

The Rodríguezes didn't kill Paul," I declared with unexpected fervor. P.J. was right about one thing. If we were a team, I'd have to share information with him.

"What makes you so certain?" P.J. was obviously irritated. He wasn't the type who liked being upstaged at anything. And certainly not by an amateur.

"I've confirmed with two reliable sources that, just prior to his murder, when Paul was meeting with the Rodríguezes in his car, a guy in a black ski mask with a gun showed up, climbed into the car, and told the Rodríguezes to get lost. They left the parking lot as fast as they could and don't know who killed Paul."

"Who told you that?" P.J. was now listening with rapt attention. I imagined this piece of information impressed him. The truth was I was impressed myself.

"I can share information with you but not sources. As a newsman, you understand confidentiality. But, I assure you, the sources are reliable. That's the story the brothers are telling, and both my sources believe they're telling the truth."

P.J. contemplated silently what I'd just told him. "Maybe they are," he mused, "but how can we be sure? We need to locate the brothers and talk to them ourselves. I'll put the word out on the street to find them. Can you put up some money? That's the universal language street people understand. For the right price, there are no secrets."

"I could and would, but it'd be a waste of time."

"What's that supposed to mean? If they're out there and we offer a few hundred bucks, we'll find them. Junkies would sell their firstborn for a whole lot less."

"It would be a waste of time, because the Rodríguezes are dead."

P.J. blinked. His jaw dropped. "How the hell would you know that?"

"I can't divulge how. An authoritative source told me they were killed, execution-style."

P.J. mulled over the information, repeating the phrase "authoritative source" several times under his breath. He finally spoke. "I assume your information is, what's the term you lawyers use, 'hearsay'. Your authoritative source didn't actually see the brothers killed."

"That's right," I acknowledged.

"Your source is either someone connected with the mob or law enforcement."

In my case it was both. P.J. was perceptive and knew his trade. Enlisting his assistance had been a savvy move.

"I should be able to confirm whether your source is correct and they're dead. I'm not without my own stable of informants. I'm grappling how to deal with the soon-to-become millionaire son. My gut tells me he's involved up to his eyebrows in his father's death. There's no other reason your friend Paul would meet with people like the Rodríguez brothers."

I told P.J. how John was coming from Chicago for the visitation and funeral and was dining with me tomorrow evening. While not outright disagreeing with P.J.'s assessment of John's connection to the meeting between the Rodríguezes and Paul, I wasn't ready to commit to the idea that John was involved in his father's death. John sounded sincere when he described his reconciliation with Paul. I found it difficult to believe it was pretense. Maybe I didn't want to believe Paul had completely misread his son.

Wednesday night's dinner would provide the opportunity to test John's credibility. Would he admit knowing Bobby Briggs and providing him drugs from the Rodríguezes? I promised to confront John and telephone P.J. as soon as I returned home that evening.

"You've done a good job in obtaining so much information. Your resourcefulness is surprising." P.J. applauded me but then admonished "Be careful, you're out of your element. These are dangerous people. Don't do anything foolish. I learned on Special Forces missions that there's a fine line between bravery and foolhardiness. It's easy to mix one up with the other. I know. I have a Silver Star for what my superiors called 'combat bravery'."

P.J.'s remarks struck a far more responsive chord than he would have imagined. Unknown to him, I was about to go undercover for the FBI to meet with a criminal whom I believed was a killer. I was way out of my element. Helping Agent Duncan, I feared, fell on the side of foolhardiness. Agent Duncan talked a good story. But I wasn't positive the FBI would be able to protect me if matters suddenly went south. P.J. was right: posthumous medals would offer little consolation.

"Thanks for your concern. I'll take your words to heart." I wondered if it was too late.

P.J. pushed back from the table and stood up. "Gotta go. I'm meeting with Detectives O'Brien and Mancini to check out whether they've developed any leads on the hit- skip driver. I'll let you know if I learn anything when we talk tomorrow evening." We shook hands. I watched P.J. stride out of the Starbucks.

I sat nursing my lukewarm coffee, pondering P.J.'s admonition.

My cell phone rang, and I answered it.

"Where are you?" I instantly recognized the loud overbearing voice of David Giacomo. I detected a note of urgency.

"You're sounding like my mother." I checked my watch. "It's only five fifteen. I'll be there on time."

"Where are you?" Giacomo repeated his question. I could tell my flippant attitude grated on him.

"Don't get your panty hose tied in a snit. Not that it's any of your business, but I'm drinking a cup of coffee in the Starbucks across from my office."

"Good. Drive your car and park in the Marriott's parking garage. Skip the valet. Remember, six o'clock at The Rusty Nail and don't be late. I admire promptness." The cell phone disconnected before I could respond.

34

As instructed, I parked my Volvo in the Marriott's garage and entered the hotel's lounge, a few minutes before six o'clock. Better early than late. Twenty-four hours had passed since I had peremptorily summoned Elizabeth to this same room. So much had happened in the interim. Now, ironically, I was returning to the location, summoned by Elizabeth's lover and probable killer.

The same tuxedo-clad, blonde twenty-something was tending bar. Two men, in their thirties, dressed in business suits, sat at the bar near the bartender engrossed in conversation. Looking around the room, I noticed an attractive, young blonde in a white sweater, with a plunging neckline, sitting at a table to the side of the bar, holding hands with a silver-haired gentleman at least thirty years her senior. He was my age. I counted only six other customers in the room. I looked at each of their faces, wondering which ones were the undercover agents. My clammy right hand continually stroked the GPS device attached to my key chain.

"Hey, Stein, over here." Giacomo signaled to join him.

I sat down across from Giacomo at a table along the wall near where Elizabeth had been sitting yesterday. His outfit hadn't changed from the morning except he now wore a beige corduroy sport jacket over his white turtleneck. A small gold cross dangled from a gold chain around his neck.

We ordered drinks; a Ketel One and cranberry for me and for Giacomo, a vodka martini with three olives.

Nothing was said until the drinks were served and the cocktail waitress left.

Giacomo broke the silence.

"I knew you'd show up."

"Let's be clear right from the start. I don't like you and haven't agreed to do anything. I'm here to listen. You've threatened to expose Paul, embarrass his family, and create a problem for the firm. I want to avoid dragging Paul's name through the mud. That's why I'm here. If you ask me to do anything criminal, I assure you I'll walk."

While this speech might sound good to someone uninitiated in the law, I was drawing a nonsensical distinction. Aiding Giacomo in his plan to flee the country was a serious federal crime that could result in considerable jail time. For a lawyer like myself to be unaware of the seriousness of what Giacomo was proposing was unfathomable. Hopefully Giacomo, an inveterate con man, would con himself into thinking he could sweet-talk me into assisting him.

"Cool it. No need for you to walk anywhere. You're going to drive me a few places. You'll be helping me pick up a suitcase. By the end of tonight, I'll be out of your life forever. You'll never see me again."

"What exactly do you want me to do?"

"Like I said, you'll drive me; we'll pick up a suitcase. Then you'll take me to the county airport and I'll be gone. You go about your life and read about me in the *Chronicle*." Giacomo drained his martini and signaled for another.

"Why do you need me? You could do those things yourself. I don't understand where and why I fit in."

Giacomo waited for the waitress to set his second martini in front of him before answering. He took a taste, ate two of the olives, and explained.

"The FBI shadows me everywhere I go. They followed me here and are waiting for me to leave. You're going to help me give the FBI the slip, pick up my suitcase, and meet a plane. Nothing dangerous. Think of yourself as a chauffeur for one of your firm's clients." Giacomo grinned, obviously pleased with this explanation. He took another swallow of his martini. He bit into the final olive.

"What's in the suitcase? Where are you going?"

Giacomo shrugged and responded, ignoring my first question. "Somewhere safe, where I won't be bothered by the authorities."

"You mean a country which doesn't have an extradition treaty with the United States," I suggested.

Giacomo laughed. "Very good counselor. No wonder they pay you the big bucks."

Catching the attention of the waitress, he requested the bill. When the waitress brought the tab, he studied it briefly and handed her two twenty-dollar bills, telling her to keep the change. Turning to me he said, still smiling, "This one's on me. That's the least I can do for your night's work."

"I haven't said I'd help," I insisted. "I want to think about it." No reason to allow Giacomo to view me as a pushover.

Giacomo's smile instantly distorted into a menacing scowl. Speaking slightly above a whisper, he hissed, "You don't have a choice."

Leaning across the table, he opened his sport jacket just enough to reveal a shoulder holster with a gun. Still frowning and speaking in a low, hushed voice, he continued. "The government's closing in. I've already lost millions to the bastards. The god damn Feds somehow got to my Hong Kong banker. This is my last chance to escape and you're gonna help. You don't have much of a choice. If you don't, I'll blow you away right here at this table. Don't test me."

"Calm down, David. I've finished thinking. I'll help, but how do I know you won't kill me anyway?"

"That's showing common sense, Stein. A good question. I'm a con man not a murderer. Help me tonight and you'll never see me again. That's a promise."

Giacomo's promise was nothing more than a gigantic con as was everything about the man. A cold-blooded killer, he already arranged Elizabeth's murder. I was certain of that. Second thoughts flooded my mind. Why had I agreed to help Agent Duncan? But it was too late. I'd have to play out the hand. I prayed Andrew was as good as he and P.J. believed.

We sat looking each other over. Giacomo was a Jekyll-and-Hyde personality. As soon as I'd agreed to help him, his demeanor again transformed. The glower disappeared. He once more smiled pleasantly as if we were best of friends. Spending an evening with this psychopath would be dangerous.

"So what's the plan?" I asked, breaking the silence.

"We'll talk about that once we're in your car. Where's your car?"

"Level 4."

"Get up and walk slowly to the door with me. Look straight ahead. Don't make eye contact with anyone," Giacomo instructed. His throaty whisper was difficult to hear. "Then we'll go out to the garage and up the stairs to your car. But first we visit the men's room."

In the men's room, Giacomo instructed me to take off my suit jacket, shirt, and tie. Then, examining me, he ordered me to lift up my undershirt and drop my trousers.

"You're clean," he announced. "No wires. I didn't think you'd have the guts, but you never can be too careful. Piece of advice, counselor, you need to hit the gym. You're putting on some extra weight – a spare tire. Now put on your clothes and let's get out of here."

We walked leisurely out of the lounge, across the hotel lobby, to the adjoining parking garage. Instead of riding the elevator to the fourth floor, we climbed up the stairwell. Once we reached the fourth floor, Giacomo stopped me from opening the door. For several minutes, we stood on the landing until he was certain no one was following.

Giacomo opened the door and ordered me to enter the garage first.

"Which is your car? I want out of the garage as quickly as possible."

Pointing to my car, I responded, "The gray Volvo directly across from us."

"You're driving. I'm riding shotgun. Now move."

With Giacomo next to me, I drove down the ramps and paid the cashier.

"Turn right onto I-93 and head for Landerbrook Heights," he directed. Landerbrook Heights is an affluent eastern suburb with multiple four-star hotels and office buildings. As I pulled out, Giacomo slid down low in the seat, invisible to anyone watching me turn onto the street.

He remained slouched in the front seat until I'd driven for about five minutes on I-93. Then he sat up, carefully surveying the highway. Now, almost 6:30 p.m., rush hour traffic had vanished.

"So far, so good." He turned to me. "I imagine if I asked your permission to light up, you'd object. So I won't ask." Chortling appreciatively at his own humor, Giacomo removed a cigarette from his diamond-and-ruby-encrusted cigarette holder and lit up. Taking a long, slow drag, he blew smoke in my direction. "I read an article how secondhand smoke is the real killer."

Ignoring Giacomo's effort to rile me, I opened the driver and passenger windows a crack to allow cross ventilation. This reaction to his smoking enormously entertained him and irritated me. To return the focus to him, I asked about his cigarette holder.

"Why the symbol of Switzerland on your cigarette holder? It's beautiful."

Better lucky than good my father always said. My admiring comment earned a home run. Giacomo's face brightened.

"You're observant, counselor. That's the Swiss flag on the lid of the holder; diamonds and rubies set in enamel. It was a gift from my mother. She was born and grew up in Lugano, Switzerland. She came to America for college and fell in love with my father, a regular Italian stallion. She never returned home. But that's enough to make me Swiss."

Now it was my turn to smile.

"You're smiling counselor. You find being Swiss amusing?"

"I have this vague recollection that Switzerland and the United

States don't have any 'extradition arrangement. That's where Marc Rich is living, the millionaire Clinton pardoned."

"'Very, very good counselor. You're a smart one. Maybe if you were my attorney, I'd hang around and beat the rap. I never heard of this Rich guy, but you're right on. I've done my homework," he explained proudly. "Switzerland doesn't extradite its citizens to the United States. I learned that gem from my uncle, my mother's brother, who lives in Lugano. Ever hear of Enrico Frigerio?"

"Can't say I have."

"'Enrico' or 'Kiko' was involved in the Pizza Connection group. That's a famous 1980s Mafia drug ring that sold heroin and cocaine and did some fancy money laundering with the cash. Kiko fled the United States and managed to reach Lugano, Switzerland. He worked some deals there with my uncle. The feds haven't been able to touch him since Kiko's a Swiss national."

"It's a long way to Switzerland. Once the feds realize you're missing, with the help of Interpol, they'll watch all the international airports."

Giacomo blew more smoke in my direction. He opened the power window and tossed the still-burning cigarette butt. "That's my problem, counselor. I suggest less curiosity. Remember what curiosity contributed to the health of the cat." Again Giacomo chortled appreciatively at his own wit. I remembered that he wasn't the first to give me that warning.

"Turn off at the New Brunswick exit," he suddenly commanded. "It's a half mile up ahead."

Giacomo directed me to a Comfort Suites hotel one mile from the exit and had me park my car in the lot outside the hotel's front door. We entered and strolled past the front desk, down a long unlit corridor and then Giacomo pulled me out a side door.

Once outside, his eyes darting furtively, Giacomo checked every direction. Seeing no one, he tossed me keys, and pointing to a red Ford Fusion parked to the right of the door, ordered, "Get in and drive. Take the side exit and get back on the freeway. Head toward Landerbrook Heights."

Giacomo slumped low in the front seat once more until we were back on I-93. After driving several miles, I glanced over and asked, "What the hell was that all about?"

"You can never be too careful. Someone might be tailing us, even looking for your car. It's my life that's at stake." Giacomo lit another cigarette. His hand trembled. He blinked. "I don't trust you." He reflected a moment, frowned, and then growled, "Screw with me, Stein, and you're a dead man." He patted his jacket where his gun was holstered.

Giacomo's chilling tone convinced me he was a cold-blooded killer. Instinctively, I dropped my left hand from the steering wheel to touch the GPS medallion in my pocket, reassuring myself it was still there. Fingering the medallion calmed my jittery nerves.

"Honestly, David, I wouldn't mess with you. You scare the shit out of me. I want you out of the country and out of my life as quickly as possible." The fear in my voice was genuine. Whether the psychopath was convinced, I wasn't sure.

"For your sake, I hope you're not bullshitting me." Giacomo shot a menacing glare in my direction, all the while taking deep drags on his cigarette. We drove like this for five minutes until he barked, "Pull off at the next exit and get on Landerbrook Drive. Keep going until you reach the Plaza."

The Landerbrook Plaza is a fifteen-story chic hotel in Landerbrook Centre, an upscale mixed-use suburban mall. With its New York-style designer boutiques and trendy restaurants, surrounding Class A-office buildings, a mini-convention center and more, Landerbrook Centre has made the mother city superfluous.

Giacomo and I entered the Plaza's fashionable lobby. Ornate furniture designed to appear antique and large vases of freshly cut flowers filled the room. Seven o'clock on a weekday night, and already a steady flow of customers streamed through the lobby to the lounge to enjoy an after-work cocktail or two, before returning to their suburban homes. Others headed toward the hotel's four-star restaurant or its Fleming's steakhouse.

Giacomo stopped at an empty bellman's station. Leaning close, he whispered hoarsely, "Walk over to the front desk and ask the clerk if a guest left an envelope addressed to Steve Stein. Don't try anything funny. I'll be watching."

Feigning nonchalance, I ambled over to one of the clerks, a young, rosy-cheeked, green-eyed brunette. Michelle from Elmira, New York, according to the badge pinned to her gray uniformed pantsuit, cheerfully greeted me.

"How can I help you, sir?"

"I'm looking for a letter a guest left at the front desk for Steve Stein."

"I'll check for you, sir," Michelle said, flashing a friendly smile. A hospitality trainer would have been proud.

Michelle returned in about three minutes, holding a white envelope with my name scrawled across it in large red ink block letters. Before turning the envelope over to me, Michelle requested identification. After examining my driver's license, she handed me the envelope. I turned back from the front desk, and walked to where Giacomo was waiting. He grabbed the envelope from my hand and tore it open. Inside was a plastic room key wrapped in a sheet of paper with the singular message: Room 713.

I looked at Giacomo and asked in a hushed tone, "how could you be so certain I'd be with you? Without me, she wouldn't have given you the envelope."

"Experience, counselor, experience. I've made a living by understanding human nature and anticipating people's reactions. You're no different than the others. I knew you'd be with me."

The hotel elevator took us to the seventh floor where we traversed an empty corridor to Room 713. I stood behind Giacomo, waiting for him to open the door to the room. He did not. Instead he handed me the plastic keycard and stood back from the door. After checking to see that the hallway was empty, he pulled the gun out of his shoulder holster.

"Open the door, counselor, enter slowly and tell me what you see."

My hands were trembling. Slipping the keycard into the slot above the door handle, I slowly pushed the door open and peeked inside. My heart was pounding. Giacomo feared an ambush and had deployed me as his point man. As I feared, Agent Duncan and his agent would be of no use.

I saw a narrow hallway that opened into a large, empty room containing typical hotel furniture including a king-size bed. A black suitcase was lying on the bed. "The room's empty," I told Giacomo, while still intently checking out the room.

Giacomo pressed the gun sharply into the pit of my back. He moved up close behind me in the doorway. I became his personal human shield as the hotel room door closed behind us. Still deploying me as a shield, Giacomo examined the bathroom and closets. Room 713 was indeed empty.

Giacomo deadlocked the door and replaced his gun in his shoulder holster. Walking over to the bed, he opened the suitcase with a key he took from his pocket. Giacomo grinned, his edginess momentarily vanishing. He took out and examined a single bundled stack of bills. As best I could tell, all were one hundred dollar bills. Returning the bundle to its place, Giacomo next removed a manila envelope from the suitcase. Tearing open the envelope, he pulled out a single sheet of paper. He scanned the handwritten message and then neatly folded and placed the paper in the breast pocket inside his sport jacket. The torn envelope was left lying on the floor.

"So far, so good. The money and instructions are here, as planned," Giacomo mumbled to himself. He lifted the suitcase from the bed, set it on its wheels, and rolled it toward the door.

"We're getting out of here. Unlatch the door and see if anyone's in the hallway," Giacomo barked. "God, I need a cigarette." Giacomo's jumpiness and impatience had returned with a vengeance. I watched as his hand, shaking slightly, slid inside his sport jacket to grasp his gun.

I unlatched and reopened the door. With Giacomo behind me, I peered up and down the hallway. "All clear," I announced, turning back to him.

We moved rapidly down the hallway to the elevator, with me in the lead and Giacomo behind, rolling the suitcase. I pressed the down button and almost simultaneously the elevator door opened. Two husky fortyish men stood inside, sporting matching crew cuts and dressed in dark business suits. I glanced back at Giacomo for direction. By a slight nod of his head, he indicated to enter. He followed rolling the suitcase. The men continued chatting about their next day's meeting as the elevator descended to the ground floor. Trying not to stare at the two men, I imagined, or more accurately hoped, they were Agent Duncan's undercover agents trailing us. I again touched the GPS medallion in my pocket for reassurance.

The elevator door opened. By another nod, Giacomo wordlessly signaled to allow our unknown companions to leave first.

"You up for a steak?" one asked the other as they stepped out of the elevator. "There's a Fleming's off the lobby."

As the two men headed toward the steakhouse, I exited the elevator and started toward the lobby door. The red Fusion was parked outside in a nearby space.

Giacomo grabbed my arm and shook his head. "No, we're leaving out a side door." He led me across the lobby, down a long corridor past multiple empty meeting rooms and out the side exit. A silver-gray, four-door BMW sedan was parked by the door. Giacomo sprung open the trunk and placed the cash-filled suitcase inside. Looking over his shoulder, I saw him move a semiautomatic weapon to one side of the trunk to make space for the suitcase.

"You're still driving." Giacomo handed me the car keys after popping open the door locks. "Get back on I-93 going east. We're going to the Richmond County Airport." A twenty-minute ride from Landerbrook Plaza, the County airport is a small, public airport with an office and several hangars, but no control tower. Executives from the city's larger corporations fly in and out of the small airport in their company's corporate jets.

Turning out of the hotel's parking lot, I drove the BMW toward the freeway. Protected by the cover of darkness, Giacomo sat erect, lighting up a cigarette. His flitting eyes betrayed his nervousness as he blinked at the glare of the headlights of the oncoming traffic.

"Your planning's impressive. Everything's happening like clockwork." I desperately wanted conversation. The weapon in the trunk made me nervous, as did Giacomo's continued silence. "How much money is in the suitcase?" I asked.

"Nine hundred thousand dollars. One million less a ten percent delivery fee, assuming it's all there."

"I've never seen that much cash before. You'll be set for life wherever you're going."

Giacomo ruminated on my comment. He puffed several times on his cigarette. "Set for life," he grunted. "Are you kidding?" He looked at me. I could feel his disdain. "The money in the suitcase is my fifty percent-down payment to get out of the country."

I said nothing in response. To my surprise, Giacomo became talkative. Money was on his mind. With the Chens now doing the FBI's bidding, the poor man was down to his last five million dollars. And two million was apparently the cost of getting to Switzerland.

"Everybody has a hand out," he complained. Giacomo was irate, sounding like some of my conservative friends bitching about big government and taxes. "You wouldn't believe how many palms need to be greased. When people know you're in trouble, they take advantage of you. The goddamned Arabs are the worst. First they charge ten percent to transfer my own money to me. And then there's another $1.8 million to fly me to Switzerland. By the time I get there, I'll be lucky if two million is left."

"I never knew Arabs had those kinds of connections."

"You ever read about Youssef Muhammad or his other brothers?"

"No," I lied.

"He's a Saudi Arabian banker connected to banks throughout the Middle East. He launders money and charges exorbitant fees. He's goddamn good. And he has brothers connected to every major terrorist outfit in the world. It's one big network, you know?"

"No, I didn't." All this information gave me a queasy feeling. He was volunteering too much, far too much more than I wanted to hear or know. Momentarily, however, curiosity got the better of me. Forgetting

Giacomo's earlier admonition about the dangerous nature of that trait, I blurted out, "What would they have to do with you?" No sooner were the words out of my mouth than I instantly regretted the question.

Lighting up yet another cigarette, Giacomo looked over at me. Speaking slowly, he said with obvious relish, "You know if I answer that, I'll have to kill you?"

"Forget I asked. I talk too much, way too much. Diarrhea of the mouth. A really foolish question. It's not my business. I don't want to know." The words poured rapidly, staccato-like from my mouth.

"It's simple, counselor. The Saudis want to finance various terrorist organizations in the Middle East, but not directly. Youssef Muhammad is an ideal middleman. He's close to the royal family, married to a princess, I think. His brothers are big-time terrorists."

"Stop," I interrupted. "Don't tell me your business."

Giacomo's broad grin persisted. Clearly he enjoyed my discomfort.

He blew smoke at me. "That's what I love about the world. It's filled with gullible people, even smart ones like you."

Giacomo pulled the gun from his shoulder holster and gingerly balanced the weapon on his lap. He flashed a broad, toothy smile. "You didn't really believe I'd let you walk away alive, did you counselor?" His laugh sent a shiver up my spine.

I didn't say a word, just kept on driving. My thumping heart felt like it would explode. I forced myself to keep my eyes on the road and ordered myself not to panic. Certainly he wouldn't shoot me while we drove down I-93. Meanwhile, my left hand slid down from the steering wheel into my trouser pocket. Just as Agent Duncan had instructed, I repeatedly pressed the yellow emergency button on the GPS medallion.

"I don't know what the hell you're doing, but it makes me nervous and I don't like it." Giacomo had noticed I was driving with one hand in my pocket. "Stop giving yourself a hand job," he sneered. "Keep both hands on the steering wheel where I can see them, if you want to make it alive to the airport."

35

The iridescent digital clock on the BMW's dashboard flashed 10:05 p.m. We pulled into the county airport. The night was cloudy without a star or the moon visible in the sky. Everything was pitch black except for the lighted runway and a lighted hangar to the right of the airport's single office building, about half a mile up the driveway.

"Drive over there." Giacomo gestured toward the lighted hangar. "And don't try anything funny." For emphasis, he pushed the barrel of his gun harshly into my ribs.

I peered through the rearview mirror. No sign of Agent Duncan's promised Cavalry was visible, just darkness. My mind raced uncontrollably, alternating between fear and anger. Paranoia paralyzed me. Perhaps the agent's promises had been a ploy to secure my participation. What if the GPS medallion in my pocket was nothing more than a placebo intended to calm my nerves? Maybe Giacomo had succeeded in shaking the FBI tail. Shit, I thought, I had gotten myself into a real mess.

A sleek Gulfstream jet was parked outside the hangar on the tarmac with its boarding stairwell down. Two large, black Mercedes SUVs were parked nearby.

"Pull over next to the SUVs, turn off the engine, and lay the keys down next to me."

I complied, praying the FBI would soon arrive.

"Pop the trunk and get out of the car." Giacomo spoke slowly, accentuating each word.

Again I obeyed, constantly gazing back at the road in hope of seeing headlights. Six men moved out from the shadows of the parked SUVs and walked deliberately toward us. Five cradled automatic weapons and protectively surrounded their apparent leader. About my height, the baby-faced leader, a handgun tucked in the waistband of his black jeans, had wavy black hair and a thick mustache with a goatee. His face was pocked from acne.

Giacomo greeted him. "Hassan, it's good to see you again. How's your father, Youssef?"

"He's fine. In Saudi Arabia with my mother right now. Where's the money?" Hassan spoke in a high-pitched voice with a hint of a British accent.

"It's in the trunk. Help me, Stein."

Giacomo walked to the rear of the BMW and lifted the automatic weapon out of the trunk. With a slight nod of his head, he signaled that he expected me to remove the suitcase from the trunk, which I did.

"It's all in the suitcase. Nine hundred thousand dollars. Do you want to count it?"

"No, David. That won't be necessary. I trust you." Hassan paused. "Besides they'll be plenty of time to count the money once we're on the plane."

"That's heartwarming, especially since I must be financing single-handedly your father's charities."

"Ah, David. How quickly you forget. Our business relationship is based on mutuality. Yes, you have money. But without us, you are—how do you American people so graphically put it, ah yes—dead meat. We're the only ones with the necessary connections to transport you to where you want to go with the money you need. We are your only friends, your lifeline. Who did you turn to only yesterday when you wanted the troublesome woman killed? Did not my man Emir handle that mission for you on short notice? That was an act of true friendship." Hassan's English had a formal tone.

"Yes, friendship and ten thousand dollars."

Ignoring the jibe, Hassan turned to one of his henchmen. "Ahmed, place the suitcase on the plane." A short, stocky dark-haired man similarly clad in black jeans and a black turtleneck, cradling an automatic weapon in his right arm, stepped forward, took the suitcase, and headed toward the plane.

Pointing to me, Hassan inquired, "Is he coming with us?"

Giacomo lit another cigarette and shook his head. "No, he knows too much. He must be eliminated."

"You request another act of friendship." Hassan spoke showing no emotion. "You know the price. I'll let you run a tab." To him my elimination was just another business transaction, and he was operating the cash register.

"That's bullshit, Hassan, absolute bullshit." Giacomo seethed. "You're nickel and diming me to death." He threw his half-smoked cigarette to the ground and crushed it with his boot.

"Emir, Joe," Hassan addressed two of his other gun-toting thugs. "What do you think? Would you discount this job for our dear friend and good customer David, say for seven thousand dollars?" Pointing to me, he added, "David's companion here doesn't look like he'll put up much of a struggle."

The two men answered their leader's question in a unfamiliar language that I guessed was Arabic. Hassan responded in kind. All three laughed.

"For you, good friend, they will do it. Do we have a deal?"

"You people . . ." Giacomo caught himself, bit his lip, and didn't finish the sentence. He took a deep breath and shook his head. "O.K. Hassan, it's a deal." Hassan and David sealed my death with a handshake. Giacomo's obvious unhappiness over the cost of my elimination did nothing to cheer me up. I kept waiting and hoping for some sign of Agent Duncan and his men. Nothing.

Emir, a giant of a man with an olive-skinned complexion and closely clipped black hair, grabbed me roughly. His huge physique resembled that of a nose tackle in the NFL. He, too, was clothed entirely in black. He pulled me to the closest of the SUVs. My arm ached from his iron grip. Joe, half Emir's size, followed behind. His menacing black eyes matched his shaggy black beard. Like all of Hassan's men he was well armed. He brandished an automatic weapon; a handgun was stuck in the waistband of his black jeans.

Joe took a roll of tape from the back seat of the SUV and bound my hands tightly behind my back. I could barely wiggle my fingers as I tried to maintain some circulation. Looking into the distance, I still saw nothing but the blackness of night. Without uttering a word, Joe shoved me into the back seat of the SUV.

"Hey, what the . . ." I started to complain.

"Keep your fucking mouth shut or I'll off you right here," he commanded in perfect no-nonsense English. He spoke with an accent I didn't recognize.

There was little to do but pray.

Hassan watched, nodding with apparent approval. "You guys take care of him. When you finish, burn the body. I'll contact you when we get to the Keys."

Giacomo looked over at me. "I'd offer the condemned man a cigarette," he chortled, "but I know you don't smoke. Give my regards to Elizabeth."

"I'll drive. We'll take the back road," Joe announced. He pulled keys from his pocket, got into the driver's seat, and started the engine. Emir climbed into the back seat and shoved me to the corner as he took up more than half the seat.

We'd not driven more than thirty seconds, maybe a half mile down a dirt road, when sirens pierced the nighttime silence. Agent Duncan's Cavalry arrived, a god damn thirty seconds too late to do me much good.

Joe momentarily stopped the SUV and took in the scene through the rear window. Flares filled the sky illuminating the hangar, the Gulfstream, and the tarmac. Huddled in the corner of the backseat, I twisted my body to look out the rear window as well. Cars were everywhere. The sound of firecrackers, which I assumed was gunfire, popped repeatedly in the distance. Another flare illuminated the nighttime sky.

"Step on it. Let's get out of here," Emir shouted. Joe floored the accelerator and we rapidly disappeared into the darkness of the night. Barely under control, the car bounced down an unpaved gravel road that seemed to lead nowhere. My body was tossed back and forth between Emir and the side of the car. Joe didn't slow up, nor did he speak.

Within five minutes, we were driving more slowly on an unlit two-lane country road. I cowered in a corner of the backseat, my hands painfully bound behind me. Emir moved over closer to me in the backseat. His large body periodically fell on top of me as the SUV bounced down the country road. He was breathing heavily. Sweat poured from his enormous body. I saw concern in his eyes.

"Something's wrong. Should we call Hassan to find out what happened?" Emir asked Joe, as he took his cell phone out from his jacket pocket. Even if decision making wasn't his strength, he recognized that Hassan's plans had run afoul.

"That wouldn't be wise, Emir. We don't know who's at the other end of the mobile. If Hassan's all right, he'll call us. The question right now is what to do with the asshole in the backseat next to you. We don't even know his name." Joe spoke calmly without the slightest hint of anxiety, all the while adding distance between our SUV and the airport.

"The name's Stein, Steve Stein. I'm a lawyer in town and have nothing to do with you guys. There's absolutely no reason now to kill me."

Emir clutched my arm with his iron grip and pulled me toward him. I could smell his unpleasant body odor. He looked me directly in the eyes. "What do you mean?"

I winced in pain. I whined, "don't squeeze so hard. You're hurting me. David wants me dead because I knew he was fleeing the country. Sure looks like the government found him before he could escape. Why kill me? You won't get the money he promised. Let me go. I promise I won't know you. Or better yet, if you want, I'll pay you twice as much to let me live." I kept talking rapidly and pleading and hoping. The longer I talked, the better the chance the FBI might come to my rescue. The GPS, if it was working, was still attached to the key chain in my pocket.

"He makes sense," Joe suggested from the front seat. "We could drop his ass off right here, in the middle of nowhere. No killing, no nothing. He'd get back eventually, but we'd be long gone."

Emir was silent. He furrowed his brow. I guessed he was trying to sort out and process this new information. He shook his head and turned to me. "We can't let you go. We gotta kill you. You know I killed that Elizabeth woman. Cops learn about that and I'm fried."

"When did you knock her off? I don't remember that." Joe's question wasn't welcome. This wasn't at all what I wanted to hear. I knew I would be better off not knowing the details about Elizabeth's death.

"Hassan called me last night. He knows I do a little freelancing. He needed a hit-skip on a broad who'd be with David when he left a restaurant. She was ratting to the FBI or something. I took care of her – firebombed the car." Emir was sweating profusely. "I've decided. Pull off at the next intersection. We'll take him in the woods, off him, and then get the hell out of here. That's what Hassan would want."

"You sure that's what you want to do?"

Emir's eyes widened. His face turned red. "I knew it. You're turning on me." As he shouted, his spittle hit my face. "I'll kill you both." His fingers visibly tightened around the weapon he cradled in his arm.

"Cool it man, I'm with you on this. We're on the same team. You're absolutely right." Joe spoke soothingly to Emir, deescalating the disagreement. "Hold on, I'm turning." He veered sharply at an intersection and began traveling down a gravel road. Emir, once again, was thrown against me.

"I wanted to make sure you'd thought everything out," Joe added. "Makes sense to me. We'll kill him. Besides, with a name like Stein, I'll bet he's a Jew. You can't go wrong when you kill a Jew. You a Jew, Stein?"

I didn't answer.

Grasping my throat in a choke hold with his right hand, his eyes bulging, Emir screamed at me, his face not more than six inches from mine. "Answer the question, you motherfucker. Are you a fucking Jew?"

Gasping for breath, I acknowledged my heritage.

Emir loosened his iron grip slightly, allowing me to gasp for breath. He gave a thumb's-up Joe could see through the rear view mirror. "You're right, Joe. It's a blessing to rid the world of another goddamn Jew. Jews stole my Uncle's land and killed two of his sons. Revenge will be sweet."

Joe stopped the SUV at the side of the road and got out. He opened the side door and looked down at me. I felt his disdain. Turning to Emir, he asked, "What's your pleasure? Do you want me to off him in the woods while you watch the car? Or do you want the privilege? Your choice. You gotta know I'm with you."

"Man, I apologize for losing my cool. You're my friend and brother." Looking over at me, he continued. "If it's my choice, I'll kill the bastard. It'll make me feel good. Like I did something for my family."

"Makes no difference to me, man."

Emir half lifted and half dragged me from the back seat. Shoving me into the woods, he flung me head first to the ground, all the while grinning. The pain was intense. "You're a dead man, Jew," I heard him say. Joe watched without emotion from a slight distance standing above me, saying nothing. I apparently now belonged to Emir. The ground was hard and damp, covered with thick vegetation. The fall split my lip. Blood dribbled from my nose down into my mouth. The pain from my tightly bound wrists was excruciating. Had I broken an arm, I didn't know. I remained silent, not wanting to let the two thugs know how much I hurt.

"What will it be, Jew? Do you want the bullet between the eyes or in the back of the head?" Emir was standing over me with his gun drawn. I lay on the ground in a fetal position in silence, my eyes tightly closed. I prayed. I prayed that Agent Duncan and the FBI would miraculously appear. I made private promises and offers to God if he would only save me.

"No answer, huh? Figured a cowardly Jew bastard like you wouldn't look me in the eye. The back of the head it is."

Every sound was magnified. I heard the soft rustling of twigs on the forest floor. My heart pounded uncontrollably. My lungs struggled for air. I imagined hearing the slightest click of a trigger being cocked. An explosion. An ear-piercing blast shattered the stillness of the night. Blood and pieces of human flesh splattered me. I felt no pain. Not the expected hurt or prelude to death. I heard a thud.

There was no pain, just a magnificent feeling when I realized I was still alive and unharmed. It wasn't my blood. I rolled on to my back. Emir in his enormity lay in a heap at my feet, blood pouring from what remained of his head. Joe stood over the body, holding the gun that had been tucked in his waistband. He reached down, took the cell phone from Emir's jacket pocket and placed it in his own. I swear I heard him look down at the body and mumble under his breath "mamzer," the Yiddish word for bastard.

36

Moments later, the woods hummed with the sounds of flurried activity. A half dozen cars, including one black and white, surrounded the Mercedes SUV. Officers examined the remains of Emir. One agent cut the tape binding my wrist with his pocketknife. Another agent ministered to my split lip and bloody nose. Emotionless, Joe stood about five feet from me, at one side of the clearing, intently watching the activity without uttering a single word to the agents or to me. No one approached or even acknowledged him.

Agent Duncan was the maestro, standing in the center of the hustle and bustle, barking orders and orchestrating the activity. Dressed in pressed gray slacks with a matching gray pullover sweater and wearing a flak jacket, he looked every bit the movie star. Seeing me now on my feet, he walked toward me, but first stopped by Joe, and the two hugged.

"Yossi, you're all right?"

"Not a scratch, Andrew. A few harrowing moments, but I'm fine."

"My man, Stein. You took care of him?"

"Like I said, a few harrowing moments, but except for minor bumps and bruises, he's no worse for the wear. He could probably use a stiff drink, but then so could I."

"Take the gray Toyota and disappear. The keys are in the ignition. We'll communicate later tonight in the usual way. Depending on how things play out, we'll decide whether to bring you in. Until we figure that out, be vigilant. I don't think you've blown your cover, but we can't be too careful."

The two men embraced a second time. Joe, or Yossi, or whoever he was, climbed into the gray Toyota and vanished into the night.

Agent Duncan walked over and put his arm around me. So only I could see, he mouthed wordlessly, "I owe you," and then whispered, "Logistically we had some problems. Things got a little too close for comfort."

I exploded. "A little too close for comfort? I was almost killed!"

Ignoring my outburst, he turned his back to me and spoke to another agent. "Johnson, put the body into the SUV and drive it back to the airport. That's where he was killed."

Facing me once more, he announced loud enough for everyone to hear, "You did great tonight, Mr. Stein, a real hero." Under his breath, he added softly, "I understand your feelings. But this isn't the time or the place. I'll meet you at your apartment later tonight."

He called over a young, heavy-set agent. "Emerson, drive Mr. Stein directly home. He's had a trying day. Find out where he parked his car and arrange to have the Volvo in his garage by the morning."

Andrew clasped my hand. "You did good Steve, better than I would have guessed – or hoped." He hugged me and said with a wink, "You're a patriot, my friend. Sarge would have been proud. I'll see you tonight."

The transformation to my apartment was mind-boggling, a reverse Cinderella effect. If Cinderella's ornate carriage turned into a simple pumpkin at the stroke of midnight, my apartment had undergone a positive makeover sometime before that same bewitching hour. Seven hours earlier, the apartment was a wreck, strewn with broken furniture and shattered dishes, a baseball bat protruding from a smashed television. Miraculously the broken furnishings and dishware had disappeared and been replaced. A forty-six inch Sony plasma television hung on the wall in the living room. The smell of furniture polish permeated the air; the carpet showed the sign of recent vacuuming. I opened the fridge to find it freshly stocked with two dozen Amstel Lights and a handwritten note: "See you tonight." I was heartened. In analyzing the over-under of my survival, Agent Duncan bet all along on a meeting with me tonight in my apartment.

For the next several hours, I unwound, drinking beer, eating chips, and watching my new tube, alternating between ESPN sports center and various late night shows. Shortly before three in the morning, the doorbell rang. Agent Duncan entered my apartment. He went from room to room, examining his colleagues' handiwork and nodding his head with approval. Then he walked back to the kitchen and took an Amstel Light from the fridge. Returning to the living room, he sat down on the couch next to me. He slipped off his loafers, placing his stocking feet on the recently polished coffee table. We tapped our beer bottles and drank.

"Who said the FBI can't get it right? Looks good to me."

"I can't believe you did this for me, and so quickly. I promise right here and now to never again cheat on my taxes. Now tell me, what's the story with David Giacomo?"

Agent Duncan took a swig of beer from the bottle held in his right hand. "Dead." After a moment's contemplation, he rotely continued, as if reading from a press release. "David Giacomo was killed at County airport shortly before midnight trying to flee the country to avoid prosecution. We recovered a suitcase filled with nearly one million dollars and a letter of instruction listing the bank account numbers and codes detailing where the rest of David's money was hidden. You'll read in this morning's *Chronicle* that he was killed together with seven terrorists including two pilots, who were helping him escape. Hassan Muhammad is from a family with known international terrorist connections." Having completed this speech, Andrew sipped his beer.

"I heard the shooting. It sounded like firecrackers popping."

Andrew helped himself to some chips from a bowl set on the coffee table. "They weren't firecrackers, that's for sure. When we arrived at the airport, Giacomo and the terrorists opened fire with automatic weapons and tried to board the Gulfstream. They had a hell of a lot of firepower. Bullets were flying everywhere. I took one on my vest. When the shooting stopped, the bad guys were all dead. All of them." He winked. "That's what you'll be reading."

Listening to and watching Andrew, I was certain there was more, a whole lot more to the story. I waited for a further explanation or elaboration. None came. When I asked, Andrew just shook his head and repeated. "As David Giacomo was trying to flee, my men killed all the bad guys at the airport including Emir. Steve, you weren't there or in any way involved. It is essential we understand each other, especially on that final point." All hint of his former joviality drained from his face. His jaw clenched, Andrew stared at me intently, waiting for my answer.

"I'm confused. Joe or Yossi, or whoever, no thanks to you and your fancy GPS medallion, killed Emir in the woods. He saved my life. I owe him. Who was he?"

"I'll explain some things you shouldn't know and don't need to know. After what you've done, I trust you. But when I'm finished, this conversation never occurred. You must promise NEVER to mention what I tell you or what you saw or did tonight to any one, EVER. Deal?" He looked at me.

"Deal," I replied.

"Yossi's an Israeli of Yemenite descent. Yemen is an Arab country. After Israel declared its independence in 1948, Yossi's family fled Yemen. Yossi was born in Israel, but he grew up speaking both Arabic and Hebrew in his home. After completing his Israeli military service, Yossi came to the United States to go to college. He joined the FBI after 9/11 when we began actively recruiting agents fluent in Arabic. He tells me that Yossi means Joey in Hebrew."

Andrew drained his beer. He stood, stretched, and headed to the kitchen, returning with a six-pack. He opened two bottles and handed one to me.

"Yossi's been working undercover for several years, infiltrating some scary groups. As I told you, we faced unforeseen technical difficulties this evening. Satellite disruption interfered with service to the GPS you were carrying. We were flying blind, operating solely on information Yossi provided. I knew he'd be at the airport which was David's point of escape. I counted on him protecting you as long as David brought you with him. Yossi didn't disappoint. Now you need to help him. I think you understand why. Emir needs to have died with the others at the airport to protect Yossi's cover. One other point: Yossi told me Giacomo never mentioned to anyone that you'd be at the airport. So you were never there. You understand."

"Giacomo could have killed me long before we reached the airport. Hell, he threatened me and I was pressing that yellow emergency button! Unexpected technical difficulties? What was the backup plan?"

Andrew sipped his beer, ignoring my question.

"You did have a backup plan, didn't you?"

Andrew slapped me on my back.

"Yossi was the backup plan. No whining now. You got a good deal. Remember, I went to law school too. I wasn't very good, but I remember a few things. In Contracts class, we learned consideration is the basis of all deals. As I figure, you suffered a bloody nose and a few scratches. In return, no one will ever know your friend Paul scammed First Mutual, his own client. His estate, Elizabeth's estate, and the mob will keep the stock they each purchased and the profit. And the mob has forgiven Paul's debt to them, including the money advanced to purchase the First Mutual stock. You have my word all this will magically occur and no one will be the wiser."

"Ah, yes," Andrew dramatically continued, raising his beer bottle toward me in a mock salute. "I almost forgot, because it's barely worth mentioning. I'll be meeting with your esteemed Blackjack. As explained to me, he runs your firm with all the power and light touch of a J. Edgar Hoover. I will personally inform Blackjack that while, for national security reasons, I can't discuss the particular details, you pulled his beloved firm's proverbial chestnuts out of the fire at great personal risk. The firm owes you. I've done business with Blackjack before. He is a patriotic American, a good Republican, and a good friend of the Bureau. I'm certain, no I can promise, Blackjack will see you are properly compensated for your fortitude."

"As I figure, you will be receiving adequate consideration for your bruises and to ensure your future silence." He paused. "There was another term we learned." Andrew was on a roll and enjoying himself. He paused. "Mutuality, yes that was the term. You would agree, Steve, there is adequate consideration and mutuality here. I think that makes a binding deal." Andrew took another large gulp of beer and looked at me with a sudden seriousness. I received his message clearly.

"Emir killed Elizabeth. He was the hit-skip driver," I volunteered, changing the subject.

Andrew reached down for a handful of chips. He ate them slowly, one chip at a time. All the time he said nothing, concentrating instead on each individual potato chip.

"You need to forget Elizabeth's death," he responded with finality. "Unless Detectives O'Brien and Mancini independently discover about Emir, which I highly doubt, Elizabeth's murder will remain unsolved. Truth be known, David and Emir are dead, so no one is getting away with murder. But Emir's role in Elizabeth's death can't come out, at least for many years. You are not to tell your journalist friend, P.J, about Elizabeth or anything else about tonight. Yossi saved your life; don't endanger his. Do I have your word?"

"Who told you P.J. is my friend?"

Andrew gave me a knowing smile and drained his beer. "It's part of my job to know things like that. For your information, P.J. covered the airport incident for the *Chronicle* tonight. He told me he hadn't seen so much gore since the streets of Mogadishu. Now do I have your word?"

"You do," I pledged. I finished my beer and opened another bottle, as did Andrew.

"Can I tell you something strange I wouldn't tell anyone else?" I felt a strong bond of friendship developing with this enigmatic man I had only met yesterday.

"As long as we agree these are our last beers. Tomorrow's a work day and believe me, there'll be plenty of paperwork."

"I really thought I was about to die tonight," I confessed. "I've never been so frightened in my life. There I was, lying on the ground, certain I was about to die, and do you know the last thought that flashed through my mind when Emir cocked his gun?"

Andrew didn't say a word. He just listened.

"I was going to die without knowing who killed Paul."

PART FIVE
SOLUTIONS

T he digital clock on the nightstand flashed noon. Nestled snugly in a quilt, clutching a bed pillow, I didn't want to get out of bed. My body told me in no uncertain terms that the previous evening's activities had taken a steep toll. Every bone and muscle ached; my chafed wrists were purple and painfully sore. A persistent sensation of anxiety and a splitting headache were uncomfortable testaments to my limited tolerance for excitement and beer. Reluctantly, I pulled myself out of bed. I needed to face the world. For a brief moment, I considered, and rejected, the idea of heading directly to the office. The thought of answering phone calls and putting out bush fires had no appeal. Besides, I was hungry. A burger and fries in McGinty's Back Room was the medicine of choice.

I shaved, showered, and dressed and headed to McGinty's, stopping at the Starbucks across from my office to purchase the morning's *Chronicle*. The front page headlined the death of suspected swindler David Giacomo, as he tried to flee the country. Scanning the accompanying story, appearing under P.J.'s byline, somehow I wasn't surprised that the narrative read exactly as Agent Duncan predicted. In addition to Giacomo, Hassan Muhammad and six other men died on the County Airport tarmac in a fusillade of bullets. P.J. described Muhammad and his family's ties to international terrorism. Sure enough, one of those killed was identified as Emir Abood, a naturalized citizen of Palestinian origin, most recently living in Detroit where he worked as a nightclub bouncer. The story neither mentioned Yossi or me. Agent Andrew Duncan, on the other hand, was highlighted and repeatedly quoted.

Striding past the wooden bar crammed with lunching customers, I marched straight to The Back Room. Charley, wearing his familiar Yankees cap jauntily tilted to one side, greeted me from his post in the kitchen.

"Mr. Stein, good to see you. It's been a couple of days. Where ya been?"

"Busy, Charley. Really busy."

"What ya goin' to want? I'll get it started."

"Hamburger platter deluxe, Charley, with all the trimmings."

"Ya want the waiter to bring the usual Amstel Light?"

"I'll go with an iced tea this afternoon."

"It'll be comin' right up, Mr. Stein."

Billy Gold waved from a corner table as I entered the room. He was sitting with Seymour Simon and Craig Johnston. Craig runs a midsize architectural firm and has been working on Seymour's recent projects. His connections to Seymour and several other major developers, and his well-timed contributions to local politicians, combine to make Craig a major force in the city's redevelopment efforts.

"Hey, Steve. Come over and join us. We got room," Billy boomed. He pointed to an empty chair. For once, an invitation from Billy was welcome. Right now, I could use an hour or so of Billy's "Me, Me, Me." I walked over and sat down next to Seymour.

"We're discussing David Giacomo," Billy informed me. "Did you read the story in this morning's *Chronicle*?"

"Yes," I replied. "Unbelievable."

"*Chronicle* says your law firm represented David Giacomo. Didn't you once tell me that Paul, before he was murdered, was set to be his trial attorney?" Seymour asked.

I nodded in agreement, not wanting to be dragged into the

conversation. Agent Duncan's admonition was my personal Jiminy Cricket, my constant conscience.

"The Right Wing is right. Terrorists are everywhere. Who would imagine? People right here in our city connected to Middle East terrorists? It's a meshuggina world." Seymour sighed and shook his head. "What I can't figure out is how the authorities knew they'd be at County Airport last night. That Agent Duncan, he's a smart one. I met him last December when Congressman Marshall took me to tour the city's FBI headquarters. We had coffee together. I'll tell you, his tentacles are everywhere. He knows everyone. I sleep better at night with a mensch like him defending our country."

"Wiretaps," Billy interrupted. "I'm sure they used wiretaps. Government always uses illegal wiretaps."

"There's more to this story than meets the eye," Craig declared from across the table. A smallish, balding man, he always wore bow ties. "You can bet an FBI informer was on the inside, like you see in the movies. That's how the FBI knew they'd be at the airport."

My deluxe platter and iced tea arrived. While munching on the hamburger cooked to perfection, I listened as the three men argued and hypothesized over last night's events. Craig was right. Last night had unfolded like a movie. I knew. I'd been there. Craig gazed at me. "You're mighty quiet, Steve. What's your theory?"

I shrugged. "How the hell should I know? Nothing's farther from the realm of my experience."

"That never stopped you before. Hell, you're a lawyer. The less you lawyers know about something, the more opinionated you become." Seymour was being Seymour. He never missed an opportunity to pull my chain or tell a lawyer joke at my expense.

"Fair enough, Seymour. Since our government's involved, I'll opt for a conspiracy theory like the *New York Times* always does." Everyone laughed.

The discussion turned to Paul's upcoming funeral. I mentioned that John was flying in from Chicago and we'd be dining together this evening.

"You're kidding. I thought Paul and his son were estranged," Billy looked puzzled. "Always bothered Paul. He told me that was the biggest disappointment of his life." Billy's comment wasn't surprising. Over the years, Billy periodically lunched with Paul. Paul made no secret of his disappointing relationship with John.

"They reconciled in recent months."

"A blessing," Seymour enthused. "No one should lose a father, or God forbid, a child. But to lose a parent or child and be estranged, eventually, I tell you, creates guilt in the living. I've seen it happen all too often. For the rest of their lives, the living ruminate over why they never said 'I'm sorry' and 'I love you.' It's a blessing that they reconciled before Paul's death."

"I wonder if they talked Friday. You know John was in town the day his father was killed?"

Craig's comment hit like a bolt of lightning. I stared at him. "In town? On Friday?"

Craig's statement didn't compute. After speaking with Babs on Friday night, I called John to inform him of Paul's death. The phone number Babs gave me for John was a recognizable Chicago telephone exchange.

"Yeah, he was at my office that morning interviewing for a summer internship at my firm."

"How'd that come about?"

"Babs arranged it. We've known each other for years, since before John was born."

Billy's cell phone rang. He answered, frowned, and stood up. "Sorry guys but I have to leave. This Mississippi lawyer's trying to screw me. I refer him a million dollar-plus class action, low-hanging fruit I tell you, and now that the case is settling, the son of a bitch is trying to cut my share of the legal fees. The teleconference is in fifteen minutes." As he was leaving, Billy looked over at me. "I'll tell you Steve, I never liked Babs. She's a real bitch. Paul was lucky to be rid of her."

Seymour nodded in apparent approval. "I don't generally agree with Billy, but he sure's got Babs's number." He checked his watch and stood up as well. "Unlike you professionals, I work for my living." Glancing at me, he added, "See you at the funeral, if not before."

Only Craig and I remained at the table. His meeting with John troubled me. Something didn't seem right. "When did Babs set up the meeting?" I suddenly was feeling that I had been had.

"At the beginning of April."

"She tell you much about what John's been doing? Mention any issues?"

"You mean his drug problem? I've known about the problem for a while. It wasn't a secret. John was out of rehab, trying to put his life back together. I've known the boy for years. Like a lot of kids, he's had problems finding direction in life."

"How does architecture fit in?"

"Architecture is his new passion. He took some drafting courses in Chicago. Babs called and asked if I could find John a summer position, or at least provide some career counseling. He was planning to stop in town on Thursday night to visit his mother on his way home from New York City. I agreed to see John Friday morning, Friday the 13th. Not a date you forget."

"Do you remember how late in the day John left your office?" I tried to maintain a non-accusatory tone, not wanting to spook Craig. I failed.

Craig peered at me from across the table. He frowned. "Your questions, Steve, they upset me, make me uncomfortable. Do you suspect John was involved in his father's murder? Is that what you're intimating? I've known John since he was a boy. A troubled, young man, yes, but not a murderer."

Craig's voice was animated with emotion. "I bit my tongue when Billy and Seymour were dissing Babs. I've never liked Billy. He's a blowhard. And Seymour, well he's Seymour. He'll never admit it, but he's not always right about everything. Believe me, there's another side to the story, and I've heard it from Babs many times. Maybe it's wrong to speak ill of the dead, but your friend Paul was no choirboy."

"You're right about that," I needed the conversation to stop being confrontational. "Candidly, though Paul's been my best friend since high school, I'm like you Craig," I lied with a straight face. "I've remained fond of Babs. She's a special lady, one of a kind." A wise lawyer once told me when someone assures you he's speaking candidly, watch the nose for sudden Pinocchio-like growth. Mine was growing by the minute.

"Friday night, after the police found Paul's body in the Wal-Mart parking lot, I was the one who informed Babs. She asked if I'd call John, in Chicago, to tell him the horrible news. She was aware of how her less-than-friendly relationship with her ex had impacted their son. Her sensitivity to John's rapprochement with his father impressed me. I really admired her," I explained. "I apologize for any misunderstanding – my sounding accusatory was unintentional. Hearing you say John was in town on Friday confused me. When I called him in Chicago, he never mentioned it."

Craig's face relaxed. The taut expression disappeared. He apparently accepted my contrition and answered my question. "Babs picked John up shortly after noon and took him to the airport to catch his flight home. By the time you called, he'd have been in Chicago. Probably in all his grief he forgot to mention he'd been in town earlier in the day."

"You're right, Craig. Makes absolute sense," I assured him. But I was skeptical. Too many unanswered questions about John continued to pop up.

S unlight streamed through the six windows of my corner office. From my comfortable perch, in an overstuffed black desk chair, on the fifty-fifth floor of the city's tallest building, my thoughts centered on John Martin and his entanglement in his father's death. My mind replayed conversations with Agent Duncan, P.J., and others. Gaps remained; pieces of the puzzle were missing.

The thump of a closing door shattered the daydream. Startled, I swiveled in my chair. Mary stood directly in front of the closed door, a look of distress on her face. A tall woman with short blonde hair, partial to high heels and colored glasses, chosen to match her varied outfits, she's been my secretary for more than fifteen years. Our relationship is limited to business. I know only she has two sons in college, and her husband works as some type of computer consultant.

She examined me for a moment. "Is something wrong, Mr. Stein?"

"No, not at all. Why do you ask?"

"You've been acting strangely the last couple days. Not that it's any of my business, but you didn't come to work today until after two o'clock. Again, it's none of my business, but you've been leaving the office without telling me where you're going. That's not you. Our clients count on me being able to locate you when they have a problem. And then that man, David Giacomo, was in your office yesterday and afterward called all day trying to find you. I even talked to him. It's spooky. I read this morning he was killed last night by the FBI."

Now it was my turn to scrutinize Mary. How much should I tell her about David Giacomo? She didn't appear upset. Perhaps she was truly worried about me.

"Mary, I appreciate your concern. I really do. Paul's death has upset me. I'm sure after the funeral is over, I'll be alright again. As for David Giacomo being here yesterday, we were reviewing his case. I can't go into the details – attorney-client confidentiality you know. But you're right. His death is downright spooky. When I read the story in the *Chronicle*, I was shocked. The firm, though, is counting on our absolute discretion."

Mary shot me a look of disapproval. "I never discuss firm business, you know that."

"Good. Any important calls this morning?"

"P.J. from the *Chronicle* called three times. He said to call back on his cell phone as soon as you got in." With that Mary abruptly pivoted, reopened the door, and walked out. She looked back over her shoulder and added unconvincingly, "I'm glad nothing's wrong."

P.J. wanted to meet right away, but not at my office. He again suggested the Starbucks as our rendezvous point. This time, as I departed, I told Mary where I was going.

She ignored me and said nothing.

The Starbucks was fast becoming a second office and I, a regular. The afternoon shift barista, a young man with shoulder length hair, nodded at me in silent recognition as I entered and ordered a black coffee. P.J. already sat at a table near the doorway sipping what I assumed was a double espresso, a *Chronicle* spread in front of him. He was intently reading his own front-page story. Black coffee in hand, I sat down.

"Mr. Front Page," I greeted him. "It's good to see a man who enjoys his own work. Last night must have been quite an adventure."

P.J. looked up. "By the time I arrived, the shooting was over. But the scene was wild. I haven't seen so much blood and gore since the streets of Mogadishu. One guy had his head partially blown off. Looked to me like he was shot from close distance."

Ignoring his description of last night, I asked, "What's the big hurry? Mary says you've been pestering her, leaving messages all morning."

P.J. neatly folded the newspaper and placed it to one side. "I've two leads to share. And we need to discuss how you'll handle your meeting with John this evening."

I sipped my coffee and listened.

"You were spot on. David Giacomo hired the hit-skip driver who murdered Elizabeth. Afterward, the driver firebombed the car to destroy the evidence. The murderer was one of the terrorists killed last night."

My response to P.J.'s information was an Oscar-worthy performance, a calculated combination of satisfaction, surprise, and admiration: satisfaction at being proved right; surprise at the news; and, admiration at P.J.'s resourcefulness in obtaining the information. P.J. beamed. Turning aside my persistent entreaties, he refused, as expected, to divulge the identity of his source. He also claimed not to know which dead thug was Elizabeth's murderer. Agent Duncan was indeed a master puppeteer. This morning, P.J. explained, Detectives O'Brien and Mancini had discovered a firebombed Black Crown Victoria. After P.J. shared his information with the detectives, they shipped the remnants of the car to the crime lab in the hope of finding DNA or some other forensic evidence to identify the killer. Otherwise, P.J. opined, the murder would never be solved. Everyone involved was dead.

"Caffeine is my addiction of choice." P.J. joked as he ordered a second double espresso. He suddenly asked, "How tall is John Martin?"

I thought for a moment and then realized I had no idea. I hadn't seen John since before he was a teenager. "He wasn't particularly big as a preteen," I answered. "Why do you ask? I don't think I've seen John in twenty years."

"This morning Detective O'Brien found a witness who claims she saw a man dressed in a black leather jacket and black jeans and wearing a black ski mask running through the Wal-Mart parking lot at around 4:30 p.m. last Friday afternoon. She says he was enormous, tall, and heavyset. The lady thinks she saw a gun."

"Anything else?" This description of the possible killer was uselessly vague. Not the basis to catch a murderer.

"Not much. The lady says maybe a minute later, she saw someone else, much smaller, wearing an oversized floppy black hat, and she thinks wearing a black leather jacket, drive away in a late model green Jaguar. No additional identification of any kind. No license plate or anything. The lady thinks there might have been a passenger in the front seat. She's not sure." P.J. gulped down the remainder of his double espresso.

"Anything new on the Rodríguez front?"

P.J. sighed. "I don't know how you did it, but you were right. I'm told reliably they're both dead and their bodies won't be found. Your dinner tonight is our most promising lead."

We'd just begun to strategize about the upcoming evening when a familiar figure in a rumpled brown suit entered the Starbucks. Detective Mancini tagged along behind, sporty as usual, in a camel hair sport jacket and beige slacks.

Standing over P.J.'s shoulder, Detective O'Brien looked down at us with a half smile. "What have we here? Looks like a party." Turning to his partner, he asked in a tone dripping with sarcasm, "Detective Mancini, did you somehow misplace the gold-plated invitation?" Mancini grinned sheepishly.

P.J.'s face turned beet red. Two blue veins in his neck expanded and began throbbing. "You sons of bitches," he exploded. "You've been following me." P.J.'s fist tightened. An involuntary twitch in his muscles hinted he was barely maintaining self-control.

Detective O'Brien flinched. His smile faded. Mancini noticeably stepped away from his partner, opting not to become collateral damage. They both knew P.J.'s Special Forces training and reputation for toughness. Recognizing he had gone too far, O'Brien wisely elected to defuse the situation rather than challenge P.J.

"Don't do anything foolish, P.J. We're just doing our job. Understand, as law enforcement, we got responsibilities to the public. After this morning's news about Elizabeth's killer, we needed to find out your source, and I think we've done that."

P.J. inhaled deeply. I saw him struggling to regain his composure. Punching out a police officer in the presence of the *Chronicle*'s labor counsel wasn't a recipe for employment security.

"What the hell are you two jerk-offs talking about?" He slammed the palm of his right hand on the table for emphasis and glared at O'Brien and Mancini. Mancini moved farther away from O'Brien.

"Only someone with inside connections with David Giacomo would know he hired an Arab terrorist to kill Elizabeth Caldwell. We've found that someone. We found your source." As he spoke, Detective O'Brien pulled over a chair and sat down between P.J. and me. Mancini silently stood behind him looking nervous.

Detective O'Brien glared at me. I reciprocated in kind. "David Giacomo, Elizabeth Caldwell, and Paul Martin, do you know what two things they have in common? They're dead, and they're connected with the attorney extraordinaire, Mr. Steve Stein, sitting next to you. Stein may have fooled you and bought you off with some information, but he doesn't fool me. He's involved. I know it. I can feel it. Where there's smoke, there's fire."

P.J. didn't react. He just stared at O'Brien. "Tell me more, detective. It sounds like you've managed to put together the pieces of this puzzle."

"Stein's with Elizabeth Caldwell and she's killed a few hours later. The next morning we interview Stein and he tells us Giacomo arranged the hit. That evening Giacomo's killed by the FBI, trying to flee the country, and you tell me that one of the thugs murdered Caldwell. And Stein's best friend, Paul Martin, who was banging Elizabeth Caldwell, also is murdered. Don't you see it? You're the great investigative reporter. Do you need a map? The common thread is your source, Mr. Stein."

I blinked at Detective O'Brien, in disbelief, wondering how I'd managed to become a suspect in so many killings.

O'Brien shifted his attention to me and asked, "Do you own a black leather jacket, Mr. Stein?"

"Yes I do. Why do you ask?"

"And where were you the afternoon of Friday, April 13?"

"Don't dignify that with an answer," P.J. instructed me. "Get the hell out of here. Now!" he commanded.

As I hurried out, I glanced back over my shoulder. P.J. was in Detective O'Brien's face, like a manager confronting an umpire after a missed call at home plate. The two men, their faces flush and crimson, nose to nose, were jawing at each other.

39

Restaurants open and then go out of business with the regularity of clockwork, with an average life of less than a year. A feature in the *Chronicle* recently described the trials and tribulations of opening a gourmet restaurant in the city's trendy Warehouse District. It's not a business for the faint of heart or someone looking to make a quick buck. A notable exception is Gilardi's Restaurante. Run by Guiseppe Gilardi, and now assisted by his two sons, Gilardi's Restaurante has specialized in mouthwatering Northern Italian fare for more than forty years. It's what's called a destination restaurant for memorable events.

Located in Bainbridge Heights, a posh Eastern suburb, Gilardi's home for its entire existence has been on the first floor of an unremarkable four-story office building at the busy intersection of Appian Way and Larchmont Boulevard. A special trademark of the restaurant is its elegant service. Tuxedo-clad waiters and busboys are omnipresent, discreetly hovering in the background, ready to refill wine glasses, bread plates, and water goblets. Giuseppe continues to personally supervise the tableside preparation of his special pasta dishes. I don't know which is more memorable, the food or the ultimate tab.

John was excited when I told him we had reservations at Gilardi's. He'd never eaten there, although his mother was a regular. Why I had chosen Gilardi's? I wasn't sure. I couldn't remember the last time I had dined there without being on an expense account. Perhaps it was the subconscious belief that no matter how my conversation with John went, this would be an occasion not quickly forgotten — a memorable event. I'd agreed to meet John in the bar at seven.

When you enter the restaurant, the bar at Gilardi's is located to the left of the main dining room. The bar was packed, running the gamut from middle-aged divorcees prowling in low-cut dresses and stiletto heels, checking out their counterparts wearing sport jackets with shirts left open to display gold necklaces and hairy chests, to gray-haired older men strutting around like peacocks flaunting their blonde trophy dates, to the businessmen on expense accounts drinking their first vodka martini while waiting for a table. A frightening thought crossed my mind. Was this the precursor of what my life was destined to become?

He was immediately recognizable. Slightly taller than his father, maybe six feet two inches tall, he had the same coal-black hair and matching magnetic black eyes. Lean and muscular, he looked like he had stepped out from a page of the GQ men's magazine, wearing fashionable blue jeans, a beige corduroy sport jacket, and a white linen shirt open at the neck. A single diamond stud glistened in his right ear.

"You must be John Martin." I clasped his hand. "I see an uncanny resemblance to your father. You look exactly like him. I'm Steve Stein."

"Good to meet you, Mr. Stein," John said vigorously shaking my hand.

"Please call me Steve."

At that moment, a well-endowed twenty-something blonde in a revealing short black dress and knee-high, black leather stiletto-heeled boots sidled up to us. An older brunette, at least thirty years her senior, in a brown leather pantsuit and three-inch heels, trailed behind.

The twenty-something blonde looked directly at John and smiled broadly. As she spoke, her hand nonchalantly touched his arm, which she squeezed gently. "How about buying drinks for two fun-loving thirsty women?"

Déjà vu. My mind drifted back to high school days, remembering how the best looking girls had swooned over his father. John possessed the same natural magnetism. His mere presence attracted and bewitched the opposite sex. I watched John closely. Like his father, he reacted to the woman's flirtatiousness as if it were his due.

John shook his head reluctantly to show obvious disappointment. "We'll have to pass, ladies. I haven't seen my uncle in years. We have a seven o'clock reservation. Our loss." The excuse was delivered with a slight nod of his head.

"Yes, it certainly is," the still-smiling blonde replied with emphasis on the word "certainly." The woman's small black purse slipped from her shoulder and fell to the ground. John picked up and returned the purse. In the exchange, I noticed the blonde wink and slip him a scrap of paper that he pocketed without comment. The blonde and her companion pivoted on their high heels and headed back to the crowd at the bar.

One of Guiseppe's daughters-in-law ushered us to a table set for two in the adjoining dining room. A painted mural of Venice, with its colorful rickety, old buildings and gondola-filled canals, adorned the wall behind us. We were no sooner seated than a busboy appeared to inquire whether we preferred regular or bottled water. We opted for the city's finest. With the water came a basket filled with bruschetta, breadsticks, and small pizza squares.

Angelo, gray-haired with a pencil mustache, stepped forward and asked for drink orders. A fixture at Gilardi's for more than twenty years, he spoke with a heavy Italian accent, as did most of the waiters. That is part of Gilardi's ambiance. Ketel One and cranberry was my drink selection. With no hesitation, John ordered tonic water with a slice of lime.

"Finally, an area where you're not your father's son. His passion was single malt scotch. He never ever drank tonic water except if it was mixed with expensive gin, and then only in the heat of the summer." Paul's philosophy of life excluded temperance.

"I'm a recovering alcoholic and drug addict," John explained matter-of-factly. "I haven't had a single drink or blow since leaving rehab in

January. I want sobriety to stick this time. I know that even one drink could be fatal. I can never be more than a recovering addict. It's taken me years to learn that. Total abstinence is my only hope. Just hearing you talk about single malts makes my mouth salivate," he lamented. John's face conveyed to me a certain melancholy.

"Did your father know about your problem?"

"Know? He was the one who pushed me into rehab and paid for it."

"How did you feel about that?"

Before John could answer, Angelo returned with our drink order. Contemplating my question, John sat, lost in thought, his eyes focused on the plastic stirrer and lime in his glass of tonic water. Brooding, he played a game with the stirrer, repeatedly submerging the lime below the ice cubes, never drinking.

"Conflicted, very mixed emotions," he finally said. "Some days I loathed him. After all these years, he reenters in my life and begins lecturing me on what I'm doing wrong, which seems to be everything. You got to remember that my whole life I'd been brainwashed to believe all my problems resulted from my father abandoning me. On those days, I saw the money he was paying for rehab as blood money, paid out of guilt. On other days, I thanked God for sending Dad back into my life. He cared for me. He really did. He had his own money problems, but still paid for my care. And believe me, the rehab was expensive. On those days, I felt lucky."

"Wasn't Elizabeth Caldwell a patient at that same rehab center?"

John stopped fiddling with his drink and fixed his eyes on me. "That's bullshit. Let's be honest with each other, Steve, and stop playing games. I'm trying to answer all your questions honestly. I really am. You knew I was in rehab. You know I met Betsy there and introduced her to Dad. Now let me tell you something I know. You were meeting with Betsy at The Rusty Nail just hours before that hit-skip driver killed her." His calm voice betrayed no annoyance.

It was my turn to gaze in astonishment. I wasn't sure how best to respond. Thinking back to the timeline, how did John know those details? Even about The Rusty Nail. Late Monday afternoon, Elizabeth reluctantly had agreed to meet me an hour later at The Rusty Nail. She rushed from The Rusty Nail to Michael's Restaurant for her date with David Giacomo. She was killed leaving the restaurant. If he was in Chicago, where and how did John fit in?

"All true," I admitted, "but it was important for me to hear about rehab from you. As for Elizabeth, she hired me as her lawyer when I met her at The Rusty Nail. Then she was killed the same night. I'm puzzled. How did you know about the meeting?"

"As I'm sure Betsy told you, she and I met in rehab. She was an older woman, but beautiful, sensitive, and fragile. She enchanted me. We talked for hours, in and out of counseling. There was a powerful attraction between us, a special connection. We became dear friends."

"After leaving rehab, we never saw each other again. For a while, we talked several times a week. But after she took up again with David Giacomo, our conversations became less and less frequent. He was deadly poison. He's the one who hooked her up to drugs in the first place. And even worse, David was insanely jealous. He mistreated her. He'd check her cell phone. If he discovered she was talking to me, he'd yell at her and sometimes punch her out. He frightened her, and for good reason."

Other than the intimation that he and Elizabeth had been lovers, John wasn't telling me anything I didn't already know. He'd validated Elizabeth's description of her relationship with Giacomo. Still, he hadn't explained how he knew of the meeting at The Rusty Nail.

"The Rusty Nail," I interrupted, "how did you know I met Betsy there?"

"Late Monday afternoon, Betsy called. The call was unexpected since we hadn't talked for more than a month. She was frantic, almost incomprehensible. You scared her. She didn't know what to do. Like all the other men in her life, except me, you were bullying her, threatening to expose her relationship with Dad to the police. She said you'd forced her to agree to meet at six o'clock at The Rusty Nail. She only promised to meet you because she feared fallout from becoming entangled in the police investigation. You created a no-win situation. Betsy feared the police, but she knew if David learned about the meeting, he'd go ballistic. She'd pay for it in spades. She wanted my opinion whether to show up or just blow you off."

"What did you tell her?"

"She showed up, didn't she? I told her you were my father's best friend. I didn't know you, Steve, but I told her to trust you. My father trusted you. That's why she showed up."

John coughed. After a sip of tonic water, he announced, "I regret my advice."

"Why?"

Before John could reply, Angelo appeared to take dinner orders. Engrossed in conversation, we hadn't yet studied the menu. Angelo suggested bringing calamari fritti and fresh mozzarella with tomatoes as appetizers for the table. We could order entrees later. I asked for another drink. Angelo disappeared back in the kitchen.

"If Betsy blew off the meeting, she might be alive today. I don't believe for a moment the hit-skip driver was a disgruntled investor trying to kill David. The jealous bastard must have found out Betsy met with you, and maybe even what you guys discussed."

John wiped a tear from the corner of his eye with his napkin. John's analysis was right on; his attitude pleased me. But I knew that I couldn't confide in him. He hadn't been fully candid with me. When I first contacted him, John told me that Paul had had a premonition of death and a client involved in a white-collar crime. Later he mentioned the guy was a broker who peddled fraudulent securities. Given what he was telling me about Elizabeth, he must have known his father was representing David Giacomo. Of that, I was certain. I decided not to confront John on the issue.

Instead, I turned to news of Giacomo's death. "You know the FBI killed David Giacomo last night. So we'll probably never know whether you're correct. The story's in this morning's *Chronicle*."

"Mom left this morning's paper on the kitchen table. As far as I'm concerned, the world's a better place without him."

"My sentiments exactly," I agreed. "Tell me though, does Babs know about you and Elizabeth and the connection with David Giacomo?"

"Mom and I are close. We have few secrets. She calls almost every day. She knew I was fond of Betsy, but not all the details," John blushed. "I don't discuss my sex life with my mother," he quickly added. "I did tell her about David's abuse."

"What about your reconciliation with Paul? After so many years of bitterness, I can't imagine Babs welcoming the news."

John paused and sipped his tonic water. After a lengthy silence, he spoke slowly, choosing his words carefully. "Mom's a good person, but she's always been totally irrational when it came to Dad. It was her blind spot. She was unhappy. Eventually I think she reluctantly accepted Dad's reentry into my life since it was making me happy. And when I told her about Dad changing his insurance trust, she was touched. That was her word. You were going to check the insurance trust for me?"

At first, this didn't ring true to me. I couldn't imagine Babs sitting quietly while Paul reappeared in her son's life. Then again, I could count one million reasons why she'd have held her tongue if she knew Paul would shortly be removed from the picture. John had shown restraint in not asking the question earlier. "The change to the trust was executed before Paul's death. You're a full beneficiary and a wealthy young man." I looked at John for his reaction. He beamed with apparent pleasure. But, I told myself that was only natural. He had just learned that all his money problems were over.

Angelo returned with my drink and the appetizers. For the next two hours, John and I chatted amiably, and shared one Italian delicacy after another. The highlight was Angelo's tableside preparation of fettuccine Gilardi, a house specialty. I amused John with stories about his father. He entertained me with tales about his mother.

Despite her being Medicare-eligible, he described Babs as attractive, the combined product of judicious nips and tucks and good genes. Her money problems, he told me, were the fault of her fourth husband, Edward Lee III, a pretentious blueblood socialite who, much to Babs's dismay, turned out to be virtually penniless. "Not a pretty picture, after the marriage, when Mom learned the truth about his lack of finances." This description gave me a perverse pleasure. From what I'd heard, his tastes and airs were every bit as outlandish and expensive as Babs's. They deserved each other. Within five years, the couple spent most of the money Babs had accumulated over the course of three successful divorces. Single again, according to John, Babs was on the prowl for Number Five, dating one target after another, living beyond her limited means. She lived in an expensive home in a prestigious suburb. A brief attempt to revive her television career floundered.

"Between us," John whispered conspiratorially, "Mom's been selling off jewelry through an agent in New York City. Truth is, Steve, when Mom learns you're about to become single, you'll become, in her terminology, an HVT, a highly valued target." John's eyes twinkled: he knew I didn't care for his mother. I shuddered at the thought.

John was likeable and seemingly sincere, with a dry wit. Discussion about drug dealing and the Rodríguez brothers remained for dessert.

40

John and I sat sipping cappuccino and picking at a large piece of tiramisu presented by Angelo as his contribution to end a perfect evening. I could feel that self-satisfied buzz that follows a great meal where you've eaten too much.

"You sure know how to pick restaurants," John enthused as he wiped chocolate from his lips. "The veal melted in my mouth. I appreciated you not having wine with your meal." Out of respect for John's temperance, I'd passed up what Angelo had described as a mellow Barolo.

"Now that I've been softened you up with good food, I've got some difficult questions for you."

John momentarily froze, but then a self-confident smile returned. "Go ahead. I'll give you honest, straight answers."

"Do you deal drugs?"

John's body stiffened. The question's direct abruptness must have caught him by surprise. The smile disappeared, replaced by a frown.

He drew a deep breath and swallowed hard, not answering. "I did," at last he inaudibly responded. Several fingers of John's right hand involuntarily drummed the table. "But, not anymore. Not since I got out of rehab." His voice had risen several octaves.

Motive To Kill • 251

"What about the Rodríguez brothers, Paco and Juan? Do you know them?"

John's face darkened further. He scowled. His fingers continued to tap the table even more rapidly. "Who told you about them? My father?"

"How I learned isn't your concern. What's important is what you tell me. Are you going to be straight like you just promised?"

John closed his eyes. I studied him. He was struggling to exude a calm demeanor. His body movements betrayed him. In addition to his fingers, his right foot uncontrollably shook back and forth.

He opened his eyes and took yet another deep breath. "O.K. Here goes." I could tell he was laboring to modulate his voice. "Paco and Juan Rodríguez were my coke dealers. After rehab, I still owed them money, over fifty thousand dollars. When I didn't pay back the money, they began threatening me; they told me they'd break my legs. I was scared shitless. So, I set them up with some friends who were looking for drugs. If I gave them some business, they promised to back off and give me some time to get the money. They wanted the money, all of it, or else. They warned me what would happen if I didn't come up with it – breaking my legs was about the nicest thing they suggested would happen. I told Dad everything."

"What did Paul do?"

"He offered to help. He didn't have the money, but agreed to meet them here in town to negotiate a solution." John closed his eyes once more. The muscles in his neck tightened. For close to thirty seconds he remained that way, apparently deep in thought. He was breathing hard, his chest heaving. He finally opened his eyes and blurted out "That's whom Dad was meeting with, in the parking lot, when he was murdered."

"My God!" I did my best to sound surprised. "They must have killed your father. Have you gone to the police?" Like many good lawyers, I've developed a flair for the dramatic.

"They'd kill me if I went to the police. But the Rodríguezes didn't murder Dad," John spoke without hesitation.

"How would you know?" I asked. I wanted to hear why John was so certain.

"Friday night, when I returned to Chicago, Paco called. While meeting with Dad in his car, he said, a man appeared, clad in black and wearing a black ski mask.. He ordered them, at gunpoint, to get out of the car, which they did. He said the man was huge. Paco knew nothing more except he repeated several times that I still owed the fifty thousand dollars."

"What do you mean by 'when I returned to Chicago'?"

This change to a less-stressful subject visibly relaxed John. "Architecture is now my interest," he explained. "Mom arranged an interview with Craig Johnston, the architect, for a summer intern position at his firm. Craig's an old family friend. The interview was Friday morning, and afterward I took the two o'clock plane back to Chicago."

"Have you spoken with the Rodríguezes since Friday?"

He shook his head and shrugged. "Surprisingly not."

"John, you're making a big mistake." And he really was. "For your own good, you need to contact the police. I know they're bozos but they need to hear from you why Paul was at the Wal-Mart parking lot. Look at it from their perspective. You were responsible for Paul being in the parking lot. You're going to profit big time from his death. Sooner or later, the police will learn about the Rodríguezes and they'll interpret your silence as evidence of guilt." I didn't bother to tell John that Paco and Juan were probably dead and wouldn't ever support or contradict his story. I kept that information to myself, wanting to see how John would react to my suggestion.

John turned pensive. He didn't reply right away. "You're right," he finally announced. "If the police learn from someone other than me about Dad's meeting with the Rodríguezes, they'll suspect I set him up. Hell, I'd be suspicious of me." He laughed one of those pained, self-conscious laughs when you know what you've said isn't funny. He thought for a further moment and added, "I'm in deep shit."

John reminded me so much of Paul. I wanted to help him. He was right. He was in deep shit. Despite some lingering doubt, I offered to introduce him to Agent Duncan, provided he agreed to take an FBI-administered polygraph test. I've always believed that willingness to take a lie detector test is a good sign of truthfulness.

John, again, did not respond immediately. This continued hesitancy bothered me and I liked his answer even less.

"Mom might not like the idea. She's paranoid about the police. I'd really like her blessing before meeting with this FBI friend of yours and taking a lie detector test. Could you call her tomorrow and explain your plan. You'll be more persuasive. She respects you."

Talking to Babs was the last thing I wanted to do. She was a woman I never liked. Besides, I was disappointed that John hadn't immediately agreed to meet Andrew and take the lie detector test. What was he trying to hide? Maybe he hadn't outright lied, but his version of his current drug dealing didn't entirely mesh with the version of P.J.'s friend Bobby Briggs. Nor had he been candid about David Giacomo.

John must have sensed my hesitancy. "Please," he looked at me pleadingly.

"You're not a child," I decided to let him know exactly how I felt. "Your decision shouldn't depend on your mother. The next few days are going to be busy with the visitation and the funeral. If you haven't made up your mind by next week, I'll talk to Babs. My hope and recommendation is that you make your own decision."

After a final cappuccino, we stood, hugged, and left the restaurant. I'd be seeing him at the visitation tomorrow afternoon. Babs wasn't coming, but she'd promised John the use of her car.

Waiting outside for the valet to bring our cars, the brisk night air refreshingly contrasted to the warmth of the crowded restaurant. The valet first brought John's car. We embraced again, and as the valet held open the car door, John climbed into the driver's seat.

"Nice car."

"Yeah," he replied, "but not really my style. It belongs to Mom."

John drove off in an immaculately polished green Jaguar.

41

Thursday morning was the kind of day that invites you to ignore the alarm clock, roll over, pull the covers over your head, and stay in bed. The previous night contributed to my lethargy. After eating too much, I returned to my apartment at midnight and called P.J. as pre-arranged. For an hour, we relived, in detail, my encounter with John. P.J. didn't believe John would take the polygraph test. He insisted John was involved in his father's death. P.J. had it figured out: John needed money to pay off the Rodríguezes. He conned his father into naming him an equal beneficiary to the insurance trust, along with his three half-sisters. Then he arranged the meeting where the Rodríguezes murdered his father.

P.J.'s theory sounded plausible, but I desperately wanted P.J. to be wrong. I didn't want Paul to have been played for a sucker. I cared too much for my friend.

My calendar was clear. I'd cancelled all meetings and appointments for the day. My plan was to play hooky from work. At noon, I'd meet Phyllis, Peter, Marti, and the girls for lunch, and go then with them to the two o'clock visitation at Brown and Schmidt.

At ten o'clock, I was still lounging when the phone rang. It was John. He needed a ride to the visitation. Babs had reneged on her promise to let him use her car. She had a doctor's appointment she'd forgotten.

Since Babs's home was no more than a ten-minute ride from Phyllis's home, I agreed to pick John up at ten minutes before noon and invited him to join our group for lunch.

"Could you come by a little earlier, like at 11:30?" John suggested. "Just stop in for a moment to say 'Hello'. Mom hasn't seen you in years. She asked to see you. She appreciates what you've done for me. Maybe you could mention your idea about the FBI agent and the polygraph test."

I felt set-up. This had the potential for ruining the day. But I couldn't say no. "Okay, if you insist. But explain to Babs it can't be more than a meet and greet. We have to be at Phyllis's at noon. Everybody will be waiting." Fifteen minutes was fifteen minutes more than I wanted to spend with Babs.

I arrived at the appointed hour, in the circular driveway of Babs's home, a large three-story brick Tudor house on a manicured lot. John was right. The upkeep of this home had to be substantial.

Parking my Volvo in the driveway near the front door, I buttoned my raincoat and put on a broad-brimmed hat and rang the doorbell. In spite of the precautionary effort, the rain splattered my eyeglasses.

John opened the door. "Come in, Steve, We'll treat you like family. Hang your coat and hat in the front hall closet and join us in the kitchen. It's straight back to your right. Mom is brewing coffee. Have a cup."

He saw the look I gave him. "Don't worry. We'll be out in fifteen minutes, I promise."

Before I could complain, John hurried off, leaving me standing alone in the front hallway to fend for myself. I dried and cleaned my glasses with a tissue that I folded and placed in my raincoat pocket.

Women's coats packed the front hall closet. Pushing a full-length mahogany mink coat off to one side, I found an unused hanger. My eyes widened. A black leather jacket hung next to the mink. I noticed a floppy black hat on the shelf above the hangers. Without comment, I hung my raincoat next to the leather jacket, placed my hat on the shelf, and walked back to the kitchen.

Babs looked great; the plastic surgeon earned his fee. The nips and tucks were not readily apparent. Her face wrinkle-free and her blonde hair in a fashionably styled pageboy, she wore a white turtleneck sweater and body-hugging jeans . She rushed toward me, hugged me like a long-lost friend, and planted a kiss on my cheek. Maybe Babs was interested in me. I shuddered at the thought.

"After all these years, Steve, it's wonderful to see you. You look good; a few pounds heavier, but not a gray hair on your head. The years have treated you kindly."

"You're the one who's still a knockout," I said, measuring her with my eyes. Babs beamed. Her love of flattery was a constant that hadn't changed over the years. "No one would guess you're a day over forty."

That compliment brought a second even more enthusiastic hug and another theatrical kiss on the cheek.

"I'll bet you say that to all the old ladies at the nursing home," she said smiling broadly. The reunion with Babs was proceeding better than anticipated.

The aroma of freshly brewed coffee wafted from a carafe on the nearby counter. John stood at the counter with a bemused look, filling three mugs with coffee. "You see, it wasn't so bad after all. It's all in the anticipation." I wasn't sure whether he was speaking to Babs or me.

"Steve, you're such a dear to pick up John. I forgot all about my doctor's appointment. It was one of those senior moments. He does so want to be part of all the remembrances for his father." Babs's sentiment surprised me. Maybe with Paul dead, she could sanction the father-son bond that during Paul's lifetime she'd worked to destroy.

After exchanging additional pleasantries, I decided to take on the matter of the polygraph test.

"Babs, there's something we ought to discuss about John."

Babs looked quizzically at her son. He nodded his head in agreement.

"John's told me you know he arranged the meeting in the Wal-Mart parking lot at which Paul was killed. And he told you about his Friday night conversation with the Rodríguezes."

I looked at Babs for confirmation.

"John and I are close. He shares most everything with me," Babs answered, although not directly answering my question. I decided to ignore her evasiveness.

"Good, then you understand John's predicament. The police know Paul was killed Friday in the parking lot but not why he was there. They haven't learned that John arranged for Paul to meet the Rodríguezes to settle John's coke debt. But, sooner or later they'll find out. When they do, they'll realize John wasn't forthcoming; there's a danger they'll conclude he was involved in the murder. Who knows what the Rodríguezes will say? Coke dealers are notorious for telling prosecutors anything they want to hear in order to avoid prison. Remember, John had a motive to kill his father — a one million dollar inheritance."

"Have the police found any witnesses who saw the gunman?" Babs asked "Anything that might support the coke dealers' story?"

"If there are any such witnesses, the police haven't told me."

"The police may not believe the Rodríguezes if no one else saw the gunman. They're coke dealers."

Babs had gone right to the heart of the problem. The Rodríguezes were not the kind of people you'd invite to Sunday brunch.

John frowned. His mother's observation troubled him. "You're right. If no one saw the gunman, no one will believe Juan and Paco. 'An unidentified gunman scares the two coke dealers away.' When you say it like that, even I have trouble believing the story. Maybe Juan and Paco did kill Dad."

John's frown turned into a scowl. "And even if a gunman exists, the police will suspect I was involved." He shook his head and looked forlornly at his mother. "Steve's right: I'm in big trouble."

"That's exactly the point." My attention refocused on Babs, I continued. "John needs to tell everything to the police. The investigators will eventually put the pieces together, and John could become a convenient scapegoat. My idea is for John to meet with one of the city's head FBI agents, a friend of mine. We need the FBI on our side. But to do that, John has to take a polygraph test."

Babs grimaced. "I read in *Cosmopolitan* that those tests are unreliable. Something about false positives and vice versa. Aren't there any alternatives?"

Babs and John needed a harsh dose of reality. "Not that I see. If John was my son, I'd have him meet with Andrew and take the test. That is if he's telling the truth."

"Can we trust your friend, this FBI agent?"

"I'd trust him with my life." Actually, I had. John hung his head and looked at his mother for her response.

"John doesn't seem to have much choice," she finally announced.

Babs's cell phone rang. She quickly answered and turned her back to us.

"Yes. Everything's set. Good. We'll be in touch." She disconnected and flipped her phone closed. She turned to face us.

"Look Steve, let's mull this over for the next couple of days; no need to rush the decision. You'll be busy with the funeral until then and won't have time to arrange anything anyway." Babs glanced down at her watch. "You guys better get moving. John said we had only fifteen minutes. It was good seeing you, Steve."

Smiling at her son, she added sweetly, "See you for dinner tonight, dear." She pecked both John and me on our cheeks. The requested meet and greet was over, and Babs seemed anxious to hurry us on our way.

The doorbell chimed interrupting John's response. He looked over at Babs. "Were you expecting someone?"

"Probably the mailman. I'm expecting a check from the jeweler. They send them return receipt requested."

Babs gently brushed John's cheek as she headed to the front door.

Fifteen seconds later, Babs shouted from the hallway, "What the hell is going on? What's this all about?"

Motive To Kill • 259

42

Babs barged into the kitchen followed by Detectives O'Brien and Mancini. Lagging closely behind were Agent Duncan and P.J. Ettinger. John and I stood motionless by the kitchen table.

"You're tracking mud all over my hallway and kitchen floor," Babs shouted, her voice rising. "Take off your shoes." Babs was right. Muddy footprints and small pools of water trailed the four men. Agent Duncan and Detective Mancini wore stylish tan trench coats. Impervious to the elements, P.J.'s combat jacket was open. Detective O'Brien's light brown suit was not only rumpled but water stained.

"We're on police business ma'am," Mancini assured Babs, as if that explanation resolved all objections. For his part, O'Brien ignored Babs's protests; dramatic entrance was his style.

The two detectives ambled over next to John and me; O'Brien was grinning like a Cheshire cat. P.J. stopped and leaned against the kitchen wall, notepad in hand. Agent Duncan positioned himself in the kitchen doorway, a strategic post that allowed him to survey the entire scene.

I glanced at P.J., then at Agent Duncan hoping to receive some non-verbal clue as to what was happening. Both men remained poker-faced.

"Well, if it isn't my good friend Steven Stein. We meet again," O'Brien greeted me with undisguised sarcasm. "Would you be so kind as to introduce me to your young companion?"

I was about to ask the good detective whether he'd learned his manners from Emily Post, when a sixth sense told me to play it straight and not respond in kind to O'Brien's hostility.

"Detective O'Brien, this is John Martin, Paul's son. Babs, here, was Paul's second wife. She's John's mother."

Turning to John, I said, pointing to the detective, "John, let me introduce you to the legendary Detective O'Brien. He is heading the investigation into your father's murder." O'Brien's immediate glare convinced me not to add that the legend existed entirely in his own mind.

Babs came to my rescue. She stepped abruptly between Detective O'Brien and her son. "Detective, this is my house," she seethed. "I understand my ex-husband was murdered. Frankly I didn't care for him."

"Mom," John tried to interrupt.

"No. It's all right," Babs hushed. "No need to pretend. Everybody knows your father and I didn't get along." Focusing her venom on Detective O'Brien, she continued in a controlled rage.

"I'm not familiar with the formalities of police protocol. There is this device called the telephone, hardly a new invention. If you wanted to arrange an appointment with me, you could have called, and I'd have found an opening for you on my schedule. Barging in unannounced at the last moment isn't considerate; it's plain rude. John and Mr. Stein are on their way to meet with the immediate family of my son's deceased father to prepare for this afternoon's visitation. I have a doctor's appointment. You can schedule your interview or whatever after the funeral on Friday. You are inconveniencing me. I would prefer you leave now and follow my protocol. Do we understand each other?"

Detective O'Brien looked bemused. Agent Duncan raised an eyebrow. P.J. jotted on his pad.

"That's not the way it works ma'am," Mancini interjected, always the polite one.

The officer's failure to follow her suggestion enraged Babs. She stuck out her chin and glared at Mancini. Mancini winked at his partner, which had the wanted effect of waving a red cape before a bull.

Motive To Kill • 261

"What he means is that I don't give a damn if you're inconvenienced. We're not leaving and we'll follow my protocol." O'Brien paused to let his words sink in.

"Do we understand each other?" added O'Brien, looking straight at Babs.

"How dare you. Such impudence," Babs snorted. "You may not know who you are messing with, officers. I'm Babs Brown, the star of *Coffee Klatch*. For more than ten years, it was the Number One program on daytime television in this city. I have important friends in high places. It's a mistake to cross me. I warn you."

A deep baritone voice resonated across the kitchen. Agent Duncan, who'd quietly been taking in the drama from the doorway, was speaking. Having gotten to know Andrew, I recognized the twinkle in his eye.

"Gosh, Miss Brown, I didn't recognize you. When I was a little boy, my Nana never missed one of your programs."

With a slight smirk, Detective O'Brien turned from Babs to face John. "Young man, don't worry. I don't hold your mother against you. We all have crosses to bear, though yours appears to be a particularly heavy one. I do need to interview you. Agent Duncan here is with the FBI. He informed me, this morning, your father was meeting with two drug dealers, Juan and Paco Rodríguez, shortly before he was killed. I'm informed they sold you coke at one time. Am I correct?"

"Yes you are, Detective."

"You arranged for them to meet with you father, didn't you, son?"

John hesitated. The nightmare scenario we had discussed was unfolding. John looked first at Babs and then at me for direction.

"Don't say another word." With that command, Babs stepped once more between her son and Detective O'Brien. "Let me call a lawyer. I don't like the direction of this man's questioning."

I can't be sure, but I'd swear I saw Andrew wink at P.J.

"Actually that would be a good idea. We'll all go to the precinct. You can call a lawyer from there. When the lawyer comes, he can talk privately to your son and then we'll sit down and chat. Young Mr. Martin has some explaining to do."

Babs looked at O'Brien with steely eyes. "That won't work. You don't listen, Detective. I told you I have a doctor's appointment in less than an hour." She now turned her attention to me. "Steve, would you be a dear and drive John to the police station. I'll call my friend, Ed Sawyer. He does criminal work. You stay with John until Ed arrives. After my appointment, I'll meet John and Ed at the station. I'm sure, by then, everything will be worked out to the detective's satisfaction."

"No ma'am, that won't be satisfactory," Mancini spoke in his usual polite tone. "We do want Mr. Stein at the interview, but he'll drive you. Your son will go with us. I know it may be an inconvenience, but you'll have to reschedule your doctor's appointment."

"You will do as Detective Mancini suggests and call your lawyer from the station." O'Brien's words were clipped; his tone commanding. His voice made it clear that his directions were not to be contravened. The patience he'd already shown Babs surprised me.

"I don't want to drive with Steve. He needs to get to the funeral home visitation with John. If you really need me, I can drive to the station in my car, that is if you don't believe that I'm a regular Ma Barker,"

"The nice one," she said pointing to Mancini, "can come with me."

"Do you drive a green Jaguar, ma'am?" Mancini asked.

"Yes," Babs answered, a slightly puzzled look on her face. "Why do you ask?"

O'Brien stepped forward and pulled a folded document from the inside breast pocket of his suit jacket. He unfolded the paper and handed it to Babs. "This is a search warrant issued by Judge Washington allowing us to seize your Jaguar. You can't drive the car. Our lab techs will be coming to remove the vehicle for forensic testing at the lab. A green Jaguar was seen leaving the murder scene."

Babs's face reddened. Her bottom lip quivered. "How dare you?" Babs screamed at O'Brien. "I'll have your job." She looked over at Mancini and added, "And yours, too."

Agent Duncan spoke smoothly from the doorway. "We have two cars. Miss Brown, I suggest you drive with Mr. Stein and me in Mr. Stein's car. The detectives will go with your son in the squad car. I'm sure the detectives will extend you all the courtesies fitting someone of your stature. If Mr. Stein has to leave for the visitation, you'll be given an escort home. Isn't that right, Detective O'Brien?"

"Of course, Agent Duncan. We'll see that Ms. Brown gets everything she deserves." Something was playing out but I wasn't sure what.

Babs stamped her foot and glared wild-eyed at O'Brien and Andrew. "I'm not driving in Steve's car with you or anyone else. I'm not. I'm not going with you. I'll take a cab to my doctor and meet you later."

"I don't think you're getting the message, Ms. Brown. This isn't an invitation to come to the station," Detective O'Brien explained coolly. "I'm tired of arguing with you. I'm telling you to get going. If you don't shut up and start moving, I'll take you into custody as a material witness."

I was confused. Why the continued insistence that Babs, Agent Duncan, and I travel to the police station in my car, while the detectives, P.J., and John go in the squad car? I started to point out the incongruity of four persons arriving at Babs's home in a single squad car, if there had already been a plan to take multiple witnesses to the police station. Andrew looked at me, tightly pursed his lips, and gave the slightest nod of his head. His actions signaled me to go along with the program. I did.

"I'll call Phyllis and tell her to have lunch without me and John. I'll go to the station and catch up with Phyllis at the visitation."

"That would be great," Agent Duncan exulted. O'Brien also seemed pleased, if not somewhat relieved, with my sudden cooperation.

I looked at John. His face showed concern. The nightmare I had warned about was becoming a reality. I saw him look over at his mother. Her face was crimson. Babs was seething. "Bullshit. This is bullshit," she kept muttering to no one in particular. She made no eye contact with John.

While I called Phyllis on my cell, I turned to P.J. "Could you get my raincoat and hat from the front hall closet?"

"No problem."

Moments later, P.J. returned and handed me my raincoat and hat. Without saying a word, he walked over and whispered into O'Brien's ear. The detective nodded and the two men headed down the hallway to the front hall closet. The rest of us followed behind. Mancini pulled Babs along, holding her tightly by the arm. A sullen look had replaced her usually haughty exterior. She was not a happy camper, apparently realizing her harangues had fallen on deaf ears.

With a flourish, P.J. opened the closet door. "Take a look, Detective, in the far corner, next to the mink coat, and up above, on the shelf with the hats." He pointed to the black leather jacket and black floppy hat that I first noticed when I hung up my raincoat.

"Are those yours, Ms. Brown?" O'Brien enunciated each word slowly.

Babs still in Mancini's grip said nothing.

P.J. looked at Detective O'Brien. "The witness you told me about this morning, didn't she see someone with a black leather jacket and floppy black hat pick up another person, also clad in black, and drive off in a late-model green Jaguar from the murder scene?"

"An interesting coincidence, P.J.," O'Brien deadpanned

"My discovery will cost you a beer, Detective," P.J. jotted notes on his pad.

"We'll have forensics check them out, or maybe we'll do a lineup with the star of *Coffee Klatch* wearing them. What do you think Ms. Brown?" asked O'Brien.

Babs didn't say a word. Mancini steered her to my Volvo. I unlocked the car doors and the detective opened the rear door. "I'm not getting into this car," Babs insisted. "I don't want to go," she pouted.

"Doesn't matter what you want to do, Ms. Brown. You don't have a choice. Now get in the car." Detective Mancini placed his other hand on Babs's back.

"Let go of me," she screamed. "I'm not getting into that car. I can't." At this point, Babs lurched loose from Mancini's grip. They struggled, and she kneed the detective in the groin and ran from the car across the manicured lawn. Her high heels sank into the soggy turf, and she fell to the ground. She jumped up in her stocking feet. To my surprise, Detective O'Brien moved with catlike quickness, grabbed hold of Babs with his left hand, and sharply slapped her across the face with the back of his right hand.

"You're under arrest, Lady, for assaulting a police officer," he growled. "Get me some cuffs, Mancini." O'Brien's partner still lay doubled over on the ground.

"The bitch kneed me in the balls," Mancini complained as he struggled to his feet.

O'Brien looked at me. "Stein," he barked, "get in your car. You're driving Ms. Brown and me to the station. The others will go with Mancini. I don't want Mr. Martin and his mother in the same car."

Babs, her tear-stained left cheek, reddened from O'Brien's blow, continued to claw, struggling to break O'Brien's grip. Mancini, still grimacing in pain, retrieved handcuffs from the squad car, and roughly cuffed Babs's hands behind her back.

"Please, please, don't start the car," Babs screamed at me. "We'll all die."

"We'll all die," she repeated. She was hysterical

O'Brien grabbed Babs by both arms, pulled her toward him, and looked her straight in the eyes.

"What makes you think we'll all die?"

"A bomb's in the car. It's set to go off when the car starts." Babs's body went limp as she sought to prevent O'Brien from seating her in the Volvo.

"And how do you know that?" he snorted, suddenly releasing Babs, and letting her fall to the pavement.

"I arranged it," she whimpered.

Babs, hair damp and disheveled, her face tear-stained and

mud-caked, lay sobbing on the ground, hands cuffed behind her back. She curled up, trembling uncontrollably. Her white turtleneck was grass stained; her designer jeans muddied. Ashen, John walked over and stood, looking down at his mother, tears welling up in his eyes.

"You'd have killed me. You told me to arrange a ride with Steve because you needed your car to get to a doctor's appointment. I'd have been riding in that car." John's hands shook and his chest heaved as he sobbed, unable to control his emotions. My hands were shaking as well. Together with John, Babs had ticketed me for a one-way visit to eternity.

Babs stopped crying. Her face hardened and body straightened. She tried to stand up, but with both hands pinned tightly behind her back, she lost her balance and awkwardly fell backwards on to the ground. After several failed attempts, she just sat on the pavement and glared up at her son.

"You little shit, you deserved to die. I dedicated my whole life to you. And how did you pay me back? After all I did for you, you abandoned me for that prick, you god damned traitor. I wish you were dead." Babs's eyes blazed as the hatred spewed from her mouth. "You've been dead to me since you took up with your father."

John stared at his mother without saying a word, his Adam's apple bulging and quivering. The depth of Babs's hatred stunned me. She was willing to kill her only son as retribution for John's overtures to his father. Only P.J., impervious to the drama, furiously recorded on his notepad the unfolding scene as the rest of us gaped.

"All I wanted was a father," John stammered. "My love for you never changed. You're my mother. I loved you."

"You sold me out for money. You, Judas. I wish you were dead." She continued without let up. "That insurance policy rightfully belonged to me. I earned it. Get out of my sight. I hate you."

Stone-faced and puffy-eyed, John stood stiffly over his mother, stunned. He was trembling. All color had vanished from his face. Detective Mancini wrapped his arm gently around John's shoulder and guided the young man into the house. John didn't utter a word. He walked robotically along with the officer.

"Give me your car keys, Stein." I tossed the keys to O'Brien as he instructed. He opened my car door and sat down in the driver sear, putting the key in the ignition.

"My God, don't. You'll kill us all." Terror in her eyes, her hands cuffed behind her back, Babs buried her face on the pavement.

My heart skipped a beat as the detective, ignoring Babs's warning, turned the key. The engine sputtered and then started.

"I don't understand. Where was the bomb?" Babs stared at my car in disbelief.

"That's right. No explosion. No bomb." Agent Duncan shook his head in mock disgust. "You can't trust hired killers these days, Miss Brown. They're so unreliable."

"Or know when they're undercover FBI agents," chortled Detective O'Brien, now also broadly smiling. "Yeah, you got to be a little more careful Ms. Brown who you confide in. It's never a good idea to confess a murder to the FBI." Andrew and Detective O'Brien were obviously enjoying a mutually shared secret.

Listening to this banter, a look of disconsolate concern settled over Babs's startled face. Wide-eyed, she stared at Andrew. "I want a lawyer," Babs demanded, still squatting on the ground.

43

Detective O'Brien left Babs sitting on the pavement, while waiting for backup. While she squatted on the ground in the rain, he Mirandized her. Despite her predicament, Babs projected her trademark haughtiness. Head held high, expressionless, she looked straight ahead, although her eyes betrayed panic. Only when the uniformed police arrived and lifted Babs up and placed her in the back of a squad car, did she break down alternately demanding, and then begging, Detective O'Brien to let her ride to the station uncuffed.

"Lady," he hissed, "you better get used to chains. When you're not in a cage, you'll be wearing them for the rest of your life, right up to the moment they strap you on to the table for the lethal injection."

Babs turned pale and her lower lip quivered. She said nothing more as O'Brien, in full game face, sat down next to her. I watched as the squad car left, transporting Babs to jail.

Detective Mancini drove with John in his car. I asked whether John needed a lawyer. The detective and Agent Duncan assured me it wasn't necessary. After John gave a statement, Detective Mancini promised to personally drive John to the funeral home. I embraced John and he drove off with P.J. and Mancini.

Andrew asked me to drive him to his car, parked three blocks away. I pulled behind what Andrew identified as his silver Lexus.

"Pretty expensive car for a public servant."

"I like it." Andrew ignored my comment.

"You've got to explain what just played out. Why the reference to lethal injection? Did Babs kill Paul?"

"Fair enough," Andrew answered. "I owe you that. Do you remember Emir?"

"I'll never forget him."

"Elizabeth wasn't his only victim. Emir ran a profitable freelance business on the side — what you might call murderer for hire. John confided everything to his mother about his burgeoning relationship with his father including how Paul added him as a beneficiary to his insurance trust. Then, fatally, John told Babs about the meeting Paul arranged with the Rodríguezes to try and settle his drug debts."

"You heard the woman today. She couldn't tolerate the idea that John and Paul were developing a father-son relationship. As revenge, she decided to kill them both, but wanted Paul dead first, so, as John's only heir, she would inherit the one million dollars in insurance money. John's death would then solve her financial problems and rid her of a son she now despised. Emir was her hit man; hired to kill both Paul and John. Babs was right there in the Wal-Mart parking lot pointing out Paul to her hired killer. She then drove away with Emir in her green Jaguar."

"But Emir is dead."

"Babs didn't know that. At least not right away. She called Emir to work out the final details of John's murder. Instead of Emir, Yossi, or Joe, as he introduced himself to Babs, answered."

"It's coming back to me," I interrupted. "I remember now. Yossi took Emir's cell after he saved my life."

"Very good," Andrew complimented me. "You've got a good memory. When Babs called Emir to complete the assignment, Yossi answered. He identified himself as Emir's business partner. Emir, he explained to her, was no longer among the living, but that anything Emir could do, he could do better. Babs bought Yossi hook, line, and sinker. She hired him to finish Emir's job for ten thousand dollars. Yossi insisted on a five thousand dollar advance that she delivered. The plan was to get John in a car rigged with a bomb set to explode on ignition.

"Did she want me dead, too?" A shiver travelled down my spine.

I'm not sure whether you were chosen to die with John because of your relationship with Paul or whether the selection was just a matter of convenience. Anyway, while you were inside, Yossi called Babs and told her he'd rigged your Volvo with a bomb. Yossi recorded all his conversations with Babs except the first."

"She's on tape admitting that she hired Emir to kill Paul?"

"We got everything. O'Brien's right. At best, Babs will be spending the rest of her life in prison."

The thought of Babs growing old in a cage was satisfying. But one concern remained. "What about John? Was he involved in his mother's plotting?"

"Absolutely not. John was another victim of Babs, just like his father."

I sighed with relief.

EPILOGUE

I am sitting in the front pew reserved for family. Jane sits to my left. Last night, she called unexpectedly, from the Las Vegas airport. Big Mama's relented at the last moment, allowing Jane to arrive early Friday morning on the red-eye flight in time for the funeral. She took a cab directly to my apartment where she is staying for the weekend. I plan to invite her to spend the July fourth weekend with me at the Bellagio in Vegas. John sits to my right, next to Phyllis, holding her hand, while her son Peter sits to Phyllis's left, next to his companion Matthew. After the visitation concluded, last night, Phyllis insisted John move into a spare bedroom in her home. Marti sits next to Jane alongside her husband and Paul's three daughters.

The deep bass voice of the black-robed minister, celebrating Paul's life and mourning his passing, resonates throughout the church. Friends and colleagues pack the hard, uncomfortable wooden pews. An overflow of mourners lines the back of the sanctuary behind the last pew. Surrounded by more than a dozen floral displays, Paul's hardwood mahogany coffin dominates the front of the church below the pulpit and the minister. Paul disliked flowers. He suffered from severe allergies his whole life. I mentally note this sad irony. He did, however, bask in being the center of attention. The massive gathering assembled to bid him farewell would have pleased him.

"Yea, though I walk through the valley of death, I shall fear no evil:

for thou art with me; thy rod and thy staff the comfort me." The minister, a tall, dignified man with an aquiline nose, recites the twenty-third Psalm. Yesterday, John spent several hours at the police station giving a detailed statement. But with Andrew present, the authorities treated John sympathetically. While John still has issues to be worked out, I think he's suffered enough. For all practical purposes, he's now an orphan. John's story has the elements of a Greek tragedy: a mother killing her son's father in a jealous rage and then trying to destroy her own son. And P.J. reported this morning that confronted with the tapes of her conversations with Yossi, Babs confessed to hiring Emir to kill Paul. Her lawyer plans an insanity defense, claiming the thought of John developing a filial relationship with Paul twisted her mind. Personally, I think the million dollar insurance trust was what twisted her mind.

The minister signals me to come forward to begin my eulogy. As I rise, Phyllis squeezes my hand. Once at the pulpit, I'm unable to focus on any of the faces in the congregation. I see only the polished wooden coffin below. It captures the profound sadness and reality of the moment. Over the last week, in death, my best friend Paul's life was opened to me, his secrets revealed. Like everyone, Paul changed over the years as his life became more complicated. How much, I never realized. The image of the cocky teenager, standing in Mrs. Henderson's Honors English class, flashes through my mind. Cherished memories of Paul will remain. The excitement of this last week, though, has changed my life forever. Paul has given me a final gift, a new zest for life.

The tears welling up in my eyes make it impossible to see beyond the family pew. All pretense of stoic demeanor vanishes.

I take a deep breath and begin the eulogy.

CPSIA information can be obtained at www.ICGtesting.com
Printed in the USA
BVOW08s2023060515

399267BV00001B/1/P

9 781480 816954